He Loves Lucy

by

Ann Yost

The Outlaws of Eden, Maine

He Loves Lucy

Cover Art by *Kim Mendoza*

The Wild Rose Press, Inc.
PO Box 708
Adams Basin, NY 14410-0708
Visit us at www.thewildrosepress.com

Publishing History
First Crimson Rose Edition, 2013
Second Crimson Rose Edition, 2016
Print ISBN 978-1-5092-0985-9
Digital ISBN 978-1-5092-1028-2

The Outlaws of Eden, Maine
Published in the United States of America

Dedication

To Ben, who loves Lucy as much as I do.

Prologue

Law offices of Claude Moore, Esq., Bangor, Maine

Nate Packer surveyed the small group gathered in his attorney's office and flashed what his ex-wife called his "Donald Trump" smile. His eyes lingered briefly on the former Mrs. Packer, Shirley, whose gray sweater and skirt and sleek cap of gray hair relegated her to the background of Nate's Technicolor life. Shirley and Claude were two of a kind—solid, dull, and devoted to Nate. He was fond of Shirley, always had been, but circumstances changed. Shirley understood.

Claude understood, too. Nate flicked a mildly contemptuous glance at his attorney, impeccable as always, in his hand-tailored gunpowder-gray three-piece suit. Claude preferred to stay in the background, using his keen mind and legal expertise to smooth the path for his best friend. This time, though, Claude had nearly written himself out of the picture. Neither he nor Shirley was still a partner at Packer, Inc., the construction company the three of them had started thirty years earlier. Nate owned it all, and he would until it was time for his son, Nate Junior, to take over. Nate glanced at Paula Binkowski, the sexy armful who would soon be his wife and Nate Junior's mother. His blood rushed southward. He'd made a good choice in Paula. Together they'd found a dynasty.

"Nate." He hadn't been aware of Shirley making her way across the small room. He lifted his glass of champagne in her direction and grinned.

"It's a great day, Shirl. A great day."

Her impassive look didn't change. Never complain, never explain. That was Shirl's motto. But this time she surprised him.

"Claude's out, too?"

Nate shrugged. "He's still my shyster, but I need sole control over Packer, Inc., so my son can take over one day. You understand that, Shirl. Claude understands it, too."

"I think it's a mistake, Nate," she said, quietly. "You need Claude."

Anger rumbled through his veins driving high color into his cheeks and causing him to clench a fist. He wanted no criticism of this new course. He'd never tolerated criticism.

"Claude hasn't objected. In any case, he adores Paula." The comment was intended to sting his ex-wife, a quick, sharp reprimand. Nate made the decisions for Packer, Inc. He always had.

"Whatever you say." Shirley sounded matter of fact, as if she were agreeing to order Chinese food for lunch. Her ready acquiescence calmed him as it always did.

"You happy with the settlement, Shirl?"

"It's fine, Nate. I'm fine."

He favored her with a wide smile and patted her hand. "I'm glad you're happy." He could afford to be magnanimous. He'd gotten what he wanted—his freedom and sole control of Packer, Inc. Some people thought he was a lucky guy, but Nate knew better. A

"...you can't keep me out of it.
This is my job, Jake. It's as important to me as your job is to you."

He ran his fingers through the short, blond hair.

"I didn't mean that, exactly." He sounded exasperated, at the end of his rope. "But let's get real about this. I'm not gonna have time to rescue your ass when you get in over your head."

"I would prefer that you not mention either my ass or my head," she said, very much on her dignity. "I would also like a copy of the autopsy results and a list of suspects and their alibis."

He barked a short, humorless laugh.

"I'd like all that, too. Look, it's way too early for any of that." She scowled at him and he shrugged his big shoulders. "I'd tell you the same thing if you were here from the *Hartford Courier*.

"I am here for the *Courier*. I'm stringing for them."

"Shit."

She didn't care for the word, but she liked the flash of respect in his eyes.

"Have you talked with anyone yet?"

"Yeah, Lucy. I have." The flash was gone; the eyes were steady and somber. "I talked with Cameron Outlaw."

"Oh."

"The guy's got a story a three-year-old wouldn't buy."

She winced at the harsh words, but he had a point.

"He didn't kill Packer, Jake."

One corner of his hard mouth tipped up.

"Whether he did or not, he's one more reason you shouldn't be involved in this story. Conflict of interest."

Praise for Ann Yost

"[*THE EARL THAT I MARRY*] was the perfect rainy-day read and the promise of further romances between the characters has me crossing my fingers that the 'Brides and Prejudice' series has a long and successful future."

~The Romance Reviews

~*~

"Ann Yost writes an intriguing story [in *ABOUT A BABY*] that keeps you entertained all the way to the end."

~Got Romance

~*~

"Yost pens a story [in *THAT VOODOO THAT YOU DO*] that's heavy on romance and suspense, but with a comedic flair in the form of some elderly ladies who are convinced they are witches."

~Romantic Times

successful man made his own luck.

It was no accident that everything always went Nate Packer's way.

Chapter One

Eden Consolidated High School auditorium,
Eden, Maine, eighteen months later

The tulips pirouetted onto the stage with smiles on their faces and bells on their toes.

Unfortunately, centrifugal force quickly turned the jingle bells into tiny missiles. Parents ducked, siblings hooted, the ballerinas shrieked, and Miss Violet Thane's annual spring recital, "Ode to the Seasons," was Armageddon. The ballet teacher planted her fists on her hips and glared at someone behind the curtain.

In the audience, Sheriff Jake Langley leaned over to speak to his six-year-old son. "Let me guess. Lucy made the costumes."

It wasn't really a question. The bell catastrophe had his nanny's name written all over it. Temporary nanny, thank God.

Sam's small face flushed with delight, and his voice was filled with admiration.

"Lucy made 'em explode! This is the coolest thing ever!"

Jake would be willing to bet his newly acquired sheriff's badge and the thirty-year mortgage on his Cypress Street Cape Cod that "cool" did not describe Miss Violet Thane's present state of mind. The elderly ballet teacher was, no doubt, ready to strangle Lucy, but she couldn't have been surprised. Lucy Outlaw's enthusiastic miscalculations were well known in Eden. During his year in the small New England town, Jake had heard stories.

Privately, he filed them under the inclusive title Lucy's Regrettable Mishaps and they included events like the explosion in the middle school chemistry lab and the addition to the annual Christmas pageant of a golden retriever who gave birth on top of baby Jesus. Most notable, perhaps, was the year that Lucy, in charge of preparing a turkey for the Thanksgiving dinner at the Grange Hall, failed to remove the plastic bag of giblets before roasting.

Lucy Outlaw was a legend in Eden, Maine. Chaos followed her the way dirt followed Pigpen, and Jake knew it. And because he knew it, he had to shoulder part of the blame for today's fiasco. He'd unleashed Lucy on the recital when he'd hired her as temporary nanny for his twins, Sam and Lillie. It was a decision he'd regretted every single day of the past two weeks despite the color and laughter she'd brought into his home.

The crimson curtain on the high school auditorium stage slammed shut, but not before Jake caught a glimpse of Lucy trying to corral the rogue bells with a broom. She was on the tall side, slender and graceful. From a distance, her short, curly hair looked black, but closer inspection revealed threads of auburn and even gold. Wide eyes that looked like pieces of a Maine summer sky were set above a small, straight nose and soft lips. Jake supposed she was pretty, but that wasn't a word often used in connection with Lucy. Her animated features suggested humor, enthusiasm, and always, always, new schemes. He searched for the right term. She was compelling. Vivid. Unpredictable. Maddening.

Mary Poppins without the umbrella or the common sense.

Sam's voice broke into the sheriff's thoughts.

"Can I go help Lucy clean up the bells?"

"Better not. Miss Violet looks homicidal." The thing was, Lucy always meant well.

Her job description did not require cooking, laundry, or housework, but she'd wanted to help. Her attempts to iron and starch his uniform shirts had turned them into corrugated cardboard, and she'd managed to lose half of every pair of socks he owned. At least three nights a week he sat down to eat some version of tuna surprise and his household now included Wiggles, a formerly stray cat and Lucy Junior, a white mouse.

But the worst part about his temporary nanny was that she'd hauled Jake's tattered libido out of mothballs.

"I wish Lucy could stay with us forever," Sam murmured.

Jake said nothing. He knew better than to argue with a man with a crush. He breathed a prayer of relief that this was Lucy's last night with them. Tomorrow his housekeeper, Mrs. Peach, would return and their lives would get back to normal.

Jake found himself counting the hours.

****

"This is the absolute limit," Miss Violet scolded.

Lucy tried to remember how many times she'd been told she'd reached the limit. Many times. Many, many times.

"I'm sorry, Miss Violet. I thought the bells were

6

sewn on tightly enough."

The older woman shook her head. The gray hair, twisted into a tight bun and sprayed to within an inch of its life, did not move.

"It's the concept of risk/reward that you fail to understand, Lucy. Bells represent a huge risk factor with very little prospect of reward. There was simply no need for bells."

Lucy didn't point out that the bells had been Lillie's idea. Naturally the six-year-old didn't understand the immutable laws of physics. But then, Lucy, a recent college grad, should have known better. She'd forgotten about centrifugal force.

"I realize you meant well," Miss Violet went on, her anger fading. "You always mean well, but it's time to think about the consequences of your ideas."

Lucy finished the thought in her head. It's time for you to stop screwing up.

"All right, now." Miss Violet patted Lucy's arm. "You go on out front. Tulips"—she clapped her hands—"line up, if you please."

Miss Violet was right. Lucy focused on the dance instructor's words rather than the amused grins on the faces of her neighbors as she made her way through the auditorium. It was time to stop screwing up. It was time to grow up, to leave home, and start a dignified career as a professional journalist, a future Pulitzer Prize winner, a war correspondent. And she would.

Just as soon as she could get a job.

Unfortunately, award-winning papers like the *Hartford Courier* tended not to hire recent college grads. Lucy knew she needed to collect some credentials. Tomorrow she intended to call Ed Stiles, owner and editor of the *Eden Excelsior*.

Tonight, though, there was still an ordeal to get through. After two weeks in their house, it would be hard to say goodbye to the twins. And it was even harder to leave their father. She slipped into the seat next to Sam. His green eyes glowed.

"I liked the bells," Sam whispered in a voice that could have been heard out on the Blackbird Reservation fifteen miles west of Eden.

She hugged the boy and peered over his head at the quirked eyebrow on Jake's lean face.

"Remind me not to ask you to sew on any buttons."

The rough drawl skittered along her nerve endings and lit a fire inside Lucy. She'd been hyper aware of the tall, golden-haired single dad since she'd met him on her return from college six months earlier. His wide shoulders, narrow hips, and long legs made her breathless. He was so…male. Around Jake she felt new sensations, yearnings she didn't understand. She admired his devotion to his kids and his job. She knew he was looking for someone to replace the wife he'd lost. Sometimes, while she was concocting the evening's tuna surprise, she pretended she was that wife, home from a hard day of reporting on the Afghanistan War, that after supper she would read a story to the twins and tuck them in and then the rest of the evening would belong to Lucy and her blond, sexy husband.

She didn't worry too much about the inherent difficulty of reporting on an overseas war while living in a small town in Maine. It was, after all, a fantasy. And, anyway, Jake had never really liked her. He'd wanted to marry her new sister-in-law and Lucy understood that. Hallie Scott-Outlaw would have made a fantastic mother for Sam and Lillie.

Jake was Lucy's Mr. Right, but she didn't kid herself. Not really. The truth was he wouldn't marry Lucy if she was the last available woman on earth.

Lucy ignored a little pang of regret and flashed the sheriff an apologetic grin. As usual, he didn't return the smile but something bright and dangerous flashed in his kryptonite-green eyes and Lucy felt a surge of longing.

One more night with the Langleys and then she could get on with her grand scheme. It would be good. It would be for the best. Somehow, though, the prospect felt like cold fingers around her heart.

****

The Cypress Street house was a sixty-year-old gray Cape Cod with a roofline pitched to shed snow and a welcoming wrap-around porch. The dwelling had always been special to Lucy. As a child, she'd spent many hours there with her best friend, Sally Carpenter and the whole friendly, easygoing family. The Carpenters, including Sally, had scattered to various points around the country, but Lucy still remembered Sunday suppers of soup and popcorn, winter nights spent giggling under warm comforters in Sally's bedroom, and talks with Sally's mother at the kitchen table. It had been a haven for a child whose household consisted of a workaholic father, a housekeeper, and her ten-years-older brother, Cameron. Their mother had taken her first born, Basil, with her when she'd left twenty years earlier, and Lucy had met Baz for the first time this past Christmas.

Lucy studied the old apple tree in the side yard as she dried the last of the supper dishes. The bare, gnarled branches bent in the wind that presaged an evening storm. It seemed like fitting weather for her last night in the sheriff's household.

She hung the dishcloth over the little rack under the sink and headed through the living room and down the corridor that led to the bedrooms. Lillie was waiting for her to read a bedtime story, *Bread and Jam for Frances*. Halfway down the hall Lucy paused at the sound of a familiar, gritty voice coming from Sam's room. Her insides somersaulted.

"Henry had no brothers and no sisters. 'I want a brother,' he told his parents. 'Sorry,' they said."

Lucy recognized the excerpt from *Henry and Mudge*.

"Lucy has a brother," Sam interrupted. "She has two brothers. Cam and the vegetarian."

"Veterinarian."

"Yeah."

Jake resumed the story. "Henry had no friends on his street."

Sam stopped him again. "Lucy's my friend."

"Mmm." Jake paused, no doubt waiting to hear what else was on the boy's mind.

"Lucy reads real good." There was a slight pause. "You read real good, too, Daddy."

Lucy's heart squeezed as Sam determinedly defended her against the vague but ever-present charge of incompetence. She heard Jake's low growl. "She reads well."

"She kisses well, too," Sam assured him.

Lucy's cheeks flushed with warmth, and she hurried down the corridor toward Lillie's room. She appreciated Sam's sentiments, but she did not want to hear Jake tell Sam he had no interest in Lucy's kisses. She knew that already.

Several minutes later the adults switched places. Lucy felt a sharp pang as she smoothed her hand over the boy's golden hair for the last time. She'd come to love the Langley twins, perhaps that much more because she identified with their motherless state. She knew Jake intended to marry again as soon as he found the perfect wife. It was the right thing to do. The twins needed a mom, and the sheriff needed a mate.

That thought caused Lucy another pang.

It was too early to go to bed, but Lucy was too restless to sit in the living room and pretend to read a book while Jake watched a pre-season baseball game on TV. She wandered back to the kitchen then out onto the porch. The humidity was high, and a powerful wind pushed thickening clouds across the sky.

April in Maine didn't bring gentle spring showers. It brought rugged weather, sometimes even a flash blizzard. Lucy listened to the steady rumble and watched the first flashes of lightning. She held onto the porch railing, leaned into the wind, and closed her eyes. She wasn't startled when she felt the railing shift. She'd known he was there even before she heard the creak of the screened door because of the way her insides clenched and the hair stood up on the back of her neck.

She opened her eyes just enough to admire the way he lounged against the porch rail, his weight braced on his wrists, the powerful muscles in his arms rippling like long grass in the wind. Not for the first time, she tipped her hat to the genius who had designed the short-sleeved khaki shirt as the universal sheriff's department uniform. And those khaki slacks were a work of art, too, the way they stretched across his flat stomach and muscular thighs. Her cheeks heated in spite of the cool wind. She drew in a deep breath and giggled.

"You smell like strawberry shortcake."

His hard lips twisted into a crooked smile. "That's what comes of sharing a bathroom with a small female. Not very masculine, is it?"

She could have told him his masculinity wouldn't suffer even if he wore ballet shoes with bells on the toes, but she knew he wouldn't want to hear a compliment from her. She was just a kid.

"Maybe not masculine but delicious. You smell good enough to eat."

Jake's eyes narrowed. She'd irritated him. Again. Shoot-a-mile. She just couldn't say anything right around this man. Suddenly a bolt of lightning creased the sky and illuminated his face. She noted the deep grooves in his lean cheeks and the lines of fatigue that radiated from his eyes and sympathy flooded her. It wasn't easy being a single parent, especially one with a brand new career. And a very trying, temporary nanny. "You're tired," she said, softly.

His gaze held hers. "Just old."

She wondered if he really felt old. He had enough experience to lend a hard edge to his carved features, but there was so much gentleness in him. She'd seen it with the kids.

Thunder growled and lightning slapped at the sky. The first drops of rain plopped on their faces.

"So much for stargazing," Jake said. "Let's go inside."

She hesitated. Somehow it was harder to be near him in the confines of the house where they'd eaten together and played Chutes and Ladders, where they'd coordinated their plans for each day just as if they were both parents to Sam and Lillie—just as if they were husband and wife.

Another bolt of lightning shot out of the sky and hit the horizon between the houses behind them on Second Street.

Jake grabbed her hand. "Come on."

His grip was strong and warm, and it sent lightning streaking through her system. It clearly had the opposite effect on the sheriff. The instant they were inside he dropped her hand as if it were radioactive.

"I don't know about you, but I need a drink. Brandy?"

He'd never offered her anything alcoholic before. She spoke before she thought. "What's up with that? Have you finally figured out I'm over twenty-one?"

"I can make it milk."

There was that sarcasm she never heard him use with anyone else. She told herself to ignore it.

One more night.

"Brandy's fine," she said, quietly. "I was just teasing because you always seem to think of me as a kid."

"You're wrong, Lucy." His green eyes gleamed. "I want to think of you as a kid. I've tried my damndest to think of you as a kid. It's getting harder and harder." He turned away from her and headed for the liquor cabinet while she stared after him. What did he mean? Did he feel the chemistry, too?

A rising sense of excitement gripped her. She had to remind herself it didn't mean anything. Jake Langley was far too responsible and disciplined, far too sure of what he really wanted to get thrown off the track by a few hormones. But the idea that he found her desirable at all made her insides feel like an amusement park.

She needed oxygen. She cracked the door. Too late she glimpsed a gray shadow as it brushed her ankles and raced out into the night. Wiggles. Dang. He paused on the top step of the porch. Thunder exploded, and the cat shot into the yard and up the tree. Horizontal rain slammed into the house as the lightning snapped and crackled.

Lucy knew the cat, paralyzed with fear, wouldn't come down until morning. Dang, dang, and double dang. She had no choice. She dashed into the yard.

****

Jake ignored the pricking of his conscience as he located the bottle of brandy in the liquor cabinet in the dining room. He filled a pair of balloon-shaped snifters. They'd have one farewell drink then go to bed. His fingers tightened on the thin stems of the glasses. Separate beds. He paused for a moment and shut his eyes remembering how she'd looked out on the porch—her short, black curls bouncing, her eyes closed, her slim figure pressed against the wind as if it were a lover. Jake's zipper tightened. It was a frustrating phenomenon that happened all too often around Lucy Outlaw.

At first he'd thought the attraction was that restless energy, the same flash and sparkle, the same butterfly magic that had drawn him to Ariel, but it was more than that. During their evenings alone together he'd discovered he was even more turned on by Lucy's stillness.

There was just something about her that he found irresistible, some combination of warmth and innocence and intrepidity. He wanted to be part of that, part of her. It was a hunger he had to ignore. She was too young for him, too young to settle down. He knew the danger. Last time he'd chosen someone too young, he'd wound up alone with two infants. Now he had Sam and Lillie to think about, and he couldn't afford to make that kind of mistake again.

Jake sucked in what he hoped was a calming breath as he shouldered his way through the swinging door that connected the dining room to the kitchen. The empty kitchen. Cold air swept in through the half-opened door. Had she gone back out on the porch? In this storm? He set the glasses down hard enough for the brandy to slosh in the snifters and he strode out into the downpour. Hard needles of rain scored his face and drenched his clothing. His better-than-average night vision was useless tonight. He shielded his eyes with one hand and bellowed into the gale.

"Lucy!"

"Up here."

Her voice was faint in the cacophony of the storm, but Jake's hearing was exceptional, too. His heightened senses and uncanny awareness of danger had helped him stay alive on the streets of L.A. So far they hadn't been of much use in rural Maine. He squinted into the apple tree that had been one of his primary reasons for buying the house. It had looked so all-American, so normal, like something Beaver Cleaver might like to climb.

"What the devil are you doing?"

"Wiggles is stuck up here."

"What?"

"The cat. He's in a panic."

Lightning exploded in front of him, and fear crowded his throat. "The tree's a lightning rod, Lucy!" He used the voice that had struck terror into the hearts of sergeants and criminals alike during his years with the L.A.P.D. "Get down from there. Now."

"I can't. I need both hands to hold onto Wiggles." She sounded scared but determined.

Jake waded into the tempest and started the wet, miserable climb. His booted foot slid on the soaked bark, and the leafless branches ripped into the thin cotton of his uniform shirt. Dammit. He'd get Lucy safely out of the tree and into the house and then he'd kill her.

He finally reached her branch. Her dark hair was plastered against her cheeks, and her eyes were huge dark bruises in her pale face. The hysterical cat arched and yowled. Lucy held onto him with both hands, relying on the tree trunk to keep her balance.

"Don't you ever think?"

"I didn't want Sam and Lillie to wake up to find their cat fried," she explained.

He glared at her. "It would be better to find you that way?"

She attempted a smile. "I'm leaving tomorrow anyway."

Fury raked through him, and he didn't trust himself to answer her.

"Give me the cat."

"But then you won't be able to climb down."

It was the last straw. "Give me the damned cat."

She stuck out her chin in a mutinous gesture but

straightened her arms. Jake jerked the wet creature under his arm and started back down the tree.

As soon as they were inside the house with the door closed, he set the animal on its feet.

"Wait. I should make sure he's okay."

Wiggles tore across the living room and down the hall to Sam's room. Lucy started to follow him. Jake knew he should let her go. Tension coursed through his veins, and his muscles bunched with adrenalin and frustrated desire. He grabbed her upper arm and realized too late that his control was fractured. He loosened his grip immediately, but instead of jerking away from him, she curled into his body like a child seeking shelter. Only she wasn't a child, and he wasn't any kind of shelter. She buried her face in his neck, and he could feel her warm breath against his damp skin. The scent of honeysuckle wafted in the air, and he felt her soft, yielding curves against his hard chest.

"Lucy."

His protest was pathetically weak and she ignored it. She slid her arms around his waist, and he felt himself pulse against her soft stomach. Jesus. This was madness. He told himself to pull away, but she felt so good, so right. He realized she was shivering, and he splayed his fingers against her back. She arched against him, and he felt the hardened nipples through her wet dress and his uniform shirt. His blood surged, and he groaned just as she slid her arms around his neck.

"Hold me," she whispered. "Just this once."

The words calmed him. She was just a kid reacting to a thunderstorm. She needed comfort. That's all. He opened his mouth, intending to whisper the right words, but suddenly her lips were under his and they were moist and wet and welcoming. She made a little gasping sound of need, and he felt himself going over some invisible edge. He parted her lips with his own and plunged his tongue down her throat.

****

Shoot-a-mile. Holy Beelzebub. Dang. Double Dang. Triple Dang. She was finally in his arms, and it was even more exciting than her fantasies. It was the Fourth of July, the Kentucky Derby, and Mardi Gras all mixed together. Her body was as warm and malleable as melted butter coating the hard planes of his body. She felt like part of him but still struggled to get closer. He parted her lips and she felt his tongue stab into her mouth and her world exploded into a kaleidoscope of pixilated color. What was wrong with her? She'd been kissed before. Not like this, though. And not by Jake. He was as hot and melt-in-your-mouth as warm maple syrup on Asia's johnnycakes. He shifted, instantly drawing her attention from his mouth to the hard jut of need that jabbed into her stomach. Holy Moly! She reached behind him to hold his slim hips, and she felt him shudder then helplessly grind against her. A harsh groan hit the air. She slid her fingers into his waistband, eager to touch and stroke that enticing male mystery. It was new territory for her, but she felt no reluctance. This was Jake and he belonged to her. Her fingers brushed the hot, hard erection. His harsh gasp was quickly followed by a high, reedy voice.

"Daddy?"

An instant later Jake's cell rang. He zipped quickly, if gingerly then fumbled his phone out of his pocket.

"Langley." He sounded hoarse.

Lucy could hear his deputy on the other end. Homer Winslow's drawl was slow and distinctive.

"Sorry to bother you, Sheriff," he said, "but we got an anonymous phone call. Seems like someone's left a body out near the rez."

Chapter Two

Jake's fingers dug into her arm hard enough to leave nail marks in the skin. Hard enough to hurt. She winced and stared into the glazed-over emerald eyes. The man needed a moment. He'd answered the phone on autopilot.

Lucy stepped away from him, crossed the room, and crouched by Sam.

"What's the matter, sweetie? Did the storm wake you up?" She thought she sounded remarkably normal.

"Your voice sounds all shaky."

"Does it?" She touched his pajama jacket. It was wet. "An accident?"

"Wiggles got in my bed. He's all wet." The green eyes were so familiar, only Sam's were clear. "You're all wet, too, Lucy."

She laughed. "That's 'cause Wiggles got out in the storm, and your dad and I went to get him." She stood and took his hand. "C'mon. Let's get you some dry sheets."

Sam glanced over his shoulder at his father who'd remained on the other side of the room facing away from them.

"Lucy, what's wrong with Daddy?" Unfortunately, nothing.

"He just got a call from Deputy Winslow," she explained.

"Why is Daddy just standing there?" Lillie had just wandered out to the living room, but even half asleep, she missed nothing. Lucy couldn't blame Jake for failing to turn around.

"He's thinking," Lucy said.

"About what?"

She smiled at the inquisitive child. "About being all wet from rescuing Wiggles and needing a hot shower." Or a cold one.

Lillie peered at Lucy.

"What happened to Wiggles? Did you let him out?"

Lucy laughed. Jake's children were just too darned smart. Lillie had jumped to the obvious—and right—conclusion.

It took about ten minutes to re-make Sam's bed and to re-settle both children. Lucy closed the bedroom door and headed back for the living room. Her heart pounded against her ribs even though she knew it was unlikely that Jake would kiss her again. The spell was broken, and he would tell himself it had been a mistake. And, anyway, there was that call from Homer.

Someone's left a body out by the rez.

It had to be an accident. People in Eden County, Maine, simply didn't kill each other. She found Jake in the kitchen with car keys in his hand.

"Look, I know you're planning to leave in the morning, but I don't know how long I'll be. Can you stick around to get the kids off to school?"

"Of course."

He nodded his thanks. "If I don't see you again, thanks for standing in for Mrs. Peach."

"You're welcome."

21

He was out the door and halfway to his white Chevy Blazer when she remembered. She rushed out into the rain.

"Jake!" He paused and turned back, the rain, now reduced to a slight drizzle, sprinkled his golden hair. "You forgot your hat."

He cursed and loped back up to the house while she ducked back inside to fetch it. She handed it over, and the green eyes met hers.

"That what you wanted to tell me?"

It was hard to breathe with him standing so close.

"Uh, no. With the recital and, well, everything, I forgot to give you a message. A Maxine Slocum called. She wants you to get back to her right away."

The sheriff's sculpted features twisted, and his eyes darkened. "She can damn well wait until Hell freezes over."

Lucy stared at him. Jake was always courteous to everyone with the exception of herself. She couldn't resist the question.

"Who is Maxine Slocum?"

"She's a snake in the grass. A Judas. My ex-wife's mother."

Lucy's jaw dropped. "You mean the twins have a grandma?"

"Not in any way that counts. The woman's a witch. She's got two goals in life: me in a body bag and custody of the twins."

A sense of disbelief swept through Lucy. "Surely not. There must be a misunderstanding."

He smiled, briefly, humorlessly. "You just keep living in Lucyworld. I gotta get back to reality."

Reality. "Do you think there's really a body out

near the rez?"

"Homer's there."

"It has to be a hunting accident."

"At night?"

"Maybe he was killed during the day, and nobody saw it until tonight."

"Dispatch got an anonymous tip."

A shiver ran down her spine. "You think it was the murderer?"

He shrugged.

"There hasn't been a murder in Eden County since, since, well, there's never been one."

Something flared in the emerald eyes, and Lucy knew he was remembering their kiss.

"Darlin', there's a first time for everything."

****

Jake's high-powered flashlight revealed the entry hole just above the T-7 vertebrae. Nate Packer, a developer from Bangor, had been literally shot through the heart, but the wound was not neat and round the way it would have been if caused by a bullet. The rain had washed away most of the blood, but there were jagged tears in his fine wool suit jacket, almost as if he'd been clawed by a very neat, very precise animal. Jake shone the flashlight around. Almost immediately he spotted the bright fletchings on the shaft of an arrow lodged in the thick trunk of a nearby oak. He blinked. The murder weapon? Cupid's arrow gone wrong? Jake peered at the look of shock on the victim's face and decided it was unlikely. The victim had been involved in the construction of a casino and resort for the Penobscot Indians on this very site. The plan had not met with universal approval. If this was murder, it probably had something to do with the project.

It looked like a professional job. The shot had killed cleanly and quickly and in the first try.

Jake rubbed the back of his neck with his palm.

Western Maine was full of hunters, but who among them would have wanted Packer dead? Someone from the rez? God, he hoped not. Law enforcement and jurisdiction issues between the rez and the county were delicate, and Jake had been careful to establish a respectful relationship with Blackbird's sole tribal cop, Davey Tall Tree. The Penobscots were part of the Algonquian band of woodland Indians who'd welcomed the European invaders hundreds of years earlier and who, for their pains, had been stripped of their rights and relegated to a reservation.

Jake had found them to be intelligent, wary, and impossibly poor. The casino they'd agreed to let Nate Packer build would have brought in much-needed cash, but the decision to build had created dissension in the tribe. There was a faction that claimed the casino and spa would increase crime in the quiet backwoods area, a claim that had suddenly proved prescient.

Jake found it hard to believe that the gentle folks he'd met out at the rez could be behind it. But if not the Penobscots, then who?

Had Packer been involved in a business deal gone sour?

Jake's hand stilled, and his stomach clenched as he remembered that Nate's partner in the Blackbird casino project was local banker Cameron Outlaw. Lucy's brother. Jake shook his head. It couldn't be Cam. The man had recently returned to his hometown, giving up a lucrative career as a Boston banker, so that he could raise his small daughter in the cocoon of a small town.

Not unlike Jake.

In any case, Cam Outlaw was not exactly the Deliverance type. If he had had a falling out with his partner, he'd have sought a legal remedy.

Could it have been an accident? Jake tried to create a plausible picture. Could somebody, desperate to put food on his family's table, have been hunting small prey near the casino site? But what about the anonymous tip?

His years as an L.A. detective had taught him the danger of trying to bend the facts to fit a preferred interpretation. He'd learned the same lesson from his short marriage. At least in crime the motives were usually straightforward.

It almost always boiled down to greed.

Jake got to his feet and paced the length of the crime scene. The body formed the third point of an equilateral triangle along with Packer's car, a smoke-gray Jag, and the construction trailer. The symmetry caught his eye. It was almost as if the killer had staged a presentation. If so, why? He blinked. The body was on county land, but the reservation border was only about twenty feet away. Had the killer wanted to keep the investigation out of tribal hands?

Jake had met Packer a few times. The guy had been short but powerfully built, ruddy-faced, with the cockiness of a born salesman. Tonight his expensive pinstriped suit was waterlogged and muddy, his body was crumpled like a downed helium balloon, and what Jake could see of his face looked waxy in the spill of light from the flashlight.

Jake had attended dozens of funerals in his

lifetime. It always amazed him to hear the deceased described as lifelike. There was nothing lifelike about the man on the ground. Whatever had made Nate Packer human was long gone leaving behind only a rotting rind, like the white flesh of a watermelon.

Death was, after all, the great leveler.

Jake knelt next to the body and searched the dead man's pockets and found a slim, calfskin wallet that included a dozen credit cards but no cash. He slid his fingers into a hidden pocket and found a foil-covered packet. A condom. That seemed odd. Jake knew Packer had recently married the delectable Paula, a trophy wife if ever there was one. Why the need for a wallet condom? Maybe he was a former boy scout and always liked to be prepared.

Or, maybe, he'd been caught messing around with someone else's woman.

Perhaps the arrow had come from Cupid's quiver, after all.

The rain started up again. Jake turned up the collar of his lightweight jacket, but not before the cold drops slid down the inside of his shirt. Homer had taken photos of the footprints in the mud, but they had to wait for the medical examiner and the forensic team from Augusta before they could get out of the weather.

Homer Winslow, short, skinny, and twenty years Jake's senior, crossed the open field, the site of the proposed casino.

"Jag's clean as a whistle."

Jake nodded. Tomorrow would be soon enough to go through the construction trailer. As soon as the boys from Augusta arrived, they'd rope off the area, examine the body, and remove it. Then Jake would have the unenviable task of driving to Bangor to alert the next of kin. And to collect alibis.

He nodded at the arrow stuck in the damp bark of one of the few trees left on the casino site.

"Got an evidence bag?"

The answer was, of course, 'yes.' The deputy had never sought the county's top law enforcement job. He'd refused even the temporary post after Sheriff Poxey's death last year, luckily for Jake, who'd answered the 'help wanted' ad in *Law Officer's Magazine*. Nevertheless, Homer took his job seriously. He was diligent and always prepared. It was unlikely any fingerprints would have survived the rain, but Homer wore plastic gloves to extract the arrow from the tree trunk.

Jake shone his light on the weapon. He didn't know a helluva lot about arrows, but he realized the arrowhead on this specimen was abnormally long and narrow, like the head of a cobra. The fletchings at the base were red, yellow, and orange. Was that significant? Probably, to its owner. Arrows were as individual as golf clubs which made this an important clue.

Jake stood with his back to the battering rain and hunched his shoulders. After a few moments, Homer spoke.

"Got to be one of them Indians."

"It's possible."

"The perp used a bow and arrow." Homer had a tendency to state the obvious.

"There are lots of crack archers in the world."

"This ain't the world. It's Eden County."

The man had a point. Eden, with its population of

twenty-eight hundred was the county seat. If there were any world-class archers in their jurisdiction someone would know. Uncannily, Homer answered the unspoken question.

"Outside of the Indians there's only one guy around here who could shoot a bull's eye into a man's heart," he said, slowly. Homer might be a rural sheriff's deputy, but he knew the power of a dramatic pause. "He was on the national team when he was a kid. Don't know if he's kept up with it."

Jake told himself to be patient. After all, he owed the man for accepting a younger boss, a city cop from L.A. And everybody deserved the occasional moment of drama. He waited.

"I think it was the Junior National team."

Who was it?

"Uh-huh."

"He usta hang around the rez, too. Cause of that girl."

Jake was getting a bad feeling about this. He ground his back teeth and kept his mouth shut.

"His daddy didn't like it none, either. Mavis, that's the wife, Mavis always thought Dr. Outlaw busted them up when Cam was away at college.

Still, he's a good boy. I can't believe he'd shoot down a man in cold blood."

A cold finger of dread worked its way down Jake's spine and his stomach roiled. "Cameron Outlaw?"

"He was a natural. Coulda made it to the Olympics, some folks said."

Cameron Outlaw, who was Packer's partner in the casino venture. Cameron Outlaw, Eden's golden boy, a widower and single dad, like himself.

Cameron Outlaw, Lucy's brother. Well, hell.

Blackbird's tribal cop appeared at the eleventh hour, some thirty minutes behind the boys from Augusta. Davey Tall Tree, big, moon-faced and slow as molasses in January wore his usual pleasant but vague expression. He reminded Jake of a recently awakened Pillsbury Doughboy, rumpled and sleepy-eyed.

"Sheriff," he said. "What's happened here?"

Jake shook the officer's extended hand and explained what he knew so far.

"Man was shot with a bow and arrow you say?"

Jake showed him the bagged arrow. "Do you recognize this?"

Davey's dark eyes widened in his pudgy face. "Yeah. It's from the museum."

Jake knew the museum of Penobscot memorabilia was located in an annex tacked onto the back of Cully's Trading Post, a general store slash-souvenir shop that was, in turn, connected to the tribe's community center which included Davey's office. Did that mean the perp was a reservation resident? Jake knew better than to jump to that conclusion.

"Who had access to it?"

The heavy shoulders lifted and fell. "Everybody. Museum's not locked when the Trading Post is open."

"If the arrow was on display it must be unusual."

Davey bobbed his head. "We say it's a war arrow from the last of the battles with white settlers."

"You say it's a war arrow?"

Davey's smile was self-deprecating. "Most of the 1800s were peaceful for us. It's unlikely this arrow's over two hundred years old. Most probably it was used for hunting fifty years ago but 'war arrow' sounds, you know, cooler."

Jake contemplated Davey's words. Had the killer chosen the fake war arrow because of its designation? Or was this an effort to cast suspicion on the tribe?

The tribal chief, Jake knew, spent most of his time jawing with a group of old men at the community center.

"Seen anyone unusual around the trading post lately?"

Davey closed his eyes and cocked his head. "Mr. Packer and Mr. Outlaw and some men from the county were out the other day."

Mr. Outlaw. Jake ignored the ripple of unease. "You have any idea when this arrow went missing?"

Davey shrugged. "I'll check with Cully. You know how it is. When you're around stuff all the time, you don't really notice it."

Jake would ask Cully, too. And he'd ask everybody else who'd been to the Trading Post in the past week.

"Did you see Packer on the rez earlier tonight?"

Davey's response was slow, but Jake didn't read anything into that. He'd observed the tendency to hesitate in many of the Penobscots. He figured it was cultural, a sign of respect, the same as the habit of pausing outside a dwelling to give the inhabitant time to adjust to the prospect of a visit.

"Mr. Packer was at the Tribal council meeting with his lawyer and Mr. Outlaw. It got out around nine."

Jake's lips tightened into a straight line. He'd talk with Packer's family first, but he couldn't eliminate Cam's name from the "A" list.

The coroner's brief examination of the body in situ elicited the information that he'd been dead a couple of hours. It was now nearly midnight. Packer must have stepped out of the Tribal Council meeting and met his death within thirty to sixty minutes. The odds were his killer had attended the meeting, too.

"What happened at the meeting?"

Davey hesitated, and again, Jake held onto his patience.

"It went pretty smooth, but afterwards there was an argument."

"Between Tribal elders and Packer?"

"No. Between Packer and Outlaw."

A pit formed in Jake's stomach. He frowned. "They argued in front of you?"

"No. Outside. Afterwards. We, that is the tribal elders, asked Mr. Packer for a list of his subcontractors. There'd been rumors the Jersey mob was involved, and we wanted to make sure we weren't getting gangsters up here. The names sounded all right to me but Mr. Outlaw looked kinda surprised and I heard them talking about it outside by the cars. Mr. Packer didn't take him serious. He laughed and said they had to get the stuff from somewhere. Then Mr. Outlaw kinda lost his temper.

He told Mr. Packer he wasn't gonna do business with a crook. It got pretty loud."

Jake ignored the ice forming in his gut. "Did you see either of them leave?"

"Yep. Packer spun out of here in his Jag and Outlaw left awhile later in his Mercedes."

"Awhile? Ten minutes? Fifteen minutes?"

"'Bout that. Somewhere's around nine fifteen, I'd guess."

So Cameron Outlaw needed a rock-solid alibi for

the hour after the Tribal Council meeting. Jake hoped he had it. He wondered if he should roust him now and decided not. The guy had a kid. He wasn't going anywhere. Morning would be soon enough.

Morning, when Lucy Outlaw would be out of his house and out of his life, for good.

The prospect should have made him happier.

****

By nine a.m. Lucy was climbing into her ten-year-old navy blue Jeep Explorer. Jake had returned to the house around three a.m., but he had not poked his head out of his room this morning, not even to see the kids off to school. He was probably trying to avoid her, Lucy thought, sourly.

It helped to be offended. It was better than dealing with the cavern of emptiness under her heart.

The gearshift tended to stick in moist weather, and she had to shove it hard. So that was that. Not that it was a surprise. Except for those few surreal moments last night, Jake had never pretended to have an interest in her. Everyone in town knew he was hunting for a stepmom for his kids. Everyone in town knew that Lucy was too young and flaky to be a parent. Besides, she had definite career ambitions. A future with Jake, well, it wouldn't have worked out anyway.

She blinked hard as her tires kicked up rivulets of water on either side of the street. The sky had cleared and the temperature dropped. Spring weather in western Maine was so wacky that while April showers could turn into May flowers, they, just as easily, could turn into a raging nor'easter.

Lucy swallowed around the lump in her throat. This morning, she was supremely uninterested in the weather.

She parked next to the carriage house behind the big, fieldstone Outlaw family home on Walnut Street. Lucy had recently moved out of her pink-and-white bedroom in the main house and into the loft apartment in the outbuilding above the veterinary clinic owned and run by Lucy's brother, Baz, and his new wife, Hallie. Regret tugged at Lucy's heart. Hallie Scott Outlaw was everything Lucy was not: mature, maternal, organized, and the kindest person Lucy had ever met. Jake had wanted to marry her before Baz swept into town and staked a prior claim.

As much as Lucy had loved getting to know Baz, and as perfect as he and his wife were together, sometimes Lucy wished he hadn't come back. Hallie would be married to Jake now and she, Lucy, would never have had the addicting experience of living in the Langley household.

She dragged herself up the outside staircase to her apartment, dropped her suitcase, and dialed Ed Stiles over at the *Eden Excelsior*.

It was time to get a real job.

"Talk about timing." Ed Stiles, red-headed, portly and very fond of putting his feet up on the desk, had been a friend of her father's. "As it happens I've just gotten an opening. Tammy Winslow quit last week after she made the junior varsity soccer team."

Lucy had no intention of becoming Ed's girl Friday, but she figured she'd tell him that after he hired her.

"Great. When can I start?"

"How 'bout last week?"

"How about today?"

"Come on over."

Forty minutes later Lucy entered the square, stand-alone building on Third Street, a block from Main, and across from the Pink Poodle hair salon that housed the *Excelsior*'s offices.

Ed swung his feet down from his desk and pushed his bulk to his feet.

"Welcome aboard," he said, around the stogie in his mouth. "Let me show you around. This is the newsroom." He swept out an arm intended to include a pair of battered desks topped with computers that looked to be nearly as old as Lucy, a hotplate and coffee pot, stacks of bundled newspapers, some reporters' notebooks, and pencils. "And that's the bathroom."

Lucy peered into a tiny dark cubicle.

"Your tasks include cleaning the toilet and coffeepot, compiling high school sports scores, checking the three funeral homes in the county, typing up the copy sent in by Esther Wheelhouse over at St. Barnabas, PTA notes from Fran Sietsma and notices from Gladys Semple at the Volunteer Fire Department

Auxiliary."

"That's it?"

"You'll be writing all the headlines and laying out pages, too. Oh, and you'll be covering the county board meetings at the Town Hall on alternate Mondays, the school board every fourth Tuesday, and the Planning Commission every third Thursday."

"Fine," she said. "What about breaking news? You know, like the body out at the casino site?"

"You already know about that? J.C., girl," he said, using his own shorthand for cursing, "you are well connected." He squinted at her. "That why you wanted this job?"

"I was going to call you anyway."

The truth was, she hadn't thought about covering the sheriff's department until that minute.

"I would like the experience, though, since my long-term plan is to become a war correspondent."

"You study journalism at the university?"

"Some." She'd also studied Russian literature, opera appreciation, classical Latin, and the Indian subcontinent among other interesting and varied subjects that had, unfortunately, not prepared her for employment.

"You think you can handle a murder investigation?"

She sucked in a breath. So it was murder.

"Absolutely," she told him.

He gave her a sideways look. His eyes were small, round, and dark brown. Like chocolate M&Ms. "Langley won't like it."

Lucy swallowed a groan. That was the trouble with small towns. Everyone knew Jake's opinion of her.

"I'll do a good job. I promise."

Ed nodded, slowly. "I believe you will. But, Lucy, I want you to stay out of trouble."

She refused to be offended. This was too important. This was her chance. She had a sudden brainstorm.

"Do you mind if I try to peddle a feature on this to the *Hartford Courier*?

"Not so long's I get my page one story first every week."

"Thanks."

When Ed cocked his head to one side he reminded Lucy of a plump, fluffy pigeon.

"A war correspondent, huh?"

While he poured them each a cup of coffee from the ancient, battered percolator, she told him about her plan to win a Pulitzer Prize covering war in the Middle East.

He leaned back in the cracked leather chair behind his big, wooden desk and parked his crossed ankles on top of it while she occupied the smaller metal desk that was so old it had a pull-out drawer for a typewriter.

"What's more newsworthy than war? I mean, it's got everything: life, death, heroism and sacrifice, danger and drama. Definitely worth writing about."

He picked up a paperclip and unbent it. Lucy noticed a small pile of similarly tortured wire bits on a corner of his desk, sort of a paper-clip graveyard. She held back a smile while he considered his response.

"There's plenty of drama in a small town, girl. The human condition is inherently dramatic. We have our share of love and hate, life and death. It's just from a different perspective. An ant's eye view, if you will. Big canvas versus small canvas. Each has its points."

A small town wouldn't work in the long run, Lucy thought. She had too much to prove.

"What made you decide to go with small canvas?"

He barked a laugh. "I was in a war, Luce. Vietnam. I'd never willingly go back to that kind of hell."

"But you've got to admit it's hard to win a Pulitzer covering the library budget and the Homecoming Day parade."

Ed had picked up another hapless paperclip. He paused before unbending it. "That what you're after?

Awards?"

"Sure. I want people to know what I can do." She heard the defensiveness in the words.

"What people?"

"The whole world. Everybody."

"You mean everybody in Eden. You worryin' about that screw-up thing? Honey, you've got to learn it doesn't matter what anybody else thinks."

She made a face. "You don't know what it's like to have people expecting you to mess up, Ed. I can't tell you how many times I've had people elbow me in the ribs and say, 'Lucy, you got some 'splainin' to do.'"

Ed smiled. "It's just because they love you."

"Huh. That makes it worse. It makes me feel like a baby, like my screw-ups are cute."

"Can't get no respect?"

She knew he was teasing her, but he wasn't wrong.

"Self-respect, Luce," he said. "That's what it's all about. When you figure that out, you'll be grown up. Just do a good job of covering the story."

Lucy's heart thumped hard. She wasn't worried about covering the story. How hard could it be? Who, what, where, when, and why, right? She was a tad nervous about stalking Jake Langley. She smiled brightly and picked up the phone. Homer informed her the sheriff was out and wouldn't be back, but he filled her in on everything he knew, including the name of the victim, the weapon, and the time of death. As soon as she hung up, she called the editor in Hartford and arranged for the freelance assignment. A moment later her phone rang again.

This time it was Hallie. The sisters-in-law had developed the habit of taking Cam's daughter Daisy and Hallie's infant son, Robert to Little Joe's Tavern and Pizza Emporium on Friday nights to meet Jake's twins accompanied by Mrs. Peach.

"Mrs. P. called to say the twins want to see us," Hallie said, "and Robert's got a cold. Since the weather's getting bad again, I don't want to take him out." Lucy understood the dilemma. Hallie was fiercely protective of her newly adopted son, but she didn't want Daisy, who was having trouble adjusting to the newcomer, to miss out on her weekly treat. "Think you could take Daisy alone tonight?"

Lucy wrinkled her nose. She'd just as soon not be reminded of how much she missed Sam and Lillie and their stubborn father, but this wasn't about her. And, anyway, she'd have to start hanging out around Jake tomorrow.

"Of course I can take her. I'll pick her up at six."

Chapter Three

Cold winds swept into western Maine on the heels of the thunderstorms, and the temperature dipped into the thirties. Lucy threw on a pair of worn jeans and tennis shoes, a paint-spattered UConn sweatshirt, and a quilted vest. She ran a comb through her short, dark curls and washed her face but didn't bother with makeup. The kids and Mrs. Peach wouldn't care how glamorous she looked. Daisy, however, looked adorable in a purple sweater and matching corduroy pants. Her blonde curls danced around a beautiful face only slightly marred by a sulkily, protruding lower lip.

"I hate Robert," the five-year-old confided, as Lucy buckled her into her car seat.

There was no question that Daisy's world had taken a direct hit with the arrival of the new baby.

"I'm pretty sure Robert doesn't hate you. I saw him smile at you the other day."

"Asia says that's just gas."

"Maybe. But I know he likes it when he sees you and Wilbur. He always kicks his feet." Wilbur was Daisy's extremely pampered potbellied pig.

"Robert likes Hallie best."

"Well, sure," Lucy said, not thinking. "Hallie's his mom."

Daisy's small face puckered.

"I don't got a mom," she announced, as if it were

39

news. "Sam and Lillie doesn't got one neither."

Oh Lord. Lucy knew she should have spoken more carefully. Neither Daisy nor Sam nor Lillie had ever known their mothers, but that didn't make the lack less painful. Lucy sifted her fingers through the pale ringlets.

"Next year I'm gonna take ballet lessons like Lillie," Daisy said. "And you can put bells on the shoes so I can shoot 'em at everybody. Especially Robert."

"Of course," Lucy murmured, hoping that sometime in the next twelve months Daisy would have adjusted to the baby. She parked on Main Street in front of the eatery, and they hurried inside, luxuriating in the warm air, the smell of pizza, and the clinking and clanking of pinball machines.

"Luuucy!"

Lillie's piping voice lifted above the din, and a moment later she and her brother launched themselves at their former nanny, each of them claiming one jeans-clad leg.

"We all missed you," Lillie spoke into the denim.

"Especially Lucy Junior," Sam added. "And Daddy."

Lucy knew the child's comment reflected his own feelings not those of his father, but her heart thumped anyway.

"I missed you guys, too."

Lillie let go first. She grabbed Daisy's hand.

"C'mon," she said. "Let's go play skee ball."

Daisy looked at her aunt. "Can I?"

"Sure, honey." Lucy dug into her purse and brought out a handful of quarters. "I'll just go hang out with Mrs. Peach at the table."

"Mrs. P. isn't here," Sam said. "We comed with Daddy."

Daddy. Lucy felt her breath stop in her chest. She looked across the room and there he was, standing by the table, looking breathtakingly tall and broad-shouldered, his sculpted features molded into a stern mask. Not for the first time she wondered about his late wife. What had possessed the woman to leave a man like Jake, much less her adorable children? Lucy realized, belatedly, that the emerald eyes were focused on her and that the sheriff was not smiling.

She straightened her spine and tried not to take it personally. Jake had never wanted her around and the mutual awareness that had made her heart sing had been a burr under his saddle. Maybe it was a good thing she looked like a refugee from an all-night study session. He wouldn't have to be irritated tonight.

Resigned to an hour of awkwardness, she threaded her way through the tables of families. It wasn't until she reached him that she realized he had traded in his khaki uniform shirt for a moss-green pullover. The color brought out the gold flecks in his green eyes. He had the longest eyelashes she'd ever seen on a man and often had the effect of softening his severe expression. Now, though, was not one of those times. She noticed the scent of strawberry shortcake shampoo was gone, replaced by something dark and sexy. Calvin Klein?

"Good evening, Lucy," he said, oddly formal. He gestured to a chair then seated himself next to a woman she didn't know.

"This is Marilyn Hart."

Lucy felt her jaw drop. He was on a date?

The woman's lush mouth stretched wide revealing

what had to be double rows of gleaming white teeth. The short, sleek style of her blonde streaked hair had come from somewhere more sophisticated than the Pink Poodle, and she wore a form-fitting gray cashmere sweater that hugged her ample curves. A strand of luminescent pearls rivaled the glow of her teeth.

"Marilyn just took over Staghorn Realty."

Lucy's eyes widened. "Staghorn Realty? What happened to Hank?"

Marilyn's laugh sounded like dozens of silvery bells, light, tinkly, practiced.

"Hank decided to spend the rest of his adolescence in the Bahamas," she said. "He's my ex, you know. Several years back."

Of course. Hank's last name was Hart. He wasn't a native, but he had sold houses in Eden for at least twenty years.

"You couldn't have been married long."

"Longest eighteen months of my life," Marilyn said. "Even though it was a long-distance marriage. I stayed in Augusta."

A horrifying thought struck Lucy. She gaped at Jake. "Oh my gosh! Does this mean you're selling the house?"

The green eyes squinted, dangerously.

"This isn't a business dinner," Marilyn said, with a coy smile. "Jake was nice enough to rescue me from a lonely evening with a frozen diet dinner of shrimp marinara." She smiled and the overhead lights bounced off the gleam of her smile. So it was a date. A date with a real-estate-peddling shark. "The evening's purely social," Marilyn added, no doubt wanting to make sure Lucy understood where things stood.

Fantastic. She'd get to spend the evening watching Hank Hart's ex audition for the role of the second Mrs. Jake Langley.

"Lucy," Jake said, baring his teeth at her, "was our temporary nanny."

Lucy had to give him credit. He'd managed to marginalize her in five words. More teeth showed, and Marilyn's beautifully lined eyes flashed as she correctly interpreted Jake's message: No competition here.

"I was just helping out while Mrs. Peach was away," Lucy said, through her teeth. "I started a new job this afternoon. At the *Eden Excelsior*."

"Ah, a news hen," Marilyn said.

Jake snorted. "News hen? You must be taking over for Tammy Winslow. Homer told me she made J.V."

Tammy was the deputy's niece. Eden didn't really need a newspaper, not with the efficiency of the grapevine.

"I'll take on some of Tammy's duties, of course, but I'll also be covering the murder out at the rez."

Jake scowled, but Marilyn spoke before he could open his mouth.

"Oh, I heard about that. It was a developer from Bangor, right? Nate Packer?"

Lucy held very still. Nate Packer was the murder victim? Nate Packer, her brother's partner? She realized she'd never even asked who had been killed.

"I must say I envy you getting to take care of such lovely children," Marilyn said, obviously wanting to make the most of her time with Jake and savvy enough to know the kids were the way to his heart. "Sam and Lillie are beautiful." She flashed a disarmingly flirtatious grin at the sheriff. "They look so much like their father."

The realtor exuded come-hither sparks. There was no question in Lucy's mind that Marilyn Hart wanted Jake Langley. Not a big surprise. Who wouldn't want the sexy sheriff?

"I should take off," she said. "And let you two be alone."

"Nonsense." Jake's voice was louder than usual. "I'm sure Marilyn wouldn't want to miss a chance to eat with Eden's Lois Lane. And, anyway, we've ordered enough pizza for an army." The realtor excused herself to freshen up.

"She seems nice," Lucy said, after she'd left.

"Hmmm," Jake said, noncommittally. He seemed disinclined to discuss his date.

"Hey, Luce." Janie Chadwick, Little Joe's premier waitress, plunked a steaming metal tray of pizza on the red-and-white checked oilcloth. A cheerleader for Eden Consolidated who had graduated a year after Lucy, Janie was short with a trim athletic figure, a blonde ponytail and an oversized personality. "When I saw the big man come in, I figured you'd be on his trail, so I decorated half of one pie with mushrooms the way you like it." She turned to Jake. "What's up with the old broad, Sheriff? You double-dipping tonight?"

Lucy braced herself for an explosion, but Jake's voice was gently teasing.

"If you want a tip you'd better watch your tongue."

Janie leaned over the man's broad shoulder until her breasts were against his back and her cute little nose was next to his.

"I'd much rather watch your tongue, Sheriff," she drawled.

"Scamp," Jake said.

Indignation rose in her throat as she watched Janie's swishing hips disappear into the crowd. Jake had made it crystal clear Lucy, at age twenty-two, was too young for a thirty-five-year-old man, and yet he'd been flirting with Janie who was even younger. What a hypocrite!

Jake focused on separating the pieces of pizza and plopping them onto the paper plates. He didn't look at Lucy.

"I know what you're thinking, but it's different with Janie."

"Different how?"

"You know how."

His voice dropped into the low, intimate register that turned her insides into a Ferris wheel. She supposed it was a compliment of sorts. He was free to flirt with Janie because there was no chemistry. Did he feel the sparks with the oh-so-eligible Marilyn Hart? She was certainly old enough, Lucy thought, uncharitably. Probably five or six years older than Jake.

"Speaking of age, isn't Mrs. Hart a little long-in the-tooth?"

Jake glanced at her.

"Stay out of my business, Lucy."

There was no way to make an early exit because Daisy was having so much fun with Sam and Lillie. Lucy devoted herself to the children as soon as they returned to the table. She tried to ignore the sound of Marilyn's pleasant small talk punctuated with suggestive hints. It was depressingly obvious that, if nothing else, the sheriff had hit the sexual jackpot.

Lucy felt a physical pain in her chest when she said

goodbye to the twins. She'd opt out from these evenings in the future. It was just too painful to spend time with the family she'd grown to love, the family that would never be hers. She hoped Marilyn Hart was fond of white mice.

"Lillie thinks her daddy is gonna marry that lady with the teeth," Daisy said, while Lucy tucked her into bed. "I wish my daddy would marry

someone."

Lucy kissed the little girl's cheek.

"He will. Just give him time to find the right mommy for you."

The child looked solemn. "Then Robert won't be the only one with a mom!"

Lucy went down the back staircase intending to head out to her apartment, but she stopped when she noticed the strip of light under the door of her father's study. Baz and Hallie were upstairs with Robert. It had to be Cam. She knocked on the door.

Cameron Outlaw, a decade older than Lucy, was a hair over six feet tall, broad-shouldered but slender. His eyes were the same sky-blue as Lucy's, but his were more striking because of his natural tan, his lean face, and his angular features. His sudden warm smile spelled danger to any nearby female heart.

Tonight there were dark crescents under his eyes and grim lines bracketed his thin lips.

"I heard about your partner," she said. "I'm sorry."

"Thanks."

Cam had stood when she entered, an example of the excellent manners they'd both learned from their father's housekeeper, Asia. He motioned for Lucy to take a seat on the old leather sofa that sagged in the middle where their late father had taken so many cat naps, while he settled himself behind the big walnut desk and dropped his head against the backrest of the leather-padded chair. Just for a moment he closed his eyes. He looked exhausted.

"I'm working for Ed Stiles," she said, knowing Cam would wonder if Ed had lost his mind hiring Calamity Lucy. "He's letting me cover the murder."

Cam's eyes snapped open, and he sat up abruptly. She braced herself for the inevitable protest.

"Good for you, Squirt." He slid long fingers through his thick, black hair. "Guess you'll be writing about me."

The warm pleasure triggered by his initial reaction disappeared as sarcasm entered his voice.

"I wasn't just his partner, you know," Cam went on, "I was the last person to see him alive and thus, the chief suspect."

Lucy's heart jumped into her throat, and she jumped out of her chair. "Is that what Jake said? That's just plain ridiculous, Cam. You'd never kill a man. I mean, you're a father for goodness sake."

"Calm down, Luce." He motioned her back to her seat. "I haven't been charged or anything. But there's only a forty-five-minute gap between when I argued with him outside the Tribal Council meeting and the time he died. Whoever killed him had to have worked fast and been more than a little lucky."

"But you were on your way home. You wouldn't have had time to kill Packer. All you have to do is have Hallie or Baz tell Jake what time you walked in the door."

She waited for him to agree with her but he was

47

silent.

"Cam?"

"I didn't leave the rez right away," he said. The words were quiet, and his sentences uncharacteristically disjointed. He was obviously reluctant to explain. Why?

"I was angry because Packer had signed contracts for inferior materials. I kept imagining the whole structure caving in from the weight of snow on the roof. We yelled at each other outside the community center, and then I took off. I drove around the rez for a while, trying to decide what to do. Finally I got sleepy and pulled off into a lay-by of some sort. It was dawn when I woke up." She stared at him.

"You didn't come home? You always come home. Because of Daisy."

Color flared on his razor-sharp cheekbones.

"I don't neglect her, of course. But Asia's here, as well as Baz and Hallie."

Lucy searched her memory. She'd lived in the house for several months after college, and she couldn't remember even one instance of Cam staying out all night.

"You said you got sleepy, but the rez is only fifteen miles from here. Surely you could have made it."

He shrugged. "I didn't want to risk an accident."

"So you slept in the car all night."

He said nothing.

"Cam, that's a horrible alibi."

"It's the truth."

She tried to think. "It won't matter in the long run. I mean, Jake will find out who did kill Packer. You can't be a serious suspect. Good grief! You're a pillar of society, Eden's golden boy. Probably Jake won't even ask for an alibi."

"Calm down, Squirt. You're right about one thing. Jake won't be able to prove I killed anyone. I'm not worried about it."

"Of course not," Lucy said, bracingly. "I'm not worried, either." But she was worried. Cam was lying about something.

"How did Packer die, anyway?" Cam's blue eyes were level on her face. "He was shot. With a bow and arrow." Lucy's heart jerked as she held his gaze. Neither bothered to mention the fact that, at one time, Cam had been one of the best archers in New England.

"A bow and arrow." Lucy frowned. "That's an unusual way to commit murder."

"Yeah."

"Was the fight really about inferior building materials?"

Her brother let his head drop back again. He closed his eyes. "That was part of it. The jackass was dealing with mob-connected subcontractors, too."

Lucy thought about the partnership between the two men, about the trust that had been violated.

"And you weren't aware of any of this until it was too late?"

There was a short, uncomfortable silence.

"I dropped the ball. Once the thing was approved, I let him carry on. I didn't want to waste time out at the construction site."

"What will you do now, about the casino and spa, I mean?"

"Assuming I'm not cooling my heels in prison, I'll find another contractor."

"You couldn't just drop the project?"

There was another silence. "No. The tribe is counting on the jobs and the revenue."

Suddenly Lucy remembered. Ten or twelve years earlier, when she'd been a child and Cam, a teenager, he'd been fascinated with Blackbird Reservation and a girl who lived there. His relationship with Molly Whitecloud, a classmate who was now the reservation's midwife, had been over for more than a decade. Was that old relationship the reason he felt such a loyalty to the Penobscot Tribe? Did it explain why he didn't want to spend any unnecessary time out at the rez?

There was something Cam wasn't telling Lucy.

"Packer, Inc. had a good reputation," Cam explained. That's why I approached Nate in the first place. I wasn't expecting any trouble from that quarter, but I should have been paying more attention. Like I said, it was my bad."

Lucy tried to think.

"Did anyone on the rez know Packer was getting them involved with the mob?"

He shrugged. "It's possible. There's definitely a younger element that doesn't want the casino at all."

Lucy brightened. "Maybe one of them killed Packer. Do you have a contact out there?"

He shook his head. "I tried to keep my distance."

"Maybe," Lucy said, carefully, "Molly Whitecloud would know."

She watched a muscle jerk in his jaw, and she knew, instantly, that her brother still had feelings for the Penobscot woman. How strong were they? Was he still in love with her? Or, had young love turned to perpetual hatred?

"I know Molly," Lucy said, "through Hallie. She's

lovely, Cam. I know she wouldn't have had a hand in Nate Packer's death."

His lips tightened. Lucy knew he didn't want to talk about his former flame, but she decided to ask the question, anyway.

"Why did you two break up?"

She held her breath, certain he'd slap away her question like an annoying mosquito. He didn't.

"She broke up with me. My freshman year at college I came home at Christmas to find her married to someone else."

A knife twisted in Lucy's heart. Poor Cam.

"It was no big deal, Squirt. A long-dead high school romance, that's all."

There was more to it than that. Lucy knew her brother. Nothing fazed him, normally, not a dead wife, or a motherless daughter, or a major career/lifestyle change. He wasn't just exhausted now; he was all but undone. Whether he was willing to acknowledge it or not, Molly Whitecloud was still important to him.

****

Jake gritted his teeth as he closed the door to Sam's room. From the moment they'd left Little Joe's, he heard a nonstop diatribe about how much each of the twins missed Lucy, how much she missed them, and why couldn't Lucy come to live at their house and be their mother?

Suffice it to say, the Lucy talk had not helped him forget about the way she'd looked when she'd thought he was dating the realtor; like he'd just drop-kicked her puppy. Or her heart.

He knew it was just a school girl's crush, but it was damn hard to resist those big blue eyes, the winsome smile, and the willowy body that didn't remind him of a school girl at all. When he'd held her softness against his hardness the other night, she'd fit him perfectly. Her body had fired a surge of need he hadn't felt in years except for the other times he'd been in her vicinity. As it had from their first meeting, her exasperating combination of enthusiasm and uncertainty had twisted his heart and sent jolts of treacherous desire through his body. He'd kept his hands off Lucy for her own good, couldn't she understand that?

He knew she couldn't. She was too damned young to understand. He fought the temptation to call her up to explain that Marilyn Hart had manipulated him into dinner at Little Joe's. It wouldn't change anything and it might give her false hope. She'd get over her crush faster if she believed he was interested in someone else.

As for himself, well, he'd just been without a woman for too long, and there was nothing wrong with Marilyn Hart. He couldn't really imagine her as the twins' stepmother, but then his instincts were unreliable. He'd never anticipated that their real mother would run off with a skydiving instructor a couple of months after their birth.

Jake felt the old anger, but it wasn't as intense this time. It had been his fault, after all, he'd been star struck and foolish, and he'd married a woman who was much too young. He'd never make that mistake again. Never.

Jake wandered out to the living room and dropped onto the red-and-green plaid sofa chosen by Lillie because "it looked like Christmas." He slumped down until he was almost horizontal then he balanced a can of beer on his belly. It had been a mistake to hire Lucy to fill in for Mrs. Peach. He'd been attracted to her from the first, even when he'd fully intended to marry Hallie Scott. He was still attracted to her. What's more, he had to find a second wife and soon. Ariel's mother, pissed that he refused to take the twins down to the farm in Texas, had threatened to haul his ass into court unless he provided Sam and Lillie with a more wholesome environment, i.e. a two-parent home.

Hell.

He wanted both Maxine and Lucy out of his life, and for that to happen, he'd have to marry someone. Marilyn Hart? Shit.

Jake reached into his pocket and pulled out the cell phone in which Marilyn Hart had playfully stored her number. He'd take her out to dinner tomorrow night and see what happened. She might not be the perfect stepmom, but she had one sterling quality that he couldn't ignore: she wasn't Lucy.

****

Saturday morning the sky was a blanket of clouds and the mercury hovered around thirty degrees. Perfect conditions for a late spring nor'easter. Lucy considered searching for a weather report on the Jeep's radio as she headed for the sheriff's office, but she decided not to bother. At the moment, the weather was not her top priority. She intended to start her coverage of Nate Packer's murder by making certain her brother wasn't on the list of suspects.

The Eden Town Hall on Main Street, a square, brick structure built in the late nineteenth century, was still used for meetings of the county board of commissioners, the library board, the school board and for town hall meetings. One small corner of it was dedicated to the Eden County sheriff.

As Lucy pulled into a diagonal space next to the sheriff's white Blazer, butterflies battled inside her stomach. The heightened awareness she always felt around Jake was compounded by anxiety over her brother, a sense of excitement about covering the murder investigation and the knowledge that, because of her jealousy, she and Jake had not parted as friends. She turned off the engine and strode through the glass-fronted doors. The sheriff's office was down the hall on the right and, as Lucy had expected, the outer office was vacant, as the dispatcher was off on weekends. If anyone called "911" today, Jake himself would answer it.

His office door was closed, and she could hear his voice. He sounded amazingly cheerful considering he had an unsolved murder on his hands. She froze as she caught his words.

"…tied up with the case. Rain check?"

He'd already made and postponed a date with Shark woman. Lucy's stomach churned. She reminded herself that Jake's love life was not her business. She was here for professional reasons, and today she'd dressed for success in her wool navy pantsuit with the voile navy-and-white polka-dot blouse. And she'd brushed on some blush and applied some lipstick, Candy Apple Red. She looked professional and at least six months older than her age. She threw her shoulders back and knocked on the door but did not wait for him to answer it.

Lucy was done waiting for Jake to notice her.

"Lucy!"

His voice was a deep, sexy growl. At least that's

how it sounded to Lucy. She felt her insides melt. And then she looked at his face. He'd aged overnight. New lines scored his cheeks and his green eyes looked dark with fatigue. He'd shoved his fingers through the thick, short blond hair and it stood up at attention. His skin looked unhealthy but that might have been the fluorescent lights.

"Wow," she said, "you look worse than my brother."

"You, on the other hand, look fantastic."

She felt the beginnings of a blush, and then she glanced at his desktop. It was littered with empty Styrofoam cups. Dozens of 'em. She shook her head. "I'll be right back."

She flashed out the door and sprinted the half block to the Corner Kitchen. Twenty minutes later she returned with a homemade-biscuit stuffed with scrambled eggs and bacon, and a large container of orange juice. Jake was on the phone again, but he didn't protest when she set the food in front of him. A moment later he hung up. His eyes narrowed on her.

"You're not my housekeeper anymore, Lucy."

She refused to take offense. The guy was dead on his feet.

"I never was your housekeeper. I was your nanny, remember? And, anyway, I consider this a form of first aid. You look like hell."

She hadn't expected a laugh, and she didn't get one. But she did get a lopsided grin.

"Thanks." He picked up the sandwich and took a huge bite. "Food of the gods," he mumbled. "What're you doing here, anyway?"

"I'll tell you as soon as you've finished breakfast."

He didn't argue, probably because his mouth was full. As soon as he'd drained the orange juice he just looked at her.

"I'm here about the murder."

He blinked, and she knew that until that second, he'd completely forgotten about her new job. "No way are you getting mixed up in this."

She narrowed her eyes at him. "I'm an official member of the Third Estate, Jake. I'm a professional whether you like it or not. And, I'd like to point out that you owe me."

"Owe you for what?" He really didn't remember.

"For taking care of your children for two weeks."

"I thought you liked taking care of Sam and Lillie."

She felt stricken but just for a minute. He was attempting to manipulate her, and he might as well find out right now it wouldn't work.

"This isn't your call. Ed Stiles hired me, remember?"

A big fist came down hard on the desk. Pencils danced in an old frozen juice can that Lillie had decorated under Lucy's supervision.

"It's too dangerous."

Her heart warmed briefly at his expression of concern. And then he ruined it.

"Besides, you don't know what the hell you're doing. I can't afford to have you screw this up."

For a moment she hated him.

"I'm not going to screw it up," she said, pronouncing each word carefully, "but you can't keep me out of it. This is my job, Jake. It's as important to me as your job is to you."

He ran his fingers through the short, blond hair.

"I didn't mean that, exactly." He sounded exasperated, at the end of his rope. "But let's get real about this. I'm not gonna have time to rescue your ass when you get in over your head."

"I would prefer that you not mention either my ass or my head," she said, very much on her dignity. "I would also like a copy of the autopsy results and a list of suspects and their alibis."

He barked a short, humorless laugh.

"I'd like all that, too. Look, it's way too early for any of that." She scowled at him and he shrugged his big shoulders. "I'd tell you the same thing if you were here from the *Hartford Courier*."

"I am here for the *Courier*. I'm stringing for them."

"Shit."

She didn't care for the word, but she liked the flash of respect in his eyes.

"Have you talked with anyone yet?"

"Yeah, Lucy. I have." The flash was gone; the eyes were steady and somber. "I talked with Cameron Outlaw."

"Oh."

"The guy's got a story a three-year-old wouldn't buy."

She winced at the harsh words, but he had a point.

"He didn't kill Packer, Jake."

One corner of his hard mouth tipped up.

"Whether he did or not, he's one more reason you shouldn't be involved in this story. Conflict of interest."

Chapter Four

The sexual tension Jake always felt around Lucy jolted him out of some of his fatigue. It was a more powerful force than caffeine. He hated that a girl who was still wet behind the ears made him ache to get her wet between the thighs. It was history repeating itself, and if he didn't watch out, he was going to wind up with yet another flighty wife who'd leave as soon as domesticity got dull.

That's what he kept telling himself, but on some level, he knew it wasn't completely true. Lucy wasn't Ariel. She was flaky, but she wasn't a narcissist. Take the mother-hen routine this morning. Ariel would never have run down to the corner to buy him breakfast. She'd had no interest in breakfast herself and couldn't imagine that anyone else was hungry in the morning, least of all her old-fogey of a husband. Anyway, Lucy would never have left her children or anyone else's. But all that being said, she was too young. And she wanted a career. He frowned, as he remembered why she'd dropped by. The murder investigation and her job as Ed Stiles' Girl Friday. He'd put a stop to that.

The fax machine whirred, and Jake forgot about his problem with Lucy while he read the medical examiner's findings.

Packer had had the normal amount of arterial blockage for a man his age. He'd have probably faced open heart surgery in a decade or sooner, but otherwise, he'd been a healthy man. Death, caused by the arrow in his heart, had been instantaneous, and it had occurred between nine-thirty and ten-thirty Friday night. Nothing new here.

Jake shoved back his chair and got to his feet. He'd driven up to Bangor yesterday to give the bad news to Packer's widow. He'd see her again this morning. He'd interview the first Mrs. Packer and Packer's lawyer, a guy called Claude Moore, and then he'd track down Cameron Outlaw and interview him again. Surely any relative of Lucy's could be more imaginative than Cam had demonstrated so far. Jake felt his face relax into a faint smile. He called Mrs. Peach, closed up the office, and went out to the Blazer.

****

Lucy drove down Main Street with no destination in mind. First she needed to get over the one-two punch of her yearning for Jake and her fear for Cam. There was nothing she could do about the former. Cam, though, was another story. She turned down Third Street and parked in front of the Eden Community Bank. She knew he'd be working. He was always working on Saturday morning. She plunged her hand into her oversized shoulder bag, searching for her cell, but came up with the box of fruit-flavored condoms she'd bought back in February after Baz and Hallie's wedding. Jake had danced with her at the reception, a slow, sexy dance that had triggered of sexual fantasy. She'd believed that he'd been as turned on as she, but it hadn't changed his mind about dating her, not even with Hallie married to someone else.

Lucy shook her head. She'd sadly misread the

situation.

She exchanged the condoms for the phone, but Cam didn't answer so she returned to her apartment over the veterinary clinic, made a cup of coffee, and sat on the chintz-covered sofa with the springs that had, long ago, given up the ghost.

Lucy found herself studying the dream catcher mounted on the wall. It belonged to Hallie, who'd lived here before her marriage. Lucy knew the willow branch that had been curved into a circle then crisscrossed with string, was intended to capture dreams through the hole in the center. The good dreams funneled down through the feathers that hung from the circle and were guided back to the sleeper. The bad ones were caught in the web.

This particular dream catcher, Lucy knew, had been a gift to Hallie from Molly Whitecloud.

Lucy's thoughts focused on the Penobscot midwife. Surely she knew something about the casino project. And, in any case, she was a walking encyclopedia on the subject of the rez. On top of that, Molly might be able to tell Lucy something about Cam and his execrable alibi.

It was definitely time for a trip to the rez.

Mindful of the wintry weather, Lucy changed into flannel-lined jeans, a crayon-red turtleneck, and matching red sweater. She shrugged into her ancient white parka with the fur-lined hood and jammed her feet into fur-topped snow boots then she headed for the Jeep.

She'd show Jake Langley. Just because he wouldn't tell her anything about the murder investigation didn't mean she couldn't attack this from another angle.

The sting of frozen crystals against her face revealed that the snow had started. Her dad had always called the first flakes "the scouting party." Lucy glanced at the opaque sky and hoped the scouts would advise their brethren to stay in the heavy clouds. In any case, she'd been raised in western Maine and wasn't afraid of a little snow.

There was no problem on M-15, and thirty minutes later, she turned onto the reservation's main road. A couple of miles later she found the single, unpaved lane that dead-ended at Molly Whitecloud's cottage.

The freshly painted white clapboard dwelling had glossy black shutters on the three front windows and a trellis arch over the front door. In summer, Lucy knew, the trellis was covered with climbing red roses.

A blast of wind slammed into Lucy as she knocked, but she forgot about the weather as soon as she saw Molly. The petite, creamy complexioned woman, always calm and collected, was pale, hollow-eyed, and disheveled. Her slender fingers were wrapped together, and her long, shiny hair, usually pulled back into a neat, French braid, looked as if it had spent the night in a blender.

There was a look of pain in Molly's beautiful indigo eyes.

The midwife grabbed Lucy's arm.

"What's happened? Has someone been arrested?"

Lucy knew instantly that she was talking about Cam.

"No. No one. I'm just here on my own," Lucy said, in a soothing voice. The other woman had let go of

61

Lucy's arms and Lucy scooped up one cold hand. "Molly, I think you're ill."

"What? Oh, no. I'm fine. Good heavens, I can't believe I've left you out here." She looked past Lucy. "It's starting to sleet. Come in. Please."

Lucy stepped into the cottage. It felt nearly as cold as the front step.

"Molly? Is your furnace on?"

The midwife's eyes widened. "Is it cold in here?" It was obvious she'd had some kind of a shock. What was supposed to help with that? Lucy searched her memory. Warm milk? Soup? Whiskey?

"Can I get you some herbal tea?" Molly's effort at hospitality was touching.

"I'd like that," Lucy replied, more for Molly's sake than her own. She followed her hostess through the small living room decorated with simple, sleek furniture and hand-woven throw rugs, all of it in earth tones, like chocolate, sand, and rust. Native-made berry baskets held magazines and knitting supplies, and carved totems served as bookends. The walls were painted the blue of the summer sky which gave the house a sense of light and laughter.

Lucy paused at the thermostat. "May I turn up the heat?"

"Sure," Molly said, absently. "Thank you."

The kitchen was tiny but well-organized. Even so, Molly stood for a long moment in front of the window that looked out onto the fallow garden.

"I'll make the tea," Lucy said, firmly, guiding her to one of the two ladder-back chairs at a small table. "You just rest."

She located a tin of loose tea, filled a pale-blue

teakettle with water, and set it on the stove. A few minutes later she set a hand-thrown rust-colored mug filled with the sugar-laced brew in front of Molly. The midwife picked up the mug with shaking hands. She took a sip and made a face.

"Lucy! You have to strain the tea leaves."

"Oh, I'm sorry!" For once, Lucy didn't mind screwing up. The incident seemed to have broken through Molly's emotional paralysis. The midwife began to ask questions about Hallie and her new family, about Daisy and about Lucy herself. She appeared to approve of Lucy's new job.

"You have a natural curiosity," Molly said. "Journalism should be a good career for you."

Lucy knew she could segue into her questions about the rez and casino, but first she needed to know whether Molly's fear had been for Cam.

"When you asked me whether anyone had been arrested, were you thinking of my brother?"

Long lashes lowered over the dark blue eyes.

"I'm worried about everybody involved. The murder happened near the casino site, and the arrow that was used came from the Blackbird Museum."

Lucy nodded and temporarily abandoned her original line of questioning. She could always get back to it.

"Tell me about the arrow."

"It was on display in the museum as a war arrow, although we believe it was used for hunting. The Abenakis, of which the Penobscots are one branch, have been a peaceful people for more than two hundred years."

"Why is it called a 'war' arrow, then?"

"It's for tourists. Not that we have that many. It is an old arrow which means it's identifiable as one of ours."

"Do you think it was used in an effort to frame someone on the rez?"

"It's possible. The whole thing seems like a set piece, you know? I mean, why shoot someone with a bow-and-arrow near the rez? There have to be dozens of more efficient ways to get rid of someone."

"The killer could be sure of privacy," Lucy suggested. "And like you said, it focuses the investigation on the tribe. What about motive? Were there folks who opposed the casino?"

Molly was hunched over her cooling tea, clearly on edge.

"Just some of the young guys. They claim it's disrespectful to the ancestors, but I really think their protest is more because of boredom and their natural combativeness. I mean, they'll all benefit from the casino in terms of jobs and a share of the profits."

"Do you think it's disrespectful? The casino, I mean."

Molly sighed. "In a way. Sure. I mean, we don't really want to encourage gambling, drinking, and whatever else goes on at a casino and resort, but we are so poor. Some people out here don't have indoor plumbing, Lucy. And we desperately need to build a medical clinic. I think the trade-off is worthwhile. And, anyway," she finished, sadly, "the old ways have been gone a long time."

"Who are the opponents?"

Molly shot her a troubled look. "There're half a dozen, but naturally, there's a ringleader. Charlie Elk.

He's eighteen, restless, unemployed." Her soft mouth twisted. "Pretty typical of the kids around here. Anyway, Charlie and his buddies are mounting protests like staging war dances at the Tribal Council meetings and sending threatening letters to the developer."

"You mean Packer?"

"He wasn't worried about it. In fact, he thought it was kind of funny." Molly made a face. "I know it's wrong to speak ill of the dead, but Packer wasn't a very nice man."

"I'm starting to get that picture." Lucy paused. "Do you think Charlie or the other boys had anything to do with Nate Packer's death?"

"No. Of course not."

"Then I don't think you need to worry. The sheriff is a fair man." It seemed natural to defend Jake. "He won't make an arrest without plenty of evidence."

Molly did not look particularly reassured.

"I get the impression you're worried about something else," Lucy said, gently. "Someone else. Is it my brother?"

Molly's eyes dropped.

"I think you're right to worry," Lucy went on. "I've heard his alibi for the time Packer was killed. A fool wouldn't believe it, and Jake Langley is nobody's fool."

Molly's head lifted. Her deep blue eyes shimmered with pain and unshed tears.

"Cam didn't do it."

"I know that," Lucy said. "But why the stupid lie about driving around then pulling into a lay-by and falling asleep?"

"It may be stupid," Molly said, "but it isn't a lie. At

least, not the driving around part. He and I met at the Tribal Council meeting and we agreed to talk."

Lucy waited, but Molly didn't continue.

"So you drove around together and then he dropped you off and went to sleep in a lay-by?"

Molly's delicate features twisted, and Lucy wished she could recall her words. She felt like she'd skewered a butterfly on a pin. It was time to change the subject.

"Tell me about the clinic."

Molly did, her eyes shining with enthusiasm. Her greatest interest was, naturally, in providing a facility for mothers-to-be.

"All right," Lucy said, an hour later. "Thank you for talking to me. I'd better get over to the Trading Post and speak with Davey Tall Tree."

But when they opened the front door, they were greeted with violent swirls of snow that had already covered the ground and started to drift against the sides of the house.

"This looks bad," Molly said, unnecessarily. "You'd better forget about the Trading Post. In fact, I think you'd better stay here tonight."

Lucy checked her watch. It was only about three p.m.

"I should get back. I promised Hallie and Baz I'd look after Robert tonight."

"It doesn't look safe," Molly protested.

"I'm used to driving in snow. But if it gets worse, suddenly, I'll come back."

"Call me when you get home, okay? Or if you run into trouble. I'll send out a dogsled."

Lucy laughed, zipped her parka, and headed out to the Jeep. Her little car, ever reliable, started immediately. She backed out of the Molly's driveway and onto the unpaved road that led to the reservation's main drag. The snow, that had looked navigable from the protection of Molly's front porch, was blowing and drifting out in the open, flat fields that flanked the road and visibility was seriously limited. Lucy inched her way along and only recognized the upcoming turn onto M-15 because she was able to make out the small cabin located near the entrance of the rez.

As she drew even with the small, wooden structure, her optimism faded, and she realized she'd made a mistake. It was hard enough to maneuver the Jeep on the slick roadway with the gusts of wind trying to knock her onto the shoulder. Worse, the windshield wipers couldn't keep up with the barrage of sleet. Lucy felt like a small rowboat in the middle of a monsoon.

She made a decision. She'd have to go back to Molly's.

With her heart thudding against her ribs, Lucy executed the world's slowest U-turn and started back toward Molly's cottage. She'd just given herself a figurative pat on the back when a sharp blast of wind forced the car sideways and caused it to slide. She remembered to brake gently, the way Cam had taught her, but as soon as a second and then a third gust of wind slammed into her, she knew it was hopeless. She felt the Jeep glide into a shallow ravine. She sucked in a deep breath and shoved the Jeep into reverse. The wheels spun, helplessly.

She stared at the wall of snow that obscured any and all vision.

Dang. Dang. And double dang.

It wasn't just a nor-easter. It was a white-out. And

she was stranded right in the middle of it.

Okay. Okay. What were the options? She wasn't far from Molly's, probably about two miles. But Molly had grown up in Maine, and she knew how easy it was to lose a sense of direction in white-out conditions. She could sit in the Jeep and wait this out but, again, a storm like this could last for hours, even overnight, and, already the ends of her fingers and the tips of her toes felt frozen.

There really was only one choice. She just hoped that Molly hadn't been kidding about the dogsled.

"Thank God," Molly said, her voice heavy with anxiety. "Tell me where you are, and I'll send someone out."

"I'm fairly close to that wooden house near the entrance to the rez."

"Okay, just sit tight. I'll get right back to you."

"I'm sorry, Molly. I should've listened to you."

"Oh, this isn't your fault. It's mine. I never ignore the weather like this. I was distracted. I'm the one who's sorry."

Lucy hung up, feeling better. At least someone knew she was stranded. It gave her a queer feeling to be alone here under the conditions, as if she'd somehow landed on the moon. It didn't take long for the howling wind to get on her nerves and the cold sensation in her extremities moved inward and upward. She began to shiver.

It was both a shock and a relief when the phone rang.

"Help is on the way," Molly reported. Between the storm conditions and the low battery in Lucy's cell, she could only hear patches of Molly's voice. She got the message that someone was coming to find her and that, when her rescuer arrived, they should take shelter at the wooden structure nearby, the Littlejohns' cabin.

"Won't the Littlejohns mind the invasion?"

"What? I'm sorry, Lucy. I can't hear you. Stay in the car, Lucy. Do you hear me? Don't get out in the storm."

The line went dead before Lucy could point out that she was nose down in a ravine. Undoubtedly snow had already covered the Jeep. The rescue party would never find her. She needed to get out, to flag them down. It was just a matter of how long to wait. She kept an eye on her watch as the minutes passed with the speed of sap dripping out of a maple tree. A half an hour later, she stepped into the storm.

Chapter Five

Jake cursed at the wintry mix of snow and sleet attacking the Blazer's windshield as he drove along Route 2 north of Eden. He'd made the hour-long drive to Bangor in dry conditions. The storm had started while he was talking with Shirley Packer, the deceased's first wife, and it had quickly gathered steam. He knew he faced a long afternoon and a much longer night of attempting to rescue clueless drivers who'd ignored all the warnings. Worse than that, his interviews had gained him nothing.

Packer's ex, Shirley, was either very clever or very lucky. She claimed that, the night Nate died, she'd been out alone at a concert where she'd run into no acquaintances. She'd returned home at ten forty-five, noticed by a neighbor who had been out at the curb retrieving his empty trash cans. The neighbor didn't know her except by sight, but he agreed that he'd seen her car turn into her driveway and disappear. Shirley's unattached garage was located behind her house. Shirley produced a ticket stub which indicated that she was telling the truth and that she hadn't left Bangor that night.

He supposed she could have obtained the ticket stub from someone, somehow managed to meet Packer after the Tribal Council meeting and kill him. She'd have had to speed back to Bangor in time to be seen by the neighbor. Alternatively, she could have hired someone to kill her ex.

Shirley Packer hadn't struck Jake as the killer type, but then, she'd been dumped for a younger woman and fired from her role in the company she'd helped build. It seemed inconceivable that she wasn't bitter but she seemed to be content in her two-story colonial, a house as unpretentious as Shirley herself.

The sleet launched itself at his windshield and Jake squinted into it.

His gut told him this was about Packer Inc. Apparently the developer and Shirley and their attorney, Claude Moore, had built it from the ground up. It had enjoyed a respectable reputation until this last project, the one out at the rez, when suddenly there were accusations of using inferior materials and hooking up with the mob. Was that because Shirley was out? Had she been the company's conscience?

He'd gotten nothing from the widow, either. Paula Packer, blonde, voluptuous, flirtatious, and living in an ostentatious mansion, was happy enough to see him, but she either knew nothing or she'd been coached by her personal guard dog, Moore, to reveal nothing.

The attorney, himself, like the first Mrs. Packer, seemed fine with his current reduced role at Packer Inc. He'd told Jake he was less involved in the day-to-day operation of the company, but that he liked having the free time, as it had given him a chance to take up some hobbies, like flying. He lived in a well-appointed, ranch-style house, dressed in hand-tailored silk suits and drove a snazzy sports car. Moore appeared to have no money worries.

A gust of wind slammed into the Blazer and Jake

had to hang onto the steering wheel to keep the vehicle in its lane. The wipers worked overtime to clear a window for him to see. Where the devil had all this weather sprung from? This must be one of those flash nor'easters he'd heard about. For the most part, he hadn't minded the change from Southern California to the northern reaches of Iceland, but this was ridiculous. He wondered if there was any chance that everyone in Eden County would use their heads and stay in. It was certainly a night for home and hearth. Jake's mind flashed on the family fun nights he and the kids had enjoyed with Lucy. They'd gathered around the table to play Chutes and Ladders, Candyland, Hearts. Lucy had made caramel popcorn balls one night, and Jake had had to spend the next day trying to get the caramel out of Lillie's hair while Lucy did the same with the cat. He hadn't laughed at the time, but he smiled at the memory now.

Lucy made even catastrophes exciting.

No wonder the kids missed her. He missed her, too.

He stopped at the service station outside Eden, filled up the Blazer with gas and his Thermos with hot coffee, just in case he got a call. He grabbed a dozen stale doughnuts including three Bavarian creams, Lucy's favorite. Which was patently ridiculous. He wasn't going to be sharing the doughnuts with Lucy.

His phone rang as he climbed back in the Blazer and he sighed. But the sighs turned to curses when Molly Whitecloud told him why she was calling.

If it wasn't just like Lucy to get herself stranded in the biggest storm of the century. This was a perfect follow-up to the jingle bell-missiles. Jake pointed the Blazer toward the rez and turned his radio up to full volume on Springsteen's "Born in the U.S.A.," but the powerful beat wasn't loud enough to drum out the reality of the situation. First, Jake had to find the little witch and then he had to spend the night with her in a deserted, unheated cabin.

By tomorrow, his entire life would be changed because of Lucy Outlaw.

Forty-five minutes later the pulse of pain that thrummed in Jake's forehead threatened to explode into a full-blown migraine. His eyes strained with the effort to distinguish anything in the impenetrable sea of white, but he knew this particular headache was due, mainly, to fear. It was not uncommon for people to die under these conditions. Lucy, he told himself, would not die. He would find her.

And then he'd kill her.

Where the hell was she?

He crept down the rez road, every sense alert. Dusk had arrived, but for once, it wasn't followed by darkness. The sky was light, pregnant with snow, and the effect was eerie.

Jake inched along the rez road scouring the landscape as best he could. Finally, finally, he spotted a jerky little movement that didn't fit in with either the storm or the snow-covered countryside. Something or someone was bouncing up and down as if riding a pogo stick, and Jake was pretty sure he knew who it was.

Jake's jaw clenched, and his fingers tightened on the steering wheel as he battled zero-visibility conditions to keep his eye on the prize. Finally, he was close enough to stop and throw the door open. "What the hell are you doing out of the Jeep?"

He was aware that the power of the wind took all

the punch out of his roar. She gave him a crooked grin and yelled something. He couldn't hear it at all, but he could read her lips.

"I'm waiting for you."

He cursed, scooped her up in his arms, and fought his way back to the Blazer. Thank the Lord she didn't try to talk while he searched for the Littlejohns'. She kept her arms locked around her waist and shook like a maraca while Jake scanned the horizon. A minute later his target rose up like a mirage in the desert. He breathed a prayer of thanks, pulled up as close as he could get to the cabin, and parked. Then he battled the storm to get to her door.

"Extend your arms," he barked at her. She didn't move. Too cold, probably. Even Lucy wasn't crazy enough to defy him under these conditions. He took her hands and pulled them away from her body, and then he loaded her up with his emergency kit, blanket, coffee, and doughnuts.

"I can't feel my arms," she said. "Or my legs."

"I know." He scooped her into his arms again and made his way through the snow that had already drifted as high as his crotch. When he reached the door, he turned the knob and breathed a sigh of relief. As Molly had predicted, it was unlocked.

"Sh-shouldn't we knock?"

He glanced down at her, a frozen popsicle, her blue eyes darkened from fear and cold. Shards of ice stuck to her dark curls. Warmth flooded his heart along with a queer tenderness he'd only ever experienced in connection with his kids. He'd been damned lucky to find her at all.

"No need," he said, his voice hoarse.

The cabin was dark, of course, with only a small window. There were a couple of wooden chairs, but no electricity and no wood for the fireplace. He figured he could break up the chairs and there were matches in his kit.

"I hope you're up for a campfire."

He set her on her feet and took the supplies out of her arms.

"I can't seem to move. I'm sorry, Jake."

He glanced at her face then started to work on the frozen zipper of her parka. She was either too cold to talk much or she sensed, correctly, that he didn't want to answer a bunch of questions. It was strangely pleasant to be with Lucy without a barrage of questions and chaos. Naturally that situation did not last long.

"Where are the Littlejohns?"

"In their winter home in Sarasota."

"Really?"

He tugged at the zipper. "No. Not really. They're gone. Moved. Dead. I have no idea."

"They don't live here anymore?"

"Right."

"So we're staying here alone tonight?"

Irritation built in his chest.

"Beggars can't be choosers. We're damn lucky to be alive."

She blinked and a small shower of snow flaked off her lashes.

"I know this is my fault, Jake. I screwed up."

There was no point in arguing with her. She was one thousand percent right.

"And I'm not complaining."

Not now. She might very well complain once she

figured out exactly what was going to happen to her tonight. As far as Jake was concerned, the battle he'd been fighting was over and they'd both lost. She'd gotten herself into this situation, and she could just damn well take the consequences. He'd known as soon as he'd gotten Molly's call that he wouldn't get out of this without making love to Lucy. He'd accepted his fate. It was time she accepted hers.

He got her jacket and boots off then pulled the red sweater over her head. It knocked some of the ice crystals out of her hair. He paused to rub her head with his hands before the ice melted and made her even colder.

"Thank you for rescuing me," she said. The words came out unevenly, as if she were too cold to speak normally.

"Don't talk."

She wrinkled her nose, a characteristic Lucy gesture, but this time it was in slow motion which didn't make it any less compelling. He brushed his knuckles against the soft, cold skin of her cheek and wished he had access to hot water. Then he remembered the coffee. Quickly, he finished undressing her down to the underwear then he wrapped her in the woolen blanket, poured her some coffee in the Thermos lid, and handed it to her. Naturally, she couldn't hold it. He held it at her lips while she took a few sips then he got to work breaking up the chairs until he had a nice pile of arms and legs in the grate.

"What about you? Aren't you cold?"

Blood pulsed through his body making it swell. He wouldn't be cold if he jumped naked into a snow bank at this point.

"Not really."

"Lucky you."

Lucky him. He was about to violate his oath, take advantage of a much-too-young woman, seal his marital fate dooming his children to the likelihood of being abandoned by another mother figure. He should be frozen deep in Dante's ninth circle of Hell, but dammit, he felt lucky.

"Yeah."

****

The sense of guilt was so heavy it almost knocked out the cold. Almost.

She'd screwed up royally, making a decision that had scared Molly and risked Jake's life and her own. She knew he was furious with her. She knew, too, he was going easy on her because she'd almost turned into the abominable snow woman and she was scared. She couldn't bear to think of him searching for her frozen corpse until he'd become one himself even though that's exactly what he would have done. She let out a little moan.

"What?" He was kneeling before the fireplace trying to coax a blaze. He still wore his leather jacket but he'd removed his hat and the blond hair gleamed in the weak light of the flames. She admired the powerful muscles in his long legs and the long fingers on his square hands. Strong fingers but surprisingly graceful for a man. As if he played the piano.

"I was thinking about what a close call that was. You might not have found me."

He turned to look at her. "I'd have found you, Lucy."

The intensity in the emerald eyes shook her to the

soul. She wished she could convince him that she could be exactly what he was looking for, but it was impossible when she kept screwing up. She knew he wanted her. She knew, too, that it was just for tonight.

She held his gaze even as her heart jerked with anticipation. She'd take what she could get.

She wished, suddenly, she'd worn the slinky black bikini panties and matching lacy bra instead of her old cotton standbys.

Jake took off his jacket and boots, but he remained dressed. He spread their wet garments out on the wooden floor with quick, efficient movements. The fire blazed suddenly and quickly took the bitter edge off the chill in the small room.

"Aren't you going to take off your pants?" The green eyes found her before he answered. "Eventually." Lucy swallowed hard.

He spread a second blanket on the floor then sat down cross-legged with her. He poured some coffee into the Thermos cap, offered it to her, and then slugged it down. He handed her a doughnut. "Bavarian cream! My favorite!" His sudden grin blinded her. "I know." She nibbled at it.

"Not hungry?"

Not for food. But she could hardly explain that.

"Still a little cold," she hedged.

"We can fix that." He moved so fast she didn't see it coming. Suddenly she was between his legs with her back against his chest and his powerful body virtually surrounding her.

"This should help."

The gruff words came out on hot little breaths that puffed against her bare neck. Lucy's temperature soared and she felt a queer achiness in her lower body that she had never felt with anyone but Jake Langley.

"It does help," she whispered.

She nibbled at the doughnut until an enormous wave of lethargy overcame her. She let her head drop back against his shoulder and the next thing she knew the fire had burned down to embers and she was still cradled in Jake's arms.

Lucy twisted to look at him. "I fell asleep?"

"Yup."

"For how long?" It must have been awhile. She felt amazingly well-rested.

"I have no idea."

"Oh, Jake. I'm so sorry. You must be paralyzed from the weight." She scrambled to get off him, a movement that triggered a sharp gasp.

"Oh, dang," she said, stricken. "I hurt you."

"Just stop moving around." The words seemed to be wrenched out of his mouth. He seemed to realize he had been too harsh because his voice softened.

"Give me a second and I'll help you up."

"Up?"

"The fire's done. We're going to have to figure out a sleeping arrangement that will keep us warm and once we do, we're not getting up again until morning. I figured you'd like a pit stop."

She grinned at him. "Spoken like the parent of small children."

He shrugged but didn't return the smile.

"That's exactly what I am, Lucy. The parent of small children."

She understood. He was telling her, again, that he was more mature than she was, that he wanted a woman on his own level.

"Is there a bathroom?"

"There's a latrine but no running water. You can deal with that or take your chances outside near the backdoor."

"Backdoor," she decided, instantly. The experience should have been ghastly, but it wasn't. She just kept thinking about bundling up next to Jake for the entire night.

When she returned, he'd arranged the blankets in a pallet on the floor. For an instant, she wondered if it would be awkward but he held his hand out to her and she took it without a word. Then he drew her down onto the blanket and pulled her against him.

"We have to share body heat," he murmured. One of his legs was between hers and even though he was still wearing his khakis, she could feel his instant erection. "We don't have to share anything more than that." His voice was firm, if a little raspy. Heat flared in her belly. This was it. Fate had deprived her of this that last night in Jake's home, but she'd been given a second chance. She didn't intend to blow it.

Tonight, for the first and last time, Jake Langley would make love to her. And she would make love to him.

Lucy spent a few seconds regretting that she hadn't gathered more experience during her twenty-two years. She'd just have to trust her instincts. What if she screwed up the screwing? And then he spread his fingers against her collar bone and the sensation nearly sent her through the roof.

She arched up into his touch and she felt his fingers on her breast. Good grief! What had happened to her bra?

"You're a magician," she murmured.

"Then we're even," he whispered. "Because you're a witch and I'm under your spell. Tell me what you want, baby."

Baby? This was seriously gonna happen, apparently. Too bad she didn't know what she wanted.

"I like what you just did."

"I removed your bra."

"Yeah. That. I liked that."

He choked back a laugh. "How about this?" He rubbed her nipples gently.

"Uh-huh."

"What about this?" He bent down and touched her breast again only this time he used his mouth. The sensation was wet, warm and mind-blowing. Her whole body shuddered and she couldn't seem to speak.

Not that he needed any coaching. Lucy was a little relieved that he'd stopped asking her what she liked especially because she seemed to have lost her ability to form words. He suckled each of her breasts then traveled down her body leaving soft, wet, seductive kisses. His hair, that golden hair that was so much softer than it looked, tickled her stomach. Her laugh ended in a sharp gasp as his right hand slipped inside her panties and shaped her buttocks and his left hand slid into, shoot-a-mile! His fingers slid inside her. Heat flared in her belly and her body clenched around him. He used his thumb to stroke her over and over again until she was coiled so tightly she thought she'd burst and she began to whimper.

"Let yourself go, sweetheart."

"Go?" She couldn't seem to focus.

"Let yourself come."

"Come? Go?" What on earth was he doing to her? She couldn't seem to catch her breath.

"That's it, baby." He rubbed harder, faster, and she twisted against his fingers, searching for something, wanting something and then his tongue darted into her mouth and his thumb found just the right amount of pressure and he muttered, "Come for me, Lucy" and she did.

Fireworks flashed and exploded around her, her head whirled and she could feel her heart pounding out a triple-time tattoo. She clung to Jake's solid frame as she struggled to breath. Finally, she collapsed in a sweaty little heap on his chest.

"What are you thinking," he murmured into her ear sometime later.

She was thinking it hadn't mattered about the cotton underpants. She was thinking that she'd had no idea at all what was meant by a female orgasm. She was thinking about how much she had wanted to be with Jake Langley and how grateful she was that she'd gotten lost in the snow.

Naturally, she couldn't say any of those things.

"I'm thinking," she said, as inspiration struck, "how much I'd like to touch you."

"Be my guest." His voice sounded deeper than usual and a little hoarse. She was lying on top of him so it didn't take long to figure out where he wanted her to touch, but she was suddenly painfully aware of her lack of experience.

"How? How do you want me to touch you?"

She held her breath, fairly certain he wouldn't make fun of her, but even more certain that he'd stop the whole business if he found out this was her first time.

He unbuttoned his shirt.

"Start up here," he said, pressing her fingers into the nest of curly light brown hair on his chest. He brushed her thumb over one flat, copper-colored nipple and she heard a sudden, sharp intake of breath. So she did it again. And then she did the same thing to the other nipple. And then she licked it and sucked it, gently.

"Jesus, Lucy."

His chest was rising and falling rapidly, and he was making no move to detach her, so she figured he liked it. The thought made her bold, and still using her tongue, she worked her way down his torso. When she reached the waistband of his slacks she hesitated. Again he helped her out, this time by unbuckling his belt and releasing the button at the top of his pants. She slipped one hand into his waistband and slid her tongue into his belly button. A moan worked its way up his chest, and she wasn't sure whether she'd caused it with her mouth or the hand that bumped against his straining fly.

She cupped him gently. He arched up against her hand and she heard another one of those ragged moans.

"Jake?"

"Huh?"

"Do you want me to touch you here?"

"Yes. Jesus, Lucy. Yes."

A strong emotion rippled through her. She loved making him react like this. It was even better than, well, maybe it wasn't necessary to compare. Sorta like apples and oranges.

"Lucy?"

He sounded desperate. "Of course, of course." She tugged at his zipper.

"Take it easy, sweetheart." He half-laughed, half-groaned. She smiled up at him then slipped her hand inside his briefs and wrapped her fingers around him. He was enormous, thick and hot and pulsing.

"Oh God that's good." It was almost a prayer. "So damn good. You have magic in your fingers."

She was glad to hear the praise. Finally, she thought, in the back of her mind, she'd found something she was good at. But she wasn't certain exactly how to proceed. She tightened her grip and he cursed and thrust upward. Maybe she should stroke him. Or maybe. She lowered her head and sucked, gently, on the velvety tip.

"Christ!"

Suddenly the world turned upside down, and she was underneath him. He ripped her panties off in one smooth motion and then he was there, between her thighs. His shoulders looked a mile wide in the shadows, and she could feel that absolutely enormous part of him pressing against her.

"Last chance, Lucy."

"I want this," she said, bracing herself just a little. "I want you, Jake." I love you.

He thrust powerfully into her and slid his tongue into her mouth which, if it didn't soothe her, at least turned her shriek into something closer to a moan.

But Jake wasn't fooled. He went perfectly still, except for the pulsing erection.

"Goddammit, Lucy! Why the hell didn't you tell me?"

She felt tears prick the backs of her eyeballs which

was ridiculous because this was all her own fault. Still, it hurt and she didn't appreciate being yelled at.

"I was afraid you'd stop."

"You're goddam right I would've stopped. Christ! Does this mean you're unprotected, too?"

"I've got condoms in my purse."

"Christ!"

The pain was starting to fade. Mostly she felt suffocated. He was much too big.

"Could you just get off of me?" She wriggled her hips.

"Stop. Stop moving, Lucy."

She felt his big hands grasping her hips as if to hold her still.

"You're too big." She wriggled her hips again. His grip tightened, and he groaned as he pulled back but almost immediately he thrust forward again. It was a funny sensation, too tight but somehow, tantalizing. His fingers were digging into her hips now, and he lowered his head so that it was jammed against the inside of her shoulder. He plunged into her over and over again, faster and faster.

"I'm sorry, baby," he gasped, "I'm sorry."

Lucy barely heard him. She arched up to bring him closer, deeper and deeper still. It wasn't the same sensation he'd created with his fingers, but it was exciting. More than exciting. She felt his sweat and heard his short, harsh gasps and she knew he felt the same coiled tension she'd experienced. She wanted to give him the release that she'd felt. She put her arms around his back and when he surged into her she deliberately tightened her inner muscles and she whispered to him.

"Come for me, Jake."

His face twisted in anguishand a groan ripped out of his throat. An instant later he'd collapsed on her, panting and shaking. She held him tightly and stroked his back.

She didn't think about how mad he was going to be when this was over or how much it would hurt her. She just threaded her fingers through his hair and luxuriated in the feel of his weight against her.

When his breathing calmed she felt a jab of regret. A minute later he'd recovered enough to speak.

"You're a virgin."

It was, naturally, an accusation.

"Not anymore."

His weight cut off her breathing as he pushed himself away from her.

"I don't want a smart ass answer."

"I didn't hear a question."

She was horrifyingly close to tears.

"Why me? My life's complicated enough, Lucy. You, of all people know that."

"I didn't do this to complicate your life. Jeez, Jake. I didn't do it at all. Do you think I planned to get stuck in a white-out?"

"No." He glared at her. "I don't think you ever plan anything. I think you just go on your merry way wreaking havoc and leaving chaos in your wake." She struggled to sit up.

"Just the words a girl wants to hear after her first time."

He scowled and thrust his fingers through his hair.

"Sorry. Sorry."

Lucy knew he meant it. He was sorry. Sorry he'd

slept with her. Probably sorry he'd ever met her.

"No harm done," she said, brightly. "I'm going to try to get some sleep."

She pulled the blanket up and wrapped herself in it even though it meant there were no covers for him. And it was on purpose. Shoot-a-mile. He didn't deserve a blanket.

****

Goddammit all to hell.

Lucy was a virgin. Had been a virgin. He should have known. He paced around the small cabin. Maybe he had known on some level. Maybe that's what had kept him away from her. The chemistry had been there from the first time he saw her. He'd done his best to ignore it, but she kept turning up and tonight was the last straw.

Worse even than the careless sex was the insidious tenderness he felt when he looked into her wide eyes. He knew she wasn't good wife material for him and he wasn't the right man for her but he'd wanted to be the guy to show her what it was all about. Well, he had. The question was, what the hell was he supposed to do now? Marry her?

The idea had some appeal, but it was a tremendous gamble. And he had the twins who would be devastated when Lucy decided she'd had enough of playing house.

Goddammit all to hell.

Chapter Six

Weak shafts of light filtered through the heavily smudged windows which meant it was morning. Lucy woke up much faster than usual due, no doubt, to the highly unusual circumstance of being cocooned in a strong masculine embrace.

She heard his deep, even breathing and knew he was still asleep. She wished she could shift enough to see his face, but maybe it was better not. She didn't need to be haunted by a vision of those long lashes against his cheeks.

Jake might be angry at her, but he had decided not to let her freeze to death.

She supposed she should be grateful.

Lucy knew Jake well enough by now to realize he would beat himself up over the events of last night. He would consider what they'd done as a mistake, a failing on his part to resist indulging in a one-night stand. And that's how he'd see it. He had made it abundantly clear that he was in the market for a mature wife because of what had happened with the twins' mother. Lucy felt a shaft of pure hatred against Ariel Langley which she realized was unworthy of her because the poor woman had died in a skydiving accident. But she hadn't died until she'd broken Jake's heart and left him with an unshakeable prejudice against younger women.

To be fair, there was an element of flakiness that

Lucy had in common with Jake's first wife.

Unlike Ariel, who had, apparently indulged herself in every whim, Lucy intended to conquer her own impulsiveness and to reverse her image, but she was fully aware that she hadn't done it yet. What would a man call a woman who got herself lost in a flash snowstorm and risked both their lives? A flake. Maybe even a fool.

On top of that, she'd disregarded Jake's expressed needs. She knew he was attracted to her but only in a physical way. She knew he would lose self-respect if he made love to Lucy but she'd lured him into it, anyway. And, what's more, she'd do it again if she could.

Good grief! What it came down to was that she was no better than Ariel. Or Eve.

The back of her throat ached with unshed tears. Lucy told herself she loved Jake Langley, but if that were true, she'd respect his boundaries. She felt the stirring of a promising arousal against her thigh and, acting on her recent, noble thought, she rolled away from him and got to her feet, snatched up her clothing, minus the panties that were a dead loss and the bra she couldn't find. She stepped into the dysfunctional bathroom, and when she emerged, she was wearing her slightly damp jeans, the red turtleneck and sweater. Jake had risen and dressed, too, and he was speaking into his cell phone. An instant later, he snapped it shut.

"That was Homer. The storm's stopped, and the sun's out. The snow'll be gone in a couple of days. Meanwhile he's sending a tow truck to dig out your Jeep."

"Thanks."

"I'll wait till he gets here then follow you back to

Eden."

"Again, thanks."

His eyes were very green in the daylight, and they were completely unreadable. He pulled something out of his pocket and let it hang from his fingers.

"Looking for this?"

She snatched the bra and felt her face flood with color.

"Where was it?"

"Underneath me."

The words were uttered in a deep, husky voice, and Lucy's blood heated.

"About last night," he started to say.

"I don't want to talk about it." Her own voice sounded breathless.

"You mean now?"

"I'd like to put it behind me."

He frowned. "Lucy, we can't just ignore what happened. I had your virginity. We've got to get married."

She gaped at him. She'd been prepared for hostility, regret, and remorse. She hadn't expected him to make himself into a human sacrifice. "No," she said. "Thanks."

Something flashed in his green eyes.

"I'm not asking," he said. "I'm a father and the sheriff. I'm long past the time for one-night stands. I took advantage of your youth and the situation. Marriage is the only solution."

Her heart squeezed with sorrow, but she scowled at him.

"I'm not marrying you to protect your reputation."

"What about your reputation?"

"Good grief, Jake. What century are you living in?"

"The one where a single man respects another man's daughter. The one where a guy accepts the consequences of his actions."

She shook her head. "I'm sorry. You'll just have to find some other way to reconcile your conscience. I have no intention of being someone's consequences, and anyway, I'm fine with what happened."

He shoved his fingers through his short hair in a movement that clearly indicated exasperation.

"You're not just a consequence. If it makes you feel any better, I knew we'd be getting married as soon as I got Molly's call."

She glared at him as hurt turned to anger.

"I am an adult, Jake. Nobody can marry me without my consent, and I'm not ready to give it. I've got a career to pursue. I'm not getting myself tied down to a readymade family in a small town in Maine."

He came close to her, so close he loomed over her and there was a bleak expression in his emerald eyes.

"We'll let the matter go for now," he said, in a quiet voice that, nevertheless, sent a shiver down Lucy's spine. "But just remember the condoms in your purse. If I made you pregnant last night, you will have to marry me."

She swallowed, convulsively. "It was just the one time."

"Lucy," he said, grimly, "how many times do you think it takes?"

He didn't refer to the matter again. In fact, he barely spoke with her during the several hours as he and Homer worked to get the Jeep out of the ditch.

Lucy's heart felt heavy when she finally arrived at her apartment then stopped in at the house to report a carefully edited version of what had happened. Later, after a long, hot shower, she stared at herself in the mirror. Everything was the same, the blue eyes, the short, pert nose, the pointed chin, and the dark, curly hair. She still had smallish, high breasts, an indentation at the waist and long legs. She was the same. Nothing had changed. Except, everything had changed. She'd crossed a threshold, passed a milestone, taken a leap into adulthood.

Lucy closed her eyes and recalled the feel of his hot breath against her collarbone, the touch of his callused fingers on her skin, the excitement of feeling his hard body against her soft one. She'd expected Jake to feel some guilt and regret. She hadn't expected the grudging proposal.

She suddenly remembered the cautionary adage, be careful what you wish for, you just might get it.

She'd wanted to make love with Jake Langley. She'd gotten what she wished for. And she'd broken her heart.

****

Jake had no time to think about the way he'd shredded his honor and his future. The awareness was there, sitting at the back of his mind like an aggravating canker sore while he rescued stranded motorists, filed paperwork, studied his notes and reports on the Packer murder, and played a few games of Go Fish with Sam and Lillie. The memories were there, too. Snapshots of the night on the rez flicked by in quick succession, inspiring both guilt and longing. He kept seeing her blue eyes, filled with shocked pleasure at experiencing her first orgasm and pain at her first penetration. He'd been responsible for both, and because of that, he'd become responsible for her. She was his, whether she chose to accept it or not.

This resistance on her part, well, it was only a reprieve. Whether she was pregnant or not, Jake intended to marry Lucy Outlaw.

On the whole, he thought it would work out just fine, as long as it lasted.

He was still catching up on sleep by Monday morning so the children had already gone to school when he arrived in the kitchen. Mrs. Peach, a ringer for Mrs. Santa Clause with her blue-rinsed curls, granny glasses and perpetual house dresses, poured him a cup of coffee.

Jake knew instantly that something was wrong. "Sheriff, I need to talk to you."

He suppressed a sigh. "Of course. Is this about your sister?"

The elderly lady nodded, unhappily.

"Esther's not recovering as well as she should. I hate to do this to you, but I'm afraid there isn't anyone else to take care of her. She needs me."

There was no choice. "You go on and go. We'll be fine."

"Thank you. I'll call Lucy," she said.

He opened his mouth to protest, but she held up a hand.

"Now, I know she's a little disorganized but the children adore her and she loves them. With Lucy in the house, you won't even miss me."

He couldn't have Lucy here. Not until she agreed to marry him.

"Let me take care of that. You just go take care of your sister."

"If you're sure. Oh, I almost forgot, this letter arrived earlier by special delivery." She handed him a thin, business-sized envelope. Jake's guts twisted as he noted the return address, a law office in Dallas.

Minutes later, in the privacy of his bedroom he read through the letter expressing the intent to file suit for custody of the twins. Maxine had finally struck.

An hour later Jake stepped into the offices of the only lawyers in town. Kirby & Kirby was located in rooms above Little Joe's. Despite the distinguished name, Josiah Kirby, round, bald and sixty-ish, was the only remaining member of the firm's founding family. In fact, he was the only remaining member of the firm.

Jake had crossed paths with him several times and found him to be a sensible man.

Kirby's pudgy lips pushed in and out as he read the letter through his bifocals. When he finished, he pushed himself away from his desk, leaned back in his large chair, removed his glasses and folded his hands over his enormous stomach.

"What's this all about, Sheriff?"

"The bottom line is she thinks the twins are not being raised in a healthy environment. She believes they need a woman's influence, and as I am single, she wants that woman to be herself."

"What did you do to make her so angry?"

It was a fair question.

"The Slocums have oil money. Maxine believes her daughter married a cop just to spite her parents."

"Was it true?"

Jake had given the matter a lot of thought.

"There was truth in it," he admitted. "I never met Ariel's parents until after she died. Maxine invited the kids and me to the ranch and she and her husband showed the kids a great time but when it was time to leave, Maxine dug in her heels. She wanted to keep them there, told me it would make my life much easier. I refused. She said I wasn't being fair to them, that they needed two parents. I told her I was working on that, but she wasn't satisfied. I knew she was contemplating a suit."

"Is it possible she just wants access to the children?"

Jake shook his head. "I think it's more than that. Her daughter turned out to be a disappointment. I believe she wants a second chance at a family."

"Can you find a way to compromise?"

Cold fingers closed around Jake's heart, and fear leapt in his stomach.

"Hell, no. They're my kids, and I don't trust her any more than I trusted her daughter. She'll stop at nothing, Kirby. She's a ruthless, determined woman."

"What are your domestic arrangements?"

Jake rubbed the back of his neck. "I work long hours, naturally, but I employ a live-in housekeeper who takes care of the children. Mrs. Peach." Josiah Kirby's broad face lit up.

"I know Elvira. Went to school with her. No fault to find there."

Jake sucked in a breath. This next part was harder to tell.

"Mrs. Peach has been taking care of her sister lately and is about to leave again. I'll need to find a temporary nanny."

95

"A temporary nanny, eh? Didn't you have Lucy Outlaw? Seems to me I heard something about that, come to think of it. Exploding bells or something at Miss Violet's ballet recital. That sounded like Lucy."

"She took good care of the children." Jake didn't know why he was defending her.

"I'm sure she did. But listen, Sheriff. It's not a good idea for you to have a young, unmarried girl like Lucy staying in your house. Sends the wrong message."

"It's not anybody's business," Jake growled.

"Neither is the fact that you sheltered together out at the rez the night of the storm, but like I said, it doesn't look good."

"Goddammit."

"It's a small town, Sheriff. The Outlaw Veterinary Clinic is gossip central." Josiah Kirby twiddled the thumbs resting on his paunch. "Seems like your best bet is to find a stepmother for those twins of yours."

"You telling me I have to get married to get Maxine off my back?" It was outrageous.

"I'm sayin' you could do yourself a favor. And, Sheriff. You could do a lot worse than Lucy Outlaw. That girl has a big heart."

Damn. He could have saved himself the effort. Kirby had just advised him to do what he'd already accepted as inevitable. Only now he couldn't give her the time to come to the same conclusion.

****

Monday and Tuesday always involved long days at a weekly newspaper, and Lucy had no time to worry about Cam's alibi or the night with Jake or anything else as she and Ed pulled together what would be the first edition of the *Excelsior* that included her byline.

She felt a thrill of satisfaction at the sight of her name under the banner headline: CASINO DEVELOPER MURDERED NEAR REZ. The story was incomplete, of course, but this was just the beginning.

Wednesday morning, she dressed in a wool, charcoal pantsuit, a white shell, and black boots. She knotted a jaunty fire-engine red silk scarf around her neck and wore matching lipstick. Her short curls refused to stay in any sort of order, but other than that, she thought she looked quite professional. She dropped by the office to meet Flynn Masters, the freelance photographer sent by the *Courier*. The two were scheduled to drive to Bangor to speak with the late Nate Packer's nearest and dearest.

Flynn's ancient Volkswagen bus was full of athletic equipment, smelly jerseys, food wrappers, and empty Gatorade cans. A native of Whitefish, half an hour away, he was tall, bean-pole thin and wore his brown hair down around his shoulders. In addition to his natural outgoing nature, he was blissfully unaware of Lucy's reputation. They immediately hit it off.

En route to the city, Flynn entertained Lucy with tales of his adventures in the Peace Corps, and she told him about her goal of becoming a foreign correspondent.

The sixty-minute drive sped by. As they turned into the open gates that gave onto a long, tree-lined driveway that led to the Packer Mansion on the West side of town, Lucy reflected on the pleasure of conversing with a man who didn't disapprove of her, a man with whom there was no sexual tension.

Flynn parked the bus in a circular driveway behind

a sleek sports car. Lucy stared at the vehicle.

"Is that mauve?"

"Wow," Flynn breathed. "It's Bugatti Veyron.

You know what those things cost?"

"I'm guessing a lot."

"Two million. There're only a handful available."

The house itself was a massive, red brick, faux Tudor with tall, stately columns. Five-foot tall yew bushes outlined the front porch and the stone walkway leading up to it. The house looked as if it had been lifted out of someone's romanticized version of the English countryside.

Lucy lifted the brass lion's head door knocker on the double-wide door then dropped it. Before the door was answered, her phone beeped with a text message. She flipped it open.

WHERE ARE YOU?

Her heart lurched ,but she closed the phone without answering. It would be just like Jake to forbid her to interview persons involved in the murder.

Flynn eyed her, curiously. "Anything wrong?"

She forced a laugh.

"Nah. You know how it is with texting. Some of my friends just have too much time on their hands."

****

Frustration ate at Jake.

He'd always faced problems head on, but he'd never run into a problem like Lucy before. Goddammit he was trying to do the right thing, but she was refusing to cooperate. By Wednesday he found himself dropping by the *Excelsior*'s office.

"Lucy's not here, Sheriff," Ed told him. "She took off with a freelance photographer. They went up to

Bangor to interview the Widow Packer."

Jake frowned. "Dammit, Ed, she shouldn't be involved in this. It's a murder investigation."

The editor raised his eyebrows.

"Lucy's not a kid," he pointed out. "I know you rescued her from the snowstorm but don't make anything out of that. She's growing up. Hell, I trust her to cover the biggest story we've had in twenty years."

"It's dangerous."

Ed shrugged. "Danger's part of life. She'll be careful. Contrary to common belief, she's got a head on her shoulders." The editor's eyes narrowed on his face. "Or is there more to this than meets the eye?"

Jake was horrified to feel heat in his cheeks.

"Can't say as I blame you," Ed said, with a chuckle. "There's somethin' damned appealing about that girl. A kind of innocence."

Jake winced.

Stiles made a choked sound which probably meant that he'd correctly deduced what had happened in the Littlejohns' cabin.

"Take care you don't hurt her, Sheriff. She sounds tough, but she's got a tender heart."

At the moment, Jake just wanted to shake that tender heart right out of her. He barely restrained himself from slamming the office door. He sent her an irritated text which she didn't bother to answer. Furious, he jumped into the Blazer and headed for Bangor.

****

Clothes make the man. And so does the car.

Lucy knew instantly that the mauve sports car belonged, not to the late developer but to his attorney.

99

She knew it from the mauve tie that Claude Moore wore with his silver-gray, hand-tailored suit.

Moore appeared to be in his late fifties. Slender and several inches under six feet, he wore his thinning silver hair neatly trimmed. His tortoiseshell retro glasses gave him the air of a 1930's dandy or maybe it was the white collar on his mauve-and-white striped shirt.

Moore had to be an anachronism in a part of the world where dressing up meant wearing a Patriots sweatshirt and cords. His polished manners matched his elegant clothing.

The attorney greeted Lucy and Flynn and ushered them into the high-ceilinged foyer with its massive crystal chandelier and through a wide corridor filled with paintings that looked like authentic grand masters. Finally, they reached a set of double doors that opened into a drawing room decorated with plush sofas, brocade drapes, and velvet-flocked wallpaper. The room was almost as large as the Eden High School auditorium.

The lady reclining on the antique crimson loveseat had platinum hair that formed a mushroom cloud above her head then cascaded down her body, rippling over mountainous breasts but carefully arranged so as not to obscure her deep décolletage. Her black widow's weeds consisted of a pair of satin lounging pajamas that clung, lovingly to her truly awe-inspiring curves. Paula Packer had "trophy wife" written all over her. Turquoise eyes between spider-length black lashes peered briefly at Lucy then settled on Flynn.

"I hope you don't mind if Flynn takes some candid shots while we speak."

"Not at all," Paula said, keeping her eyes on the young male. Flynn shivered. Lucy glanced at his suddenly flushed face.

Paula Packer fluttered her eyelashes and stretched her collagen-enhanced lips into a cat-that-ate-the-cream smile.

"Be my guest," she murmured in a smoky voice.

Flynn didn't move. Lucy suspected he couldn't move. She spoke his name.

"Huh." He couldn't seem to take his eyes off the vision on the loveseat. He reminded Lucy of a fly stuck in amber.

"You can start shooting anytime."

"Oh, um, yeah." Flynn lifted the digital camera out of his satchel and started clicking. Paula lit up like a Christmas tree. She arched a bit, giving the photographer an excellent view of her majestic chest and probably a hard-on. Lucy decided not to look.

"I'd like some background on your husband." Lucy switched on her tape recorder. Paula didn't seem to hear her. Lucy cleared her throat and raised her voice. "I'd like the readers to see him not just as a victim but as a person, a husband, and co-worker."

"Mmm," Paula said. She licked her lips and fluttered her lashes at Flynn. The camera clicked a little faster.

"Can you tell me about your marriage?"

"It was a wonderful marriage," Paula said. Her voice was thick, like warmed honey. She lifted one manicured hand to her cheek revealing a diamond the size of Gibraltar.

"Ah," Lucy said. What was she supposed to say? Nice going? "How did you meet?"

"Someone introduced us."

"Someone?"

Paula's shiny lips spread to reveal sparkling teeth which reminded Lucy of Jake's shark woman. "Yes. Someone. I can't remember who it was." She paused to reply to Moore who had asked if she'd like to serve tea. Lucy took the opportunity to speak to Flynn.

"Probably a professional escort service."

"Huh?"

Good grief.

"I know people think Nate married me for my looks," Paula said, dismissing Moore with one fluttering hand. "But it wasn't just that. I can be a lot of fun."

"Nate was devoted to you, Paula," the attorney chimed in. "Everyone knew it."

So much for the debonair, man-about-town image. The legal eagle was a suck up. Was he dependent upon Paula to maintain his job? Or had he fallen for her blatant sexuality? Lucy suspected the former.

"Nate wanted to take me to Africa on safari," she went on, "but we decided to stay in our little nest for the next year or so."

"Nest" wasn't the term Lucy would have used to describe the Packer mansion, but she didn't argue.

"Nate didn't mind," Paula went on. "He was happy here." She glanced at the attorney who responded promptly.

"I knew him for fifty years. Never saw him happier."

"Not many people know this, Ms., uh…"

"Outlaw," Lucy supplied.

"Right. I know your brother." She leaned forward,

and the fabric of her lounging pajamas strained to control its bounty. "He's super hot with that dark coloring and the blue eyes."

Lucy nodded. "What don't many people know," she prompted, trying to get the widow back on track.

"Oh, that Nate wanted an heir."

"Good heavens," Lucy said, startled into rudeness. Was that why Packer had divorced a wife of more than thirty years and married a much younger woman? Had the developer had a Napoleonic complex?

Paula did not appear to be offended. Lucy suspected she didn't much care about women's reactions.

"Naturally I was happy to comply. What is more romantic than a man begging you to have his child?"

Lucy thought a distinction could be made between a man who wanted to create a family with a woman and one who just wanted to leave his biological footprint on the world but she wasn't here to insult Paula Packer. She was supposed to be gathering material for a story.

"I can't think of a thing."

A set of chimes produced the first bars of the William Tell overture. Moore excused himself to answer the door.

"Mrs. Packer," Lucy said, "can you tell me who your late husband's beneficiaries are?"

"Oh, well, Claude's the money man. You'd have to check with him for the details, but I get to keep the house and the cars. And, of course, all the money."

What else was there except the house, cars, and money? Lucy tried to analyze the answer, but she got distracted when the hair prickled on the back of her neck and her stomach somersaulted. She knew it was

Jake even before she spotted the big, blond man or inhaled the familiar scent of strawberry shortcake.

The kryptonite eyes met hers, and she felt lightheaded even before she got around to admiring the way his khaki uniform shirt outlined his powerful shoulders. She gazed at his flat stomach, remembering the ridged muscles and below that, the thick, smooth evidence of his desire. Her eyelashes fluttered shut and when she opened them, there was a woman on his arm. Literally. Paula had wrapped her long, manicured fingers around his bicep and her huge, virtually unconfined breasts rested on his forearm.

"Sheriff." Paula's voice took on a lower, more husky tone. "How lovely to see you again so soon." So soon?

"Please, come sit by me." The widow drew him across the room and onto the crimson sofa. She continued to hold onto his arm, a calculated move, Lucy thought, because she was able to gradually let go of it and let her fingers fall on his thigh.

The whirring camera had stopped, and Flynn's mesmerized gaze was as admiring as a dog eyeing a juicy steak.

Lucy glanced at Jake who winked at her.

"I'm being interviewed," Paula explained to the man on the sofa beside her. "It's all very exhausting." She allowed her head to drop against his shoulder. Her hand started to trail down the plain of his muscular thigh, but he scooped it up and held it.

"I'm sure Lucy is nearly finished," he said, to Paula.

Lucy was momentarily speechless and fury swept through her. How dare Paula Packer manhandle Jake?

"Uh, I just have one more question, Mrs. Packer. Did you sign a prenuptial agreement?"

Paula frowned and Lucy braced herself for an offended response but the widow didn't seem to mind the question.

"I believe I did sign a prenup. Claude would know." She glanced at the attorney who nodded. Then she glanced back at Jake as if he had asked the question. As if he were the source of life. "It seemed like the right thing to do."

Lucy's eyes narrowed on Jake. What would the voters of Eden County think if they could see their sheriff twisted into a pretzel with the sexy widow?

"Why do you want to know?"

"I imagine Ms. Outlaw is trying to figure out whether you had a reason to want your husband dead," Jake drawled. "Inheritance is often a motive."

"Not in this case." The attorney sounded apologetic but firm. "A prenup is set up to protect the parties in the event of divorce. Nate didn't fear that. His only worry was fertility. Paula's prenup provides a guarantee that she will inherit all of Nate's personal holdings in the event of death with the only provision that she was to provide him with a son. Otherwise she gets nothing."

Lucy blinked, astonished. "So you inherit nothing?"

Paula's smile was filled with triumph.

"I was fortunate enough to make Nate's dream come true, and I was able to let him know the good news before his unfortunate death." She rubbed, lightly, against Jake's arm. "I will deliver his heir on January first."

Lucy gaped at her. "January first?"

"Guaranteed. It's a scheduled C-section. Going through labor was not part of the bargain."

"You already know it's a boy?"

"We went the designer route. No point in going through any of this otherwise." Just for a moment she sounded like the practical soul that she probably was under all the sexy camouflage. "He's already named, too. Nate Packer, Junior."

Lucy was aware of Jake's gaze on her. Was he thinking about the slim possibility that she was pregnant? Or was he thinking about her namesake, Lucy Junior?

"Congratulations," she said, finally.

Paula nodded but her attention was now fully engaged in her own fingers which were playing a version of the Eensie Weensie Spider going up Nate's arm.

Lucy did not like the surges of jealousy that ribboned through her body. She'd already turned down his lame proposal. What business was it of hers if Jake wanted to flirt with a murder suspect? Although, she had to admit, she wasn't certain that Paula was a suspect. Nor was she certain that Jake was flirting. He didn't seem to mind the attention, though.

"Mrs. Packer, one last question. Where were you the night of your husband's death?"

"Lucy." Jake's deep voice held a warning.

"You're not a cop."

"Why, Sheriff," Paula sparkled up at him. "I don't mind answering. I was right here, Ms. Outlaw.

Upstairs in bed. Pregnant ladies need their sleep, you know. Isn't that right, Claude?"

"You were here in the house, Paula," he said, with

his precise diction. "The servants can corroborate that."

"The servants? Could I talk to them?"

Jake stood, dragging Paula, who was still attached to his arm, to her feet. "The interview's over."

Lucy ignored him but she stood, too.

"Mrs. Packer, before we leave, could we take a few pictures of your lovely home?"

"Certainly. Claude, could you give the guests the grand tour?" She smiled at Lucy. "Is your name really Lucy? Are people always saying, 'Lucy, you got some 'splainin' to do?'"

"Yes."

"Come along, Ms. Outlaw, Mr. Flynn." Moore gestured toward a door then he waited until Lucy and Flynn had preceded him. She couldn't help noticing that left Jake along with the Black Widow. He probably hoped she'd bite him. Lucy wrinkled her nose. She realized she was being ridiculous on so many levels. Lucy might not make it to Jake's short list but neither would pregnant Paula.

Probably.

The trio climbed the wide center hall staircase, and Flynn shot photos of the master bedroom's purple walls, gold-toned fixtures, and the massive canopy bed held up with posts carved into the shapes of naked women. Then they descended a back staircase to the large, square kitchen full of gleaming appliances and state-of-the-art equipment worthy of a five-star restaurant.

"The late Mr. Packer loved his food," Moore said, by way of explanation. "The first Mrs. Packer was a gourmet chef. Of course she never lived here. The mansion was built six months ago for Nate and Paula."

He'd provided an excellent opening to talk about the victim's ex and Lucy took it.

"I understand that the first Mrs. Packer helped her husband found Packer Inc."

"That is correct," Moore said. He spoke in a calm, deliberative manner as if he carefully considered everything that came out of his mouth. The opposite of herself, Lucy thought, ruefully. "The three of us grew up together. Shirley was intimately involved in Packer Inc. right up until the divorce."

"And you, too?"

The question bordered on rudeness, but Lucy reminded herself she had an excuse. She was, after all, a member of the fourth estate.

"Oh, yes. I am still involved, of course, in a somewhat different role."

Lucy nodded. It appeared that Moore had taken on the task of guarding Paula Packer's interests. The question was, why? Had he fallen under her spell? Lucy could detect in him none of the sexual awareness that was so evident in the other males. Was it the money? Loyalty to his lifelong friend? She glanced at the lawyer's pleasant face and decided that it was probably a combination of the two.

Moore appeared to read her thoughts.

"Paula insisted we dissolve the three-way partnership at the time of her marriage and neither Shirley nor I objected. We understood Nate, you see, and we didn't begrudge him his last chance for immortality."

"I find it a little difficult to believe neither of you minded being given the boot.'

"It wasn't 'the boot,'" Claude said. Did she detect

just a whiff of irritability there? "He bought us out. I remained his personal attorney, and I will do everything I can for his widow."

"And the first Mrs. Packer was equally understanding?"

"Shirley is not one to wear her heart on her sleeve. Neither does she dwell on regrets. I believe she has adjusted well to her new life."

"And you?" Once again Lucy knew her question was impertinent.

An odd expression flashed in the pale gray eyes.

"I miss the old days. How could I not? We were partners for more than thirty years. But things change and people must change with them, Ms. Outlaw."

It was a logical, reasoned response. The attorney, Lucy thought, was a man who knew when protest was useless.

They arrived at a corridor that contained three closed doors. As they were about to pass, a uniformed maid stepped out of one of the rooms. She paled, apparently as startled to see them as Lucy was to see her and, after a mumbled apology, she sped down the hall.

"What's in there?" Lucy asked the attorney.

"It's a trophy room," Claude said. "Probably best to bypass it. People are often disturbed by the heads."

Lucy repressed a shudder. But she had a job to do, and there was no time for squeamishness.

"I'd like to see them," She said, with a bogus smile.

Claude seemed to hesitate, but in the end, he didn't try to change her mind. He unlocked the door and stood aside to let her enter. It took most of her courage to step inside and as soon as she did, her stomach lurched. She'd forgotten Flynn was with them until she heard his horrified whisper. "Holy Mother of God."

Chapter Seven

Hundreds of lifeless but, somehow, accusing eyes stared at Lucy and she had to curl her fingers into fists to keep from screaming and/or sprinting back down the corridor.

Every instinct told her to get away from the room, and the house, pronto, and yet there was an equally insistent bell ringing in her head. This room was important. This room could tell her something about Nate Packer, something about why he'd been shot through the heart on the casino site near the rez. Lucy forced herself to step into the heart of the room.

She forced herself to look at the heads.

"Do you notice anything weird about this," she asked Flynn.

"Apart from the fact that they're dead?"

Suddenly she realized what it was. Instead of the traditional deer, elk, bear, and moose the animals were exotic. Many of them had spiral horns and some had striped faces.

"These are all types of African antelope," Moore explained. "Kudu, enyala, cape buffalo, gensbuck. There's a cape buffalo and leopards, lions, hippos, a zebra."

Lucy's heart twisted at the sight of the lion and the zebra. She much preferred to see them in a zoo or, better yet, in a storybook.

"Rhinos are off limits these days," Moore continued, "and that's all you can bring home from an elephant." He pointed to a pair of large dumbo-like ears, tusks, and a tail mounted on a board.

The room felt like the setting for a horror movie.

"Is this, is this a crocodile," Flynn asked, his voice faint.

"That's right. And here's a white tiger."

She felt tears prick the backs of her eyes. All this killing. All this death. If life were fair, Packer would have been shot by an avenging kudu. "Did Mr. Packer shoot all these himself?"

"Every single one," Moore said.

"With a rifle?"

The attorney shook his head. "Nate was more sporting than that. He shot them, believe it or not, with a bow and arrow."

The breath caught in Lucy's throat. Was there a message in that?

"Ironic, in its way."

"If he only hunted with a bow why all the other weapons," Flynn asked. He indicated a wall full of antique weapons including long rifles, pistols, a Samurai sword, a rapier, and a foil. There was a crossbow, too, as well as a quiver of arrows.

Moore shrugged his elegant shoulders.

"Nate liked weaponry, but these are just collectibles. He hunted only with the bow as that made the effort more sporting. A bowman must get within thirty feet of his prey whereas a rifleman can hit a target from a distance of hundreds of feet.

Bow hunting requires skill, finesse, and courage."

Pride in his late friend was evident in his voice.

Lucy had been born and raised in Maine, and she knew that many in the state hunted for sport but also for food. The idea of pursuing these African creatures just to show off their dead faces felt cruel.

She noticed a section on the wall of photographs. They were all of one man, the same man, dressed in bush clothing, including an Ernest Hemingway-styled hat. The man's face was only partly visible because of the hat and a bushy beard, but Lucy could see the massive grin, and she had no doubt at all that it was Nate Packer. The Great White hunter.

Flynn leaned over her shoulder. "Who's in the background of that picture?"

Lucy squinted at a figure so small she hadn't noticed it at first. It was a second hunter dressed similarly.

Claude's voice had a smile in it. "Believe it or not that's Shirley. She always accompanied Nate on the trips."

"She's a hunter, too?"

"Oh, no. We were just his entourage."

"You were there, too?" Somehow, Lucy hadn't put that together.

"Who do you think shot the photos, Ms. Outlaw?" The attorney's voice sounded amused.

"I hadn't thought."

"I wasn't just the photographer, of course. I have a pilot's license. That's how we traveled from one venue to the next. And, of course, I conveyed the kill to the taxidermist. Nate was a touch squeamish about that."

It was hard to reconcile the grinning hunter in the photograph and the dozens of dead eyes with a man who was "squeamish."

The trio really had been the Three Musketeers, their lives intertwined for thirty years until Paula showed up. Lucy just didn't understand why Shirley and Claude had accepted the change so easily.

When they returned to the salon, it was empty and Lucy felt the now-familiar surge of jealousy. Had they gone up to the decadent master bedroom? Paula had seemed ready to throw down and consummate and Jake, well, Lucy knew very well how attractive he was. Suddenly, she wanted to get out of the mansion. She thanked Moore and tried not to mind when she saw that white Blazer still parked in the circular drive.

Thirty minutes later, the VW bus pulled up in front of a neat, tidy, clapboard home on Cherry Street on Bangor's north side. Flynn pulled part way into a paved drive that led around back to a garage.

The Cape Cod topped with a widow's walk was more of a bungalow than a house, and it should have looked cozy with its protective eaves and stone walkway. Despite the curtains at the windows and the rhododendron bushes that flanked the stone walkway, the house appeared just a bit forlorn. It took Lucy a minute to figure it out. The entire house was gray, including the shutters. There was no white trim, no jaunty front door.

This time there was no dapper lawyer to open the door just the first Mrs. Packer, slim and fit with cropped salt-and-pepper hair had a long nose and a narrow face whose lines were unsoftened by makeup. She dressed much like Lucy herself, in a pair of worn blue jeans and a green-and-white checked blouse. There was a direct look in her faded blue eyes. She'd never been a beauty, Lucy decided, but she'd probably been a force of nature, one who had helped her husband to success. She seemed to be the antithesis of the Widow Packer, and yet Nate had married them both.

How had it felt to be cast aside after thirty years?

"Ms. Outlaw?' Shirley's voice was polite, if not welcoming. "Please come in."

After granting permission for photos, Shirley appeared to ignore Flynn as he moved around her small, shadowed living room snapping shots.

Lucy explained again that she was trying to flesh out the characters in the murder.

"I want to show your ex-husband as a multidimensional human being, a normal man." She was rather proud of her explanation.

"Except that," Shirley said, dryly, "normal men do not get murdered—with bows and arrows. But then, that makes it a better story, doesn't it?" Lucy ignored the undertone of sarcasm.

"Well, let's just say it makes it a story. Do you think the weapon was significant? Do you think it could be related to your late husband's passion for big game hunting?"

Shirley's mouth twisted in what might be amusement. "I thought you were interested in the everyday Nate Packer, not the murder."

"I'm interested in both," Lucy admitted. "And I would imagine my readers are, too."

Shirley nodded. "That's honest. I can't tell you why he was killed or who did it. Nate was sixty years old, wealthy and often ruthless. He was not overburdened with principles, and he could rub people the wrong way. I believe your brother hated him."

Lucy's heart almost stopped. She'd almost

forgotten about Cam's involvement in all this.

"Hate is a strong word. I think Cam was disappointed in Mr. Packer, but only recently."

"Coincidentally, the murder occurred recently, too."

Lucy's eyes narrowed on the other woman. "Are you accusing my brother of killing your ex-husband?"

"Not at all."

Lucy blinked. "Because he didn't, Mrs. Packer.

Cam would never have killed another human being."

Shirley surprised Lucy by agreeing.

"I don't know your brother well, but I would be surprised if he'd murdered Nate."

"Were you surprised your ex-husband was murdered?"

She appeared to think about that.

"Yes and no. As I said, he had some enemies."

"Was it true he was mixed up with the New Jersey mob?"

The late developer's ex-wife waited an instant too long to answer.

"I wouldn't know. I haven't been involved in the business for well over a year."

Lucy nodded. "You seem to have adjusted to the change very well. It had to be upsetting to be, well, ousted from the company."

"To say nothing of being ousted from the marriage," Shirley said, without a smile. "It wasn't flattering, but I'm a realist, Ms. Outlaw. When something's over, it's over. Nate got a bee in his bonnet about what he called creating a dynasty. It was time for me to bow out."

"That's a very generous attitude."

She shrugged. "I knew Nate very well. He was fun and outgoing and he could be great company but he was never much of one for delayed gratification.

There wasn't any point in being bitter."

"Did Mr. Moore feel the same?"

The notch deepened between Shirley's eyebrows.

"Claude was devoted to Nate. He'd never denied him anything, and Nate kept him on, in a somewhat altered capacity."

"Have the two of you remained friends?"

Shirley held Lucy's gaze long enough for the younger woman to recognize her own impertinence. Lucy tried to ignore the rush of heat. This was her job.

"We don't see each other much. Our mutual interest was Nate." She paused. "I can tell you're confused. People are types, you know. Nate was charismatic, a whirlwind of energy and charm very attractive to us worker bees. The flip side of that temperament is often carelessness."

"Could he have been killed because of his carelessness?"

"I would think so."

"But you don't know who killed him."

"I know who didn't kill him, Ms. Outlaw. I know it wasn't me."

"Do you think it could have been the current Mrs. Packer?"

The light eyes were knowing.

"This isn't really a story behind the man, is it?

You're hoping to build a career by finding a scandal."

"I want to find the scandal if there is a scandal,"

Lucy said, taken aback by the woman's forthrightness. "I definitely want the story about
Nate Packer _ his life and death."
Shirley Packer looked mildly amused.
"Why did he suddenly want a child? I mean, at this late date?"
"Who knows? Maybe he really just wanted a younger, different woman, and the child was the excuse." She suddenly seemed to lose interest in the whole conversation.
"Do you think he loved Paula?"
It was a very impertinent question, and Lucy knew it.
"I have no idea. I'm not sure Nate knew what love is. I'm not sure anybody knows what it is. 'Love' is a concept for the very young, you know." Her smile was not unkind.
Lucy felt as if the former Mrs. Packer was trying to tell her something. Maybe if she could keep the conversation going she'd find out what.
"What about the business? Did you mind giving up your part in it?"
"It was necessary. I'd been in the captain's chair for too long to accept a demotion. I got a reasonable settlement, and I have what I need."
She was very understanding, Lucy thought. Almost unbelievably so.
"Let me give you a piece of advice from an older woman to a younger one. You can't force respect or affection. If you hang on to a man who doesn't really want you, you will lose your self-respect in the long run."
Lucy eyed her, grimly. She'd figured that out for

herself.

Lost in thoughts about Jake, Lucy didn't think of the last question until they'd reached the door.

"Do you know about the baby?"

Something flashed in the pale eyes, but it was gone so quickly Lucy couldn't identify the emotion.

"I knew it was in the works. So there is to be a baby, after all," she said. "Nate must have been pleased."

The sun had stayed behind the clouds most of the day, but now in the late afternoon, it was strong enough to cast shadows on the snow-covered lawns. Lucy started down the front path but stopped in her tracks when she spotted the white Blazer that had pulled in behind the van, corralling it the way a sheepdog would have herded an escaped lamb. Flynn was standing on the sidewalk arguing with an equally tall, much broader figure. Jake's hat was pulled down low over his eyes. With his feet apart and his hands on his hips, he looked like a gunslinger facing down an enemy at high noon. He glanced over at Lucy and his green eyes flashed.

Lucy's stomach flipped.

"Get into the Blazer," he growled.

She glared at him. How dare he order her around? "Flynn's taking me home."

"Flynn won't be able to get out of the driveway unless you cooperate."

She searched his face. The dark circles under his eyes had deepened in the past few days, and there was a new vertical line running down each of his lean cheeks. Jake Langley looked like a man at the end of his rope. She decided to cut him a break.

"Flynn," she said, "I'll ride back with Jake."

The photographer nodded. "No worries. I'll see you tomorrow."

****

Jake drove with singular concentration until they reached the interstate. He didn't bother to try to analyze why he was so angry. He knew why. He'd lost control of the investigation, and he'd lost control of his life.

He blamed both of the losses on the woman in the seat next to him.

Dammit. He knew he was making excuses. It wasn't Lucy's fault he wanted her. It wasn't Lucy's fault she was too young. It wasn't even her fault that she wanted to interview the two Mrs. Packers for her story but it had made him furious to find her in—with another guy.

Worst of all, he found himself halfway hoping she'd turn up pregnant so she'd have to marry him soon.

Hell.

She sat beside him looking out the window.

"You have nothing to say?"

She turned to face him. "You're the one who insisted I ride with you, Jake."

He glanced at the wide sky-blue eyes. She was right.

"What's tomorrow?"

"Thursday."

"I mean," he said, with exaggerated patience, "why are you seeing that photographer tomorrow?"

"Flynn? We're going out to the casino site so he can shoot some photos."

"Not alone."

"Not alone. With Flynn."

Jake felt a surge of temper. "You tell camera-boy if he messes up the crime scene I'll have his job. And yours."

Her blue eyes opened wide. When had he turned into such an ass?

"Listen," she said, "I know this is a frustrating time for you but you'll catch whoever killed Nate Packer."

"Yeah."

"Or I'll catch him. Or her."

Fury coursed through his veins.

"You need to stay out of this."

"I'm a reporter, Jake."

"Your job is to find out from me what's going on in the investigation. It is not to gather evidence or witness statements." He thrust his fingers through his short, biscuit-blond hair. "You could compromise the case, Lucy. Do you understand that?"

"I'm just talking to the people involved. I'm not trying to gather evidence or build a case. We're on the same side."

"Sometimes it doesn't feel that way."

Lucy laughed, and the tension eased. They rode in silence for a few minutes. It felt almost companionable.

"You know what, Jake? I think Nate Packer may have deserved what he got."

He glanced at her flushed cheeks and the clear blue eyes. The words surprised him. Lucy might be young and impulsive but she wasn't judgmental.

"What makes you say that?" He really wanted to know.

"He may have been a psychopath. At the least he was a self-centered jerk. He used Shirley and Moore, and I don't think he ever did much for Paula, either."

"He made her pregnant."

"A good example of what I'm talking about. Who does that designer baby business? Megalomaniacs."

"Why shouldn't people get to choose the gender of their children?"

She laughed. "There speaks a man who ended up with a boy and a girl with one toss of the dice." Then she sobered up. "There's just something creepy about fertilizing an egg and then rejecting it because it has no 'Y' chromosomes."

There was another silence, and Jake knew they were both thinking about their failure to use birth control at the cabin.

"Lucy," he said, finally.

"What do you think about Paula?"

She didn't want to discuss it now. All right, he'd wait.

"Paula?"

"As a suspect, I mean."

"You think Paula murdered her husband?"

"She's the only beneficiary. This way she gets the fortune and the baby, and she doesn't have to put up with Nate."

"I think we can rule her out. I've shot a bow and arrow before, and I'm not sure she has the right, uh, physique to be an effective archer. Too many obstacles in the way."

Lucy giggled. "There is that."

"Anyway, she's got an airtight alibi."

"She's a bombshell," Lucy pointed out. "She'd have been able to get a guy to do it for her."

"Like who? Moore?"

Lucy appeared to consider that.

"He's too fastidious and not a sportsman. Besides, by all accounts he was totally attached to Packer. But there have to be men in Paula's past."

"Scads of them, I'd guess."

Lucy sat up a little straighter, her spine stiff.

"She may even have a partner who's expecting to get half of the Packer estate."

"Like Bonnie and Clyde."

"Why not?"

"It seems a little melodramatic."

Lucy shrugged. "Paula Packer's not exactly the queen of subtlety. Think about the timing. She has to provide an heir if she's going to inherit and she's barely pregnant when he's killed."

He cast her a look.

"You think I'm right, don't you?"

"I think there's no such thing as 'barely pregnant.' Once that train's out of the station it's on its way. There's no stopping it."

She was quiet a moment. He'd have bet a month's wages she was trying to figure out how to change the subject.

"Jake, did you get a look inside that trophy room?"

"I've been all over that house."

She looked out the window as if his answer troubled her. Why? What had he said?

"What about the trophy room?"

"I don't know. It bothered me. All those dead eyes. All that blood. What kind of a guy kills all those creatures for fun?"

"A guy with something to prove. The same kind of

guy who wants to start a dynasty."

"Maybe. It's just that everybody who knew Nate Packer seemed to like him so much—even my brother. I can't imagine being charmed by a coldblooded killer."

"Most con men are charming. It's what makes them effective."

"I guess."

"Lucy."

She looked directly at him, and he felt a familiar tightening in his gut.

"You have that warning note in your voice," she said. "The one that always leads up to 'Lucy, you've got some 'splainin' to do.'"

"Not this time. I found out that the contract between the Eden County Community Bank and

Packer Inc., had a death clause. If either dies before the project is finished, the other gets full control. It was put in there to make sure the Blackbird Reservation gets its casino and resort."

The color drained out of her face, and the blue eyes looked huge in her small face.

"Cam didn't do it, you know, Jake," she spoke quietly. "I know he didn't do it the same way I know you didn't do it."

He was unexpectedly touched by her faith in him, but he didn't admit it. And he couldn't relieve her mind about her brother. The guy had means, motive, and opportunity and an alibi as full of holes as Swiss cheese.

Forty minutes later they pulled up in front of the *Excelsior*. She unbuckled her seatbelt and looked at him.

"You texted me earlier. What was that about?"

Christ. He'd almost forgotten. He told her about Mrs. Peach's sister.

"I've got a kid coming in for the afternoons, but she can't sleep there. And besides, I've got to have an adult in the house to satisfy my mother-in-law."

"Jake, why don't you just make peace with her?"

"Out of the question. I tried the friend route. She tricked me into bringing the twins to the ranch, and then she seduced them. I had a helluva time getting them to leave."

"They were younger then. They would never choose a ranch over you now."

He shook his head. "Give Maxine an inch and she'll take away your children. Trust me on this."

"I can't be your nanny again."

He clamped his jaw shut. He'd asked, she'd answered. Same as with marriage. She didn't want to be an instant mom any more than Ariel had, and in Lucy's case, these weren't her children. He had to respect her wishes.

"I've got the job at the *Excelsior*. I couldn't be there for them after school."

"Like I said, I don't need you after school. I've got Moonbeam for that."

"Moonbeam?"

"It's her name du jour. A small teenage rebellion. Mary Ellen's actually a good kid." If you ignore the dyed black hair, the pierced nose, and the eyeliner that made her look like a raccoon.

"What about the tuna surprise? I haven't learned to cook in the last week. I was kinda busy."

He flashed on the memory of her eager little cries, the soft but resilient feel of her small breasts, the sense of homecoming he'd felt embedded in her sweet depths. Yeah. She'd been busy. She didn't have time to be his nanny anymore, either, but she was considering it. Soft-hearted Lucy.

"I could have Moonbeam pick up a coupla cans of Chicken of the Sea before she comes over this afternoon."

He felt like Nate Packer. All he wanted was for his kids to be safe from Maxine. He wasn't thinking about inconveniencing Lucy. He wasn't thinking about putting her in the much-too-vulnerable position of sleeping just down the hall from him.

Or maybe he was. He wanted her. He wouldn't like to himself about that.

"I'll do it," she said, quietly. "But only until you can get someone permanent."

Gratitude swept through him along with a sudden realization that Lucy wasn't like Ariel at all. His wife had been a taker while Lucy was not. He didn't share his conviction that she belonged to him, that when there was someone permanent in his household it would be Lucy herself.

"Great," he said. "Thanks."

Chapter Eight

Lucy stared at the ceiling. It felt right to be back in the double bed in the Langley's guestroom. It had felt right to share another tuna meal with Jake, Sam, Lillie, Wiggles, and Lucy Junior. It felt wonderful to hear all about school and the upcoming first-grade play, Parade of Presidents. It felt fantastic to read a bedtime story to Lillie while Jake read one to Sam.

It also felt surreal. And dangerous. She'd agreed to come here again knowing the price she'd have to pay. She was facing more heartache. This wouldn't end well. Not even if, in a moment of weakness, she agreed to marry the studly sheriff.

If you hang onto a man who doesn't really want you, you'll lose your self-respect in the end.

That he didn't really want her was evidenced by the fact that she was here and he was in his own room down the hall. She flipped over onto her stomach and told herself it was for the best. More sex would just mean more complications, and neither of them needed that.

She flipped onto her back.

If they maintained a professional distance, Jake could continue to search for the perfect second wife and she, Lucy, could continue to work on her long-term career plans.

She was here for the children, whom she loved.

And for Jake, whom she loved even more.

Lucy grabbed the pillow and hauled it over her head.

The next morning was so warm that there were only small islands of snow in the grassy earth of the construction site. By late morning the sun had pushed the temperature above sixty degrees, and the breeze was practically balmy.

Lucy and Flynn tramped around the mud while he shot photos of the cordoned-off area where the body had been found, the construction trailer, and the fringe of trees behind it.

Until the land had been cleared, this area had been home to balsam, maples, elm, and wild apple trees, as well as assorted evergreens. Every Maine fourth-grader learned that the state was ninety percent forested, more than any other state in the Union, and Lucy had been no exception. The woodland Indians of a century ago, including the Penobscots, the Abenaki, the Passamaquoddy, the Mi'kmaq, and the Maliseet would have been shocked to discover that a chunk of the forests that had nurtured them was being ripped out by the roots to make way for hot tubs, craps tables, and slot machines.

On the other hand, the Penobscots could no longer live off the land. They needed jobs, and they needed a clinic.

It still seemed sad.

Lucy inhaled the fresh scent of the earth. It was May first, and spring was finally on its way. Around the edges of the cleared land, she could see tender green shoots on the deciduous trees, and she could hear a few of the birds that had returned early from their southern retreat. Lucy had been so busy fighting her reputation and her feelings for Jake that she'd forgotten how much she loved springtime in western Maine. She said a quick silent prayer that the season would bring peace and happiness to everyone on the rez and in town, too. Especially to Jake and his kids.

While she waited for Flynn to finish snapping photos, she walked back to the site outlined in yellow tape. The morning sun reflected off of something on the ground. Was it dew? Or was there something embedded in the mud? A shiver ran up her spine as she knelt for a closer look. Not dew. A shiny object. She scooped it up in her hand and gasped. It was an earring, a tiny silver feather, and she'd seen it before, last February, the day Hallie had brought her out to the rez to meet Molly Whitecloud.

Had Molly been here the night of the murder? Lucy's heart beat fast. Surely not. It was entirely possible the earring didn't even belong to Molly. There had to be dozens if not hundreds of pairs of silver feather pierced earrings in western Maine.

Molly thought back to the weather of the past week. The area had suffered a series of cloudbursts up through the night of Miss Violet's recital which was also the night of murder and the night of The Kiss. Warmth flooded Lucy, and she momentarily lost her train of thought. The nor'easter had struck the very next day so that if the earring had been dropped that night it would have been buried under the snow and only surfaced now because of the melt.

It seemed likely the earring had been dropped here recently. Lucy shivered. Surely Molly hadn't had anything to do with Packer's murder. She was a woman of peace, a healer. And, in any case, she'd been with Cam.

Unless they'd both been out at the casino site.

Lucy's heart thumped harder. The earring was clearly evidence. She should turn it into Jake, but she knew she wouldn't. This was one lead she would follow up on alone.

"I'm done unless there're more shots you want."

Flynn's voice, much closer than she'd imagined, startled Lucy. She bounced up to her feet in a nervous movement.

"You okay there, Ace?"

"Fine. Great. I was just thinking."

The photographer grinned at her. "It's too nice a day to think."

"You're right. You ready for the picnic?"

"Hell, yeah. Ground's kinda wet though. Let's sit in the van."

Lucy agreed. Minutes later she was unpacking the basket prepared by Asia in the Outlaw kitchen.

"Oh my god!" Flynn stared at the drumstick in his hand. "Fried chicken, homemade potato salad, and brownies. Sweet tea. I'm in heaven."

"I know. Asia's a fantastic cook. I'm pretty much a one-dish girl."

"What's the dish?"

"Tuna surprise."

The photographer laughed. "These days I'd be happy with any version of tuna, but it makes my girlfriend sick. She feels too lousy to cook, and all she ever wants to eat is Ben & Jerry's Red Velvet Cake ice cream. In a cup, not a cone. She can't even stand to have me cook anything."

"Sounds like she's pregnant."

"She is." He sounded self-conscious and proud at the same time. His eyes twinkled.

"Oh, wow! Congratulations!"

"Thanks. The timing wasn't perfect. I was about to take a gig with National Geographic, and Marcia planned on spending a year doing Teach For America but, hey, what're you gonna do?"

"It must have been hard for both of you to give up your dreams."

The photographer shrugged. "Life's all about choices until you make a kid. Luckily, impending parenthood is exciting, too. We've already got a name. Jessie Augusta for our mothers. I can't wait to see her."

Lucy felt tears prick the backs of her eyes. "It's a beautiful name. She's a lucky little girl."

"I guess she will be if her parents ever learn to cook."

They ate in companionable silence until Lucy spoke.

"What did you think of those trophy heads?"

"Weird, man. I spent a summer interning for National Geographic in Kenya. I'm pretty sure it's illegal to kill some of those critters."

"I wondered about that. Was there anything else that struck you as strange?"

Flynn closed his eyes as if trying to reconstruct the scene. "The lawyer told us he and Packer's first wife just went along on safari as extras. That role made sense for him, I guess, but Mrs. Packer struck me as the type who'd go off on her own adventure rather than tagging along behind her husband."

"I think she was pretty devoted to him at one time."

"Maybe people change, but there was something weird about that three-amigos-on-a-camel scenario."

"We don't know when the safaris ended. I got the impression Shirley came to see him more as a son than a husband, so when he wanted to take off and marry someone else, it must have seemed almost natural. Although I wonder what she really thinks of Paula."

"Whew. Paula." He waved his hand across his forehead, pretending to wipe away sweat. "She's one hot number."

"Is it possible she married him for anything but his money?"

"Who knows? Maybe she was looking for a father figure. I'll tell you something about women like Paula. They use their own attractiveness as a tool to get what they want."

"Well, duh."

"No, what I mean is, she uses her sexuality, but she may not enjoy it."

"Would that bother you if you were the man?"

Flynn appeared to think.

"Probably not. It's kinda hard to think around her."

"Do you think she really is pregnant?"

"I wondered about that, too," he said. "I guess time will tell. Speaking of that, don't let me forget to stop at the Stop and Shop on the way home."

"You out of ice cream?"

"Always."

Lucy poured him more tea then lifted her paper cup in a toast. "To your little family."

He clinked cups with her just as the hairs rose on the back of her neck again and a harsh growl made her jerk enough to slosh the tea out of her paper cup.

"This is a murder scene, Lucy. Not Jellystone Park."

Flynn held up a brownie. "Dessert, Sheriff? We've got plenty."

Jake's eyes never left Lucy. "I gave you permission for a photo shoot, not an orgy."

"I gotta brush up on my definitions," Flynn said. He appeared blissfully undaunted by the snarling lawman. "I thought an orgy was something else entirely."

"Don't mind him," Lucy told Flynn. "He's just a little sleep deprived."

"As you're in a position to know."

The provocative tone shocked her, and she searched the scowling face at her elbow. Was Jake jealous?

"We were toasting Flynn's family," she said, mildly. "He and his girlfriend are about to become the parents of a little girl."

The harsh lines in the sheriff's face eased.

"Welcome to the wars," Jake told the photographer.

"Thanks. I think."

"It's the hardest job you'll ever do, but trust me, there's nothing better."

Lucy felt a sudden lump in her throat. All three children were lucky to have such caring dads. Flynn's baby would be lucky enough to have a mother, too. Suddenly Lucy understood why it was so important for Jake to marry the right person and soon.

Jake slapped his hand on the windowsill of her door.

"See you at home," he said. As the Blazer

disappeared down the dirt road Flynn turned to Lucy.

"You want to explain that?"

She hesitated, briefly, considering the complicated relationship that existed between the sheriff and herself.

"I'm his temporary nanny."

"Uh-huh."

Later that afternoon Lucy met Moonbeam for the first time. Her goth looks were a little startling, but she turned out to be responsible and good company. Over the next few days they developed a workable routine to make sure the kids were cared for, the meals cooked, and the laundry completed. It was easy to begin thinking of the little group on Cypress Street as a family.

Jake always came home for supper despite the added work of the murder investigation, but most nights he went back to the office afterwards to catch up on his routine paperwork. Lucy got into the habit of sitting cross-legged on the living room sofa and working on her laptop, reviewing her notes and shaping her stories. One evening a few days after she'd returned to the sheriff's home, the phone rang. Lucy flinched. No one in Eden called after eight p.m. Not unless it was an emergency. Fear shot through her. Had Jake interrupted a robbery? Had he been shot? She picked up the phone.

"Sheriff Langley's residence."

"Who is this?" The caller was female, peremptory and irate. Lucy suppressed her natural desire to withhold information. It was, after all, Jake's house.

"This is Lucy Outlaw. May I ask who's calling?"

"My name is Maxine Slocum," the woman snapped. "And I wish to speak with Sheriff Langley. Immediately."

Maxine Slocum. The troublemaking grandma. Lucy's heart kicked. She shouldn't meddle in Jake's life, but her interception of this phone call seemed like fate. And somebody had to fix this family's problem.

"Hello, Mrs. Slocum. Jake isn't here at the moment."

"Who are you? The girlfriend?"

"No. I'm the temporary nanny, but I'm also a friend. Do you have a minute? I've been hoping to talk with you."

****

Jake stopped at the light on the corner of Main and First Streets and watched, with growing impatience, as Miss Clara Atwater, Eden's eldest resident and sole member of the D.A.R., supported by her walker, inched across the two-laned thoroughfare. At one point she stopped to rest, looked over at him, and beamed. He waved, ashamed of his impatience. He had no call to take out his frustration on her.

The fact was, he'd stalled out on the Packer investigation. All the leads had fizzled out.

The young turks out on the rez who opposed the casino had been playing pool at the community center at the time of Packer's death, and there were no Packer employees who would benefit from their boss's demise. Packer had definitely cut corners in his purchases and he'd signed contracts with mob-linked vendors but Jake hadn't been able to find anyone but Cam Outlaw who'd been outraged about that. There was no reason for the mob to rub him out.

Jake's gut told him the wives were at the heart of the matter, but both they and Moore had solid alibis, backed by a neighbor in Shirley's case and by servants for the other two.

Moore had been in the right spot at the right time, since he'd joined Packer at the Tribal Council meeting, but testimony from Davey Tall Tree and Cam Outlaw had him leaving directly after the gathering and his arrival back in Bangor substantiated that fact.

There was only one suspect with no alibi at all.

Cam Outlaw.

Miss Clara finally reached the opposite curb. Jake waited until she'd lifted the walker and then herself to the sidewalk.

Damnation, he didn't want it to be Outlaw.

He liked the guy. And sympathized with him, raising a child alone. Outlaw was also a member of the town's leading family, and he'd done more for the local economy in the past year than anyone else had for the past decade.

And then there were the other complications. Outlaw was Hallie's new brother-in-law, and of course, he was Lucy's brother.

It would ruin Jake's plans to arrest him. He'd be out of a nanny immediately and out of a wife in the long run.

None of that mattered, of course.

Time had run out for the banker. Unless he coughed up a reasonable alibi and soon, Jake was going to have to arrest him.

With a final wave to Miss Clara, Jake turned onto Walnut Street, drove to the end, and parked in the wide driveway in front of the house. He'd visited here a few times due to his friendship with Hallie. This time he'd be much less welcome.

Hallie opened the door to his knock, and as always,

he responded to her quick smile and kind warmth. He'd thought she'd make the perfect stepmother for the twins. He still thought so, but as much as he liked her, he realized the chemistry had never been there.

"I've come to talk to Cam."

Hallie asked no questions, and her smile didn't falter. She led him through the big, comfortable house to the late Jesse Outlaw's study.

"Stop to see me in the kitchen before you go, will you?"

"Sure."

Cameron Outlaw stood when Jake entered. The banker was nearly as tall as Jake, but his build was lean and wiry rather than solid. His hair, the same inky color as Lucy's, was arranged in a neat, businessman's style, and he wore a white button-down shirt with the sleeves rolled up to his elbows, charcoal slacks, and a tie striped in charcoal and the blue of the Maine summer sky. It was the color of his eyes—and Lucy's.

Cam's chiseled features were a more masculine version of his sister's. The two younger Outlaws barely resembled their elder brother, Baz. Cam was only thirty, but Jake noticed a network of lines that crisscrossed his forehead.

Cam Outlaw looked like a man with something eating him. Jake hoped to God it wasn't a guilty conscience.

"Have a seat, Sheriff. Drink?"

Jake wished he could accept the offer. Two guys with drinks in their hands, well, there was an instant camaraderie. But this was an official visit, and he needed an official answer.

"No. Thanks."

Jake sat on the battered leather sofa and glanced around the book-lined room while Cam resumed his seat behind the heavy walnut desk. A latticed window looked out onto the courtyard that led to the old carriage house that was home to the Outlaw Veterinary Clinic and Lucy's apartment.

"We haven't changed the room since Dad died." The death had been sudden and rather recent. "It was a loss for all of us, but I think it hit Lucy the hardest. As a kid she followed him around to the farms to doctor the large animals. For a long time, we thought she'd study veterinary medicine, but in the end she didn't. I think it reminded her too much of growing up without a mother. And Dad, well, his job always came first. What was your father like?"

"I never met him," Jake said, briefly. He didn't add that, due to his mother's early death, he'd been on his own before he was sixteen. Just for an instant Jake allowed himself to picture Lucy here as a small child, playing under her father's desk, pelting him with questions, her blue eyes round with curiosity and mischief.

Cam interrupted his thoughts.

"I know you're not here to talk about Lucy but…"

Jake lifted one eyebrow.

"I can't help worrying about her. She's an adult and all that, but I know how impulsive she can be, and as you undoubtedly know, she's developed a huge crush on you."

It crossed Jake's mind that Lucy would hate having her brother talk about her like this. "The crush is mutual."

Cam's dark eyebrows lifted.

"Are you afraid I'll take advantage of her."

Outlaw's gaze was steady. "Hell, no. You're the sheriff," he said, quietly, "and a father."

The vote of confidence was flattering if misplaced, and he couldn't accept it.

"I'm a man, too. You know your sister and I spent the night together at that cabin out on the rez."

What a damn fool. He'd handed Outlaw a shotgun and the bullets he needed. All the man had to do was aim and fire. In fact, Cam's eyes narrowed.

"I've asked her to marry me."

The frown subsided.

"I didn't know. What'd she say?"

"Told me to take a hike." Jake's lips twisted.

Outlaw hooted. "That sounds like Lucy. You must've done it wrong. If I remember correctly, she's expecting a down-on-one-knee rendition."

"It was more than that. I haven't given up hope."

This time only one dark eyebrow lifted.

"You wanted to marry Hallie."

That, of course, was true. At least he'd thought that was what he wanted.

"None of my business," Cam said. "And I suspect you aren't here to talk about that. I imagine you're here about my alibi."

Jake nodded.

"There's nothing I can add. I told you about driving around, pulling over, and falling asleep."

"I let it go before because there were other leads to follow. The leads have run dry. This time I need the truth."

"I'm sticking to my story."

Jake leaned forward, elbows on his thighs,

frustration in his voice.

"Who the hell are you protecting?"

"No one. Unless I'm mistaken, no one else in my family is a suspect."

The guy had a point.

"Let's go at this from another angle. Who do you think wanted Packer dead?"

Cam shrugged. "The guy could be a prick, and ethically he skated pretty close to the edge. The money goes to the widow and, of course, to the casino project of which I have control. I guess you could pick a motive out of that."

"So the choices are Paula Packer or you."

"Looks that way."

"You're the expert archer. You're also the one with no alibi."

Cam said nothing.

Jake searched the lean, tanned face. "What d'you know about Shirley Packer?"

Cam's smile was ironic.

"Trying to clear me, Sheriff? Why? Because of Lucy?"

"I'm trying to get to the truth," Jake bit out, "and with damn little help from you."

Cam sighed. "I'm sorry for that. And, I'm sorry to say, I've never met the first Mrs. Packer, but I now understand the reputation that got me interested in Packer Inc., was mostly due to her efforts. And those of the attorney, Moore. They were involved when we signed the contract, but Packer shook things up shortly thereafter. That's when the casino project went to hell. As you know, I was unhappy with the inferior quality of the building materials he was getting from suppliers."

Somehow it didn't surprise Jake to learn that Shirley was the brains of Packer Inc.

"If Shirley was so valuable, why didn't he try to keep her as a partner after his remarriage?"

Cam shook his head. "Probably her choice. It seems to me it would have added insult to injury to keep Packer Inc. afloat for the offspring Nate intended to have with Paula. I imagine Shirley wanted to leave. I'm not so sure about Claude. Nate told me once, after a couple of drinks, that neither of them suffered financially. And, of course, Claude was devoted to Nate."

Jake's ears pricked up. "Devoted. That's an interesting word to describe a male relationship."

"I'm not an expert on these things, but I don't believe it was romantic. More like brothers. They'd known each other all their lives." Cam shrugged. "And like with most relationships, it wasn't equal.

Claude appeared to be the giver."

"And Packer, the taker?"

Cam nodded. "I never got the feeling Packer was malicious. He was used to being the center of attention and accepted it as his due. In retrospect, I'd say he had an inability to put himself in the other guys' shoes."

"A sociopath?"

Cam seemed to think about that. "Maybe. He just didn't have much of an ethical barometer. He liked people and expected them to like him back. For the most part, they did."

Jake thought about the guys he'd put behind bars in L.A. Some of them, the con men, for example, had been friendly and likeable. Conscience, he thought, was a useful thing, albeit an uncomfortable one.

"I finally figured out that Moore was the one who kept up appearances after Shirley left."

"Are you saying the company's going bankrupt?"

"I finally got a copy of their financial report. They've botched a few jobs and had to make big restitution settlements during the past year. Meanwhile, fewer jobs are coming in. Ironic, isn't it? Packer triggered the company's decline by getting rid of Shirley so he could spawn an heir. Packer Inc. will be a dim memory before Packer Junior is out of the nursery."

"What about the casino?"

Cam sighed and leaned back in his chair.

"I'll make sure it gets built." He shot Jake a look. "Even if I have to do it from a jail cell."

"What about Paula Packer's inheritance?"

"She gets the house and cars. She won't realize much out of the company, but she won't be liable for the debts, either. I wouldn't worry about her too much, though. I think the Widow Packer can take care of herself."

Jake thought about Paula's super-sized sex appeal and decided Outlaw was right. "If Packer had lived, he'd be facing bankruptcy?"

Cam nodded.

"Seems like he died just in time."

"That's one way of looking at it."

The man was cool, Jake would give him that. Frustration welled up inside him. Outlaw was holding something back. What was it?

"I'd hoped this interview would clear you."

"Sorry, Sheriff. You gonna arrest me?"

The light tone in his voice belied the awareness in the blue eyes. Outlaw knew he was in danger. Jake got to his feet.

"Not yet. Let me know if you decide to cooperate."

"And don't leave town, right?"

Jake stared at him for a long minute. He knew just how intimidating his green gaze could be.

"Means, motive, opportunity," he repeated. "You've got 'em all."

Cam's mocking smile faded. "Let me walk you out."

Jake waved him back to his chair. "I told Hallie I'd stop by the kitchen to say hello."

Hallie stood at the sink. Her light brown curls were disheveled, and her pretty cheeks were flushed as she painstakingly juggled a baby on her shoulder and prepared a bottle of formula at the same time.

Jake grinned.

"Hey," he said, softly, "need some help?"

Hallie held a protective hand against the boy whose body was balanced against her shoulder as she flashed Jake a welcoming smile that reached the depths of her hazel eyes.

She peeled the baby off and handed him to Jake.

"I know you've met before, but I'm not sure he remembers you. Robert," she said to the baby, "this is your Uncle Jake." She looked at the man. "If you've got time to give him a bottle, I'll be forever in your debt."

He didn't have time. He had a murder to solve and domestic problems up the ass. But he'd never been able to say no to the sweet-tempered veterinarian. She motioned him to a padded rocking chair in one corner of the big country kitchen. A moment later she handed

143

him the warmed bottle then she sat in one of the Windsor-style kitchen chairs. He nudged the nipple between the baby's rosebud lips.

"I adore a man who knows what he's doing," Hallie breathed.

"It's like riding a bike. It comes back to you."

"He seems so happy. I think he feels more secure in a pair of strong arms." Robert began to suck, his small cheeks blowing in and out in a way that reminded Jake of his own children. A gentle sense of nostalgia wafted through him and he could feel himself relaxing.

"Parenthood's exhausting," Hallie said, "but it's the best."

"Yeah." The baby obviously heard Jake's rumbling voice. His long lashes parted for a minute, and eyes the color of blueberries stared up into his.

"Tell me about Sam and Lillie. I missed seeing them last Friday. What're they up to?"

"They love Lucy," he said, realizing it was true. "They would never eat anything but macaroni and hotdogs for Mrs. P., but for Lucy, they'll try tuna with pickles, tuna with ketchup and even tuna tacos."

Hallie laughed. "Lucy's inventive. Just imagine what she'll come up with once she gets over her tuna fixation."

"She's working on the costumes for the first grade end-of-the-year play. No bells this time." He grinned at Hallie then shook his head. The baby swayed with the movement but did not stop eating. "I don't know what I'd do without her. Lord knows I don't have the time or expertise to sew costumes or organize the other moms to plan a program or to gather neighborhood kids in the backyard to hold an impromptu festival to celebrate

May Day. She does it all while holding down a job."

"You sound like a fan," Hallie said, mildly.

Robert paused and looked up at Jake.

"Good looking kid."

Hallie grinned and scooted her chair close enough to put her head next to Jake's and join him in the admiration of her child.

"He's gorgeous and I'm beat."

"Put your head on my shoulder."

"Really?"

"Why not? Just consider me a pillow."

"Nice pillow," she said, with a yawn. Her head drifted back against his shoulder, and a minute later she was asleep. It felt good to have a woman depending on him again. Her weight and the scent of baby powder relaxed him even more. He let his own head fall back against the curved back of the rocker. His eyelids drifted shut. He smiled, faintly, just before he conked out.

A sharp intake of breath brought him upright. His lashes lifted and he registered three things: Robert was still sucking on the bottle; Hallie was still asleep on his shoulder, and a pair of stricken blue eyes stared into his.

"Damn." The soft curse woke Hallie, and she lifted her head.

"Luce!"

Jake saw her dilemma in those clear eyes. She wanted nothing more than to sprint out of there, but she wouldn't wound Hallie for the world. She stayed put.

"I was gonna call you," Hallie said, getting to her feet and stretching her back. "I just wanted to make sure you were planning to bring the twins to Little Joe's tomorrow night." She smiled. "Daisy's pining to see all three of you and so am I."

Lucy glanced at Jake. The new shadows in her eyes caused him a physical pain.

"Is that okay with you?"

She didn't want him to come along. For some reason that hurt.

"Knock yourself out. I have other plans, anyway."

Lucy nodded then disappeared through the back door that led to the clinic and her old apartment.

Hallie exchanged a look with Jake.

"What's going on between you two?"

She wasn't stern, exactly, but Jake got the definite impression she held him accountable for Lucy's odd reaction.

"Chemistry," he said.

"I think she's in love with you."

He shrugged. "I'm too old for her." He waited for her to contradict him, but she just gazed at him with a gentle expression.

"Lucy is warm and loving, and she adores the twins. You could do a lot worse, Jake."

He thought about how his careless affection toward Hallie must have hurt the younger woman, Hallie's sister-in-law. He really was a horse's ass.

"I've gotta go."

Chapter Nine

Lucy stared into the Langley's side yard. The apple tree no longer looked like something out of an Edward Gorey print. Green buds softened the twisted branches, and in a matter of days, pink blossoms would dress the tree in its yearly finery. Finally, spring had sprung.

Jake hadn't come home for supper, and she suspected, he wouldn't come home until everyone, including Lucy, was safely in bed. She rested her forearms on the porch railing and watched the children playing in the yard.

She thought she'd done a pretty good job during her second tour of duty as temporary nanny. She'd enjoyed taking care of the kids, and if she hadn't gotten over her feelings for Jake, she'd kept them hidden. No more mooning around. No more trying to set up an "accidental" meeting in the narrow hallway. No more night-time visits to the porch in the hope that he'd follow. She no longer pretended to herself that she was Jake's wife or the twins' mother. She kept her fantasies under wraps until she was alone in her own bed.

She'd thought she had the obsession under control, but it wasn't true. One look at Hallie's head on his broad shoulder and Hallie's baby in his arms had sent an arrow through her heart. They'd looked so Norman Rockwell. So perfect. So exactly what Jake wanted. He couldn't have it, of course. Not with Hallie. But he couldn't have it with Lucy, either. She simply couldn't be his consolation prize.

Out in the yard Sam waved from his seat in the rope swing Jake had mounted in the apple tree. Lucy grinned and waved back, her heart in her throat. She'd miss the little boy so much. She'd miss Lillie, too. She knew they needed a mom, and she sent up a prayer that they'd get one soon. Someone just like Hallie. In the meantime, Lucy intended to end the estrangement between Jake and his in-laws.

Sam and Lillie needed their grandparents. Jake needed them, too.

Lucy gazed up at the darkening sky. The spear of pain she'd felt this afternoon had subsided into a dull but persistent ache in her chest. Jealousy was as strong a force as love or hate or loyalty. Maybe stronger. Was it possible that Shirley Packer had felt this way when she'd seen her husband of thirty years with the younger woman? Was it possible that Paula had happened upon a similarly tender scene between the two who had spent most of a lifetime together? Had one or the other of the two wives killed their mutual husband?

It was possible. Likely, even. What, after all, was an alibi in the face of the green-eyed monster that had the power to turn a person inside out?

After she put the children in bed, Lucy phoned Shirley Packer and asked for another meeting. "Why?"

An excellent question.

"I'd like to talk with you about your experiences on safari."

"Ah. Because the great white hunter was killed with the same weapon he used to bring home all those trophies, right?"

"I think my readers will be interested in the irony."

"I imagine so. I can see you on Saturday."

In the meantime, Lucy would have her hands full trying to come up with an alibi for Cam. She knew he was lying to protect Molly Whitecloud for some reason, and she knew he would continue to lie. Lucy would have to get Molly to talk to Jake.

Jake. Just thinking about him brought back the suffocating feeling of jealousy.

Her cell phone rang and she hesitated. She wasn't ready to discuss what she'd seen, but then maybe it wasn't Jake. She answered it. "Luce, I just wanted to check if you're all right."

"I'm fine." She knew her voice sounded stiff.

"Listen, honey, I'm not trying to butt into your life, but I need you to know there's nothing going on between Jake and me."

"Because you're married."

"That's right. Because I'm married. And because there never was that much going on between us." A white lie to soothe her feelings.

"It doesn't matter," she said, hoping she could end the conversation before the tears that had gathered behind her eyes began to make their way down her cheeks. "I can't stay here, Hallie. I'll be home tomorrow."

****

The bedroom was dark and tiny, a cubicle in a modest, overheated mobile home. A woman writhed on the bed, trying to find some kind of relief from the pain wracking her body and the sweat that poured into her eyes. Every once in a while, a tortured groan escaped her, and Lucy's heart squeezed in sympathy.

"You're making good progress, Winnie," Molly Whitecloud murmured to the sufferer. "This is transition, the worst part. You're almost there." The dark eyes gazed, unseeing, at the midwife. "Almost there," Molly repeated. She laid a cool, wet washcloth on Winnie Deer Killer's forehead. "Just a little while longer and it will be time to push."

Molly stepped back as Rain Deer Killer, gray hair pulled back in a long braid, face as wizened as a dried apple, appeared with a homemade poultice which she spread on her daughter-in-law's swollen belly.

"What about drugs?" Lucy whispered.

"Winnie's going natural," Molly said, in a normal voice. "She's doing what's best for the baby."

Winnie's body twisted as another contraction hit.

"I'm guessing she'd like to re-think that decision," Lucy said.

"There's little choice for women of the rez," Molly explained. "We have no clinic and no doctor and thus no anesthetic. To have a medicated childbirth, a woman has to check into Eden Memorial Hospital. Even an overnight stay costs thousands, and most of our folks are uninsured. Winnie's healthy and young, and the child is in the right position. The pain will disappear as soon as she delivers her child. She'll forget all about this part."

Molly was a professional midwife and, no doubt, knew best, but it was hard to believe Winnie would ever forget this morning. And it seemed inhuman to put her through it when a mere insurance policy could have brought relief.

Molly stroked the young woman's forearm. "I can tell the poultice is working."

The moans subsided somewhat. Did the smelly glop on Winnie's belly really cut the pain, or was it a placebo? Lucy guessed it didn't matter which.

"I want Ray," Winnie whimpered.

"A man does not belong here," her mother-in-law said.

"This is his baby, too," Molly pointed out, gently. "If Winnie wants him, he should come." The older woman clearly respected Molly's opinion. She opened the door and disappeared down a narrow hallway. When she reappeared she was followed by a tall, thin, very young man who looked like he should be in his bedroom finishing his algebra homework, not witnessing the birth of his child. He reminded Lucy of a cat being dragged by the scruff of his neck even though no one was touching him. He looked scared to death.

"Sit here," Molly told him, in a no-nonsense voice. "Just hold her hand. Your mother will stay in the room, and I'll be back in fifteen minutes."

"Yes, ma'am."

Molly motioned to Lucy. They walked through the tiny living room stuffed with chattering female relatives and friends and found a seat outside on the front stoop.

Molly sank onto the concrete with a sigh. She smoothed her hands over her jeans-clad thighs. With her pink-flowered T-shirt and thick braid, she looked like a teenager except for her air of calm confidence. She made a face.

"I hate it when they call me 'ma'am.' It makes me feel like Methuselah."

The words shocked Lucy. "You're not old."

"Thirty. Sometimes it feels old."

Lucy didn't know the midwife well, but she'd

never seen her anything but calm and cheerful. Except the night of the storm.

"Forgive me if this is too personal," Lucy said, "but you love people and babies. Why do you have no family of your own? Don't tell me all this natural childbirth stuff scared you off."

Molly chuckled. "The midwife gets all the fun of the birthing process and none of the pain."

It was a good answer but not a complete one. Lucy waited. Molly's silence made Lucy ashamed.

"I'm so sorry. That was unpardonably nosy. I shouldn't have asked."

Molly smiled, briefly, as if to reassure her. "Childbirth doesn't scare me off," she said, evenly. "My life just hasn't worked out that way." Emotion was crouched beneath her even tone. What was it? Disappointment? Regret? Loss? Was she sorry she'd given up her young love? And what had happened to the man she'd married when Cam was away at college?

Lucy couldn't bring herself to pry any further.

"It can still work out for you," Lucy said, comfortingly. "You're young."

Molly smiled her thanks. "Don't worry about me. I have a good life. Now, you came out here for a reason, right?"

Lucy had almost forgotten. She nodded and pulled the silver earring out of the pocket of her windbreaker.

"I found this, Molly. At the construction site."

Color burned in Molly's dreamy cheeks. "When?"

"Two days after the storm. It was half-buried in the mud right near where they found the body." She held it up, and the shiny feather glittered in the morning sun. Then she took Molly's hand, turned it palm up, and dropped the earring in it.

"Why didn't you give this to the sheriff?"

Lucy shrugged. "I didn't see any point in getting you involved if you dropped it there last summer or something."

Molly's fingers closed around the trinket. "I didn't lose it last summer. I lost it last week. I didn't have anything to do with Nate Packer's murder, Lucy, but I was there—at the casino site. You should give this to Jake."

Lucy studied her. She'd felt fairly certain Molly wouldn't lie and she'd been right.

"I'm giving it to you."

Molly looked at her a long moment. "Do you have any idea where he is in his investigation?"

Lucy shivered in spite of the sun's warmth. "I think he's stuck. As far as I know he's still looking at Cam as the chief suspect."

Molly's indigo eyes widened, and Lucy read the fear in them.

"But he didn't do it."

"I know. The trouble is, everybody else has a credible alibi, and Cam had motive, means and opportunity."

"Ms. Molly! Ms. Molly!" Ray Deer Killer's voice had shot up into an adolescent register. "You gotta come! Ma's suffocating Winnie!"

Lucy expected the midwife to jump to her feet, but she didn't.

"Go with Ray," Molly directed Lucy. "Make sure Winnie's all right. I'll be there in three minutes." She pulled a slim cell phone out of the pocket of her jeans while Lucy hurried inside to see to the mom to-be.

Lucy stayed with Molly. She got to see Winnie Deer Killer's child and the subsequent huge grin on the new mother's face.

"What color are your eyes," Winnie asked Molly. "Dark blue. Some people call it indigo."

"Indigo," Winnie repeated. "That's what I will name her. Indigo."

"That's quite an honor," Lucy said, when they were back in her Jeep and headed toward Molly's cottage. "To have the baby named after you."

Molly nodded. "This is a very rewarding job."

A few moments later Lucy turned down Molly's lane. There was a white Blazer in front of the cottage and, leaning against it, a tall man, wearing khaki uniform slacks, a brown leather jacket, and a sheriff's hat tilted over his eyes. Lucy's heart jerked.

"What's he doing here?"

"I called him," Molly said, calmly. "I asked him to come."

Lucy parked in the driveway, and they got out of the Jeep. Jake followed them into the house, his entire attention on the midwife. He seemed comfortable in her small home, as if he'd been there before.

Lucy felt the flicker of jealousy, and she was disgusted with herself. She straightened her spine and forced herself to block out the compelling masculine scent of Jake.

"I'll make the tea," she said, forcing herself to turn away from the sight of those long lashes. "Thank you for coming," Molly said to Jake. "I apologize for the wait."

"No problem," Jake said. The undertone of impatience in his words irritated Lucy.

"She's been a little busy," Lucy pointed out, without turning around. She spooned the tea leaves into the pot. "She delivered a baby this morning."

She could feel his eyes on her back. He was probably wondering at her hostility. She wondered at it herself.

"Boy or girl?"

Molly told him a little bit about the Deer Killers and their baby. When Lucy had served the tea, Molly cleared her throat.

"I'll get to the point. Cameron Outlaw has an alibi for the night of Nate Packer's murder. We were together after the Tribal Council meeting. We drove over to the casino site. That's where I dropped this earring." She produced the silver feather. "We talked for a while then got back in his car and came here."

Jake nodded slowly. "When did he leave?"

Lucy noticed two bright spots of color along Molly's cheekbones.

"He didn't leave. Not until morning."

"Ah," Jake said. "So he was protecting you."

"My reputation, I think. It probably didn't occur to him that I'd need an alibi for the murder." She made an oddly helpless gesture. "In any case, it doesn't matter. I'm thirty years old. No one is worried about who I spend my night with."

"Are you and Outlaw dating?"

"No. No, nothing like that. We're old friends. We were just catching up."

"Who found the earring?"

The question was so low key it took Lucy a moment to understand its significance.

"I did." Molly spoke too fast. Naturally, Jake

wasn't fooled. His gaze shifted to Lucy.

"Then what are you doing out here?" Lucy threw Molly an apologetic look.

"Molly's trying to protect me. I found the earring. Yesterday. When I was at the murder site with Flynn."

"And there was no chance to tell me about it."

She opened her mouth to defend herself, but it wasn't necessary. There hadn't been a chance to tell him. He hadn't come home last night. But she wouldn't have told him, anyway.

"I wanted to speak with Molly first."

Jake's angry expression assured her he'd have something to say about that later. He transferred his attention back to the midwife.

"So you'd gone out to the casino site to talk, and while you were standing there, right where a man would be killed minutes later, you just happened to lose an earring."

"That's pretty close." Molly didn't look at him. "We heard a car coming down behind the trailer so we left."

"What time was that?"

"Between nine forty-five and ten."

"Good grief!" Lucy gaped at her friend. "The driver must have been the murderer!"

"Or Packer, himself," Jake said. "Unless they were together."

"Maybe the murderer was already on the premises," Lucy said. "Maybe he or she was listening to you and Cam talk!"

A telltale color burned in Molly's cheeks. Good grief! Cam and Molly hadn't been just talking out here. They'd been...Lucy refused to finish the thought.

"Did you hear anything?"

"No. I don't know. I thought I heard something. A kind of rustling," Molly told Jake, "but it could have been a breeze."

"Then you came back here to finish your discussion."

"Yes," Molly said. There was so much emotion in her voice that Lucy knew she was telling the truth. They'd come back here. And talked. Nothing more.

"Are you certain Outlaw stayed the whole time?"

"Until at least three. That's when I fell asleep. He left sometime after that. He was gone when I woke up at six."

"Why did he feel he needed to protect your reputation?"

"There was a lot of gossip about us years ago. I imagine he didn't want to stir it up again. I understand he's dating someone in Eden. The innkeeper."

"So he kept quiet to protect himself," Jake said.

Molly shrugged.

"Pretty big risk," Jake said. "He could be charged with obstructing a murder inquiry."

"But he didn't really obstruct it," Lucy put in. "You continued to interview people and collect evidence."

"Thank you for your expert legal opinion," Jake snapped. His voice softened when he spoke to Molly. "Why did you come forward now?"

"I didn't want the old gossip resurrected, either. I should have contacted you right away, I know. I was a coward. Not for the first time."

Minutes later Jake and Lucy walked outside.

"They were trying to protect each other," Lucy

said.

"They were obstructing the investigation," he said, without heat. "So were you."

Suddenly Lucy felt bone-weary. "Well, now you know."

"Like hell. They're still lying."

"What do you mean?"

"There's something going on between your brother and Molly Whitecloud."

"They're just friends."

"Are you blind, Lucy? You ever notice the color of the walls in her cottage? All the walls?"

She didn't understand. "They're blue, aren't they?"

"They're the blue of the summer sky, Lucy."

How many times had people used that description for her eyes and those her brother?

Lucy felt another slash of pain, this time it was for Cam and his star-crossed lover.

****

Lucy's emotions were on overload. She didn't need to be at work, and she didn't have to get back to Jake's house until dinner time. What she needed was to get away—up, up and away. She pointed the Jeep toward Bangor and headed to the airstrip outside town.

This was only her second lesson. She'd taken the first, thinking that familiarity with a small plane might be useful when she got her dream job reporting overseas, plus there was the indisputable fact that people did not consider pilots loose screws. Tacked on was her hope that learning to fly a plane might cure her fear of flying.

It was too soon to tell whether she'd achieve any of her goals, but the afternoon of gliding above the woods and fields of springtime Maine in the competent hands of the instructor, had been soothing. She felt decidedly more mellow when she turned the Jeep toward home while she watched the crimson sunset. She wasn't needed at Jake's until suppertime so she decided to stop in at her apartment for an hour. She turned down Walnut Street, parked the Jeep in the empty clinic lot, then climbed the outside stairs. It wasn't until she reached the small landing that she realized there was someone huddled outside her door. The last rays of the sun illuminated the golden curls.

"Good grief! Sam!"

The boy's thin arms reached for her, and his lower lip trembled as he tried to bite back tears. Lucy scooped him up and held him against her. Six-year-old legs locked around her waist, and he buried his face in her shoulder.

A million questions raced through Lucy's head, but she held her tongue and held onto the sobbing child. Finally, he released his grip enough for her to locate her key, and a minute later, they were seated on the worn chintz sofa.

"What's this all about, sweetie?"

He sniffed and sat back. Her heart twisted at the sight of his red and blotchy face.

"Me and Lillie thought you wasn't coming back."

"Why would you think that, sweetheart?"

"Lillie heard you talking on the phone. I comed to bring you home."

Guilt sleeted through Lucy. Lillie must have overheard her conversation with Hallie. Dang. She should have been more careful. She should have known the children would be confused by the o-again, off-again arrangement. They needed stability, and Jake and she had failed to provide it. Lucy made an instant decision. She wouldn't bail on Jake. Not until Mrs. Peach was home to stay. And she'd urge Jake to step up his second wife search. This situation was utterly unfair to the children.

Lucy hugged the boy and dried his eyes. "Does anybody know where you are?"

"Jus' Lillie."

Lord. Jake must be out of his head.

"Okay, pal, here's what we're going to do. I'm going to take you home, and I'm going to stay there with you, okay?" He nodded. "But first I have to call your dad."

"Is Daddy gonna be mad at me?"

"Probably. A little. Because he's worried. You can't go off on your own again, honey. It's just too dangerous. But he'll be so happy to see you."

"Are you happy to see me, Lucy?"

"More than you know."

"Are you goin' to stay with us forever?"

It would have taken a harder heart than Lucy's to hint at the truth. That she couldn't stay forever.

"I'll stay, honey. I'll stay as long as you need me." She meant it, too.

****

It gave Jake a queer feeling to watch Lucy's Jeep disappear down Molly's lane. He didn't want to let her go. He knew it had hurt her to see him with Hallie and the baby. Hallie must be right. She must care about him. She probably thought she was in love. Twenty-two-year-old women always thought they were in love. He sighed. He didn't know what to say to her. He was

160

no longer sure that it was right to marry Lucy. She'd made a good point. She had her whole life in front of her. Who was he to tie her down?

At least her brother was off the hook.

He drove over to the Trading Post-slash community center to touch base with Davey Tall Tree who hadn't yet figured out who had taken the war arrow off the display. He spoke, once again, to several of the young males who gathered there to play pool. They were typical, bored kids, underemployed and a little rowdy. He couldn't convince himself that any of them had a motive to kill Nate Packer.

Jake handed Davey a few bills for a sandwich and a soda and got some advice back with his change.

"You might want to talk to Molly Whitecloud," he said.

"Already did. Just now."

The chief's pudding face creased into a thoughtful look.

"She's a fine woman, Molly. Been single a long time." He paused. "You single, Sheriff?"

Single. Widowed. Divorced. Jake didn't try to explain his marital situation. He nodded.

"I heard you got a coupla kids."

"A boy and a girl."

"Molly'd make a fine mama."

Good Lord. Why hadn't he seen that coming?

He nodded, not wanting to encourage the conversation.

"Don't look like Cam Outlaw's gonna do nuthin' about her. Thought mebbe they'd get together, but it seems like they're finished."

Jake nodded again, but he didn't agree. Whatever

was going on between Cam and the midwife, it was far from finished. He drove out to the casino site, got out of the Blazer, and leaned against it as he ate his lunch. It was so quiet out here. He closed his eyes and imagined that it was two hundred years earlier, that the wooded area was still filled with tipis and campfires and the sounds of building canoes and children playing. What had Molly heard out here that night? Birds? Maybe an owl? Or had the murderer been waiting for Nate, either in his own car or in the construction trailer? Why had Packer stopped here in the dark, after the meeting? He was the kind of guy who might have had a woman on the side, but Jake thought that was unlikely considering his apparent devotion to Paula.

He might have had a deal on the side, too.

If he was working with the Jersey mob, he might have met a representative out here, but Jake didn't think so. Packer wasn't the sharpest arrow in the quiver, but he knew how to look out for himself. He'd have known better than to plan a clandestine meeting with a mobster.

Jake opened his eyes and gazed at the budding leaves on the deciduous trees on the site's perimeter. Budding leaves. He could hear birds singing and chirping, but there was no rustling sound.

Damn. If Molly was telling the truth, she had heard somebody out here. It had to be someone who'd arrived in his or her own car and departed the same way. It had to be someone Packer had arranged to meet. Not Cam, apparently. Not Moore, who'd been with him at the Tribal Council. Paula? Shirley? X?

Jake unlocked the construction trailer and took a look around. Nothing had been touched since last week when he and Homer had searched it thoroughly. Not that there had been much to search as construction hadn't yet begun.

He stepped outside and drew in a deep breath of fresh air. The area had been gone over with a fine tooth comb, but Jake did it again, this time pretending he was stalking a victim who'd parked not far from the trailer. The murderer could have gotten to the site by driving up to one of the deserted dirt roads that ran behind the woods and walking up under cover of the trees to hide behind the trailer.

They'd found no tire tracks on either of the dirt roads, but the heavy rain followed by the next day's snowstorm would have obliterated any trace.

Once again Jake closed his eyes, and taking advantage of the afternoon's peace, he employed a trick taught him by his mentor back in L.A., one Patrick McGillicuddy. Mac had said that to solve a murder, study the victim. Jake let his mind drift and swirl, focusing generally on what he knew about Nate Packer.

The guy was sixty, outgoing, charismatic, and self-centered. He flaunted his wealth with a gaudy mansion and an even gaudier trophy wife. He flaunted his athletic prowess, too, with those safari kills. He'd wanted a son to carry on his name badly enough to jettison a smart and loyal wife and to humiliate his lifelong best friend. The weird thing was, neither of those two seemed to have put up much of a fuss. Why?

Jake had thought from almost the beginning that the murder seemed personal. Claude's role in Packer, Inc. had changed, but he was still Packer's personal attorney and friend. Shirley Packer was the woman scorned. She'd struck him as a sensible woman with a

163

somewhat chilly personality. Had that extended to the bedroom? Had Packer wanted a more enthusiastic sexual partner? If so, he may have been disappointed. In Jake's experience, overtly sexual women tended to be bored or boring when push came to shove. That's the way it had been with Ariel.

His mind kept reverting to the first Mrs. Packer. She was lean and fit. What if the legend of the great white hunter was just that? What if Shirley had been an archer, too, but, to placate her husband's ego, she'd lied about her own participation in the safaris?

The same could be true of Moore, although Jake considered that less likely. The attorney did not seem athletic in the least, and in any case, he'd shot the photos.

The case was coming together. It was like working a jigsaw puzzle. If you stared at the shapes of the pieces and the slight variations in color long enough, a picture began to emerge.

At the moment, Jake's money was on Shirley. She had an alibi, of course, but they all had alibis. That's what he'd check next. Those alibis.

The sun dropped below the tree line, and sunlight splintered across the site. Jake realized he'd been out here for hours. Time to head home. The prospect filled him with a warm anticipation which he knew was only partly because of the children. Lucy would be there tonight. Lucy would be in his home.

With Lucy there, they seemed like a family.

He needed her, dammit, and the kids needed her. Suddenly he didn't care that she was only twenty-two and had her whole life in front of her. He wanted that life to be spent with him.

Suddenly, at five-fifteen on a May afternoon in the middle of M-15, Jake Langley faced the truth.

He was in love with Lucy Outlaw.

The sun had disappeared beneath the horizon by the time Jake turned off Third Street and onto Cypress. It was that mystical time when day was ended but night had not yet begun. The neighborhood was quiet, the children back in the houses getting ready for bed. Parents were getting their second wind and looking forward to an uninterrupted evening of television or reading or talking or making love. Jake felt breathless, strangely alive and, to tell the truth, turned on. He was going to tell her tonight. He was going to propose again.

And this time he was going to do it right.

He pulled up in front of his house and blinked. Everyone in Eden seemed to be on his front lawn. He looked around for Lucy, but it was Hallie Scott Outlaw who caught his eye. Her face was gray with worry.

An uneasy fist pounded into Jake's gut.

Something was very wrong.

Chapter Ten

It was Moonbeam's tear-streaked face that converted Jake's uneasiness into pure terror. The sobbing girl, her fingers gripping Lillie's hand, stuttered an explanation he couldn't begin to understand.

Luckily, Hallie was right behind her.

"Sam didn't come home from school." The veterinarian was trying to keep her voice calm. "Homer, Baz, Cam, and half the town are out looking for him. We've checked with all the neighbors and all his friends."

Sam was missing.

Jake heard a buzzing in his ears, and Hallie's voice receded. It was the sensation he'd had back in L.A. while he watched a teenage drug kingpin pull a gun on him. This couldn't be happening. Only it was.

Where the hell was his son?

"Daddy?"

Lillie's small voice cut through the clouds of panic.

Jake scooped his daughter into his arms. It wasn't anxiety he saw in the green eyes. It was guilt. Jake sucked in a breath and deliberately softened his expression.

"Where did Sam go after school?"

"We was upset about Lucy."

Jake frowned. "What about Lucy?"

"She went away."

"She went to work, like she always does."

Lillie's curls bounced as she shook her head. "She's not coming back."

Jake frowned. "What makes you think so?"

"We heard her talking on the phone."

He ignored the wrench in his heart. He couldn't think about that now.

"We'll talk about that later. Tell me about Sam. Where did he go after school?"

He watched her thought process. Her eyes, like Lucy's, were easy to read. He knew she was trying to calculate what the truth would cost her, and he forced himself to wait.

"We want Lucy to come back," she said.

The cell in his pocket rang and he answered it. "Langley."

"It's Lucy." She spoke quickly. "Sam's here with me."

He felt a bolt of knee-weakening relief, but it was quickly followed by fury. He deliberately enunciated his words.

"At my apartment. We'll be there in a few minutes. And, Jake, I know you were scared out of your wits, but don't be too hard on him. They overheard something I said to Hallie on the phone and thought I was going to leave. This was our fault."

Fear and frustration flashed into fury. His arms tightened around his daughter, and he lashed out.

"Sounds like it was your fault."

"Daddy, you're hurting me."

He hung up the phone and reported the news to the others. Hallie contacted her husband and the other searchers then sent the neighbors home. Jake stood next to the road. He couldn't wait to get his hands on Sam and Lucy. He wanted to strangle them both.

Jake watched her park the Jeep, unbuckle the child's seatbelt, and hold his hand as they crossed the street. He didn't think he'd ever been this angry in his entire life. Not even when Ariel decided to take off leaving him with the babies.

He ignored Lucy and knelt down to speak with his son.

"I'm glad to see you," he said, annoyed to hear the tremor in his voice. "Tell me what's going on here, son."

Sam's eyes were swollen from crying, but his grin was proud.

"I brung Lucy back."

Dear God. Sam thought he'd rescued the little witch. Like father, like son. And Lucy, well, she should be ashamed of herself. What kind of a mother figure needed to be rescued all the time?

"All right, Sam." He hugged the boy and kissed him. "We'll talk about this later. Let's go inside and get some supper."

Jake knew he needed to talk to both of the twins. He needed to explain exactly why it wasn't safe for them to take off without telling the adult in charge. He needed to make clear to them that the stunt they'd pulled was unacceptable behavior. He knew he couldn't have that conversation tonight.

He was too damned mad.

He met Lucy outside Lillie's room after the twins had been tucked in.

"On the porch," he said.

She lifted her little pointed chin, but she didn't argue. They stood at the railing, side-by-side, and gazed into the backyard. There was enough light from the house to give the trees a pleasant glow. The evening air felt welcome against Jake's heated skin. In more than a dozen years as a cop, he'd learned how to be cool in a crisis. This afternoon he'd felt like Mount Vesuvius in the days of Pompeii.

Not cool at all.

He turned his back to the railing and studied his temporary nanny. Her dark curls were wind-tossed and her cheeks were as pale as the new moon rising behind the apple tree. Another wave of fury swept through him. Jake's fingers curled around the railing, and he fought for control and waited for her to speak.

"The twins made a plan. After school, Sam was to go to Walnut Street to find me, and Lillie was to cover for him. Only I wasn't there. He waited on the landing outside the apartment for more than an hour. The clinic was closed, and I guess it didn't occur to him to go up to the house. I am so terribly sorry."

He heard the genuine remorse and his anger softened. Slightly.

"Why did you tell Hallie you were going to leave?"

The big eyes met hers. He couldn't see the summer sky-blue tonight, just the clarity and youth. It made his heart ache.

"I was frustrated. This situation is difficult for all of us, Jake. But I made a mistake. The twins need stability."

"They have me."

"They need more than that."

He controlled the flare of anger. She was right, of

169

course. They needed another parent.

"We should have made it clear to them, right from the start, that I'm only here to fill in. I was pretending that I belonged to them and to you, and of course, they sense all of that."

He was unaccountably hurt, partly because he knew she was right. He and Lucy had been playing at being a couple, and the kids had misunderstood.

"The obvious solution is for you to remarry."

He struck his forehead with the heal of his hand. "I never would have thought of that!"

Lucy ignored the sarcasm.

"I'll stick around until you figure out a permanent arrangement."

"You're gonna live with me while I'm dating the next Mrs. Sheriff Langley?"

"This isn't about us, Jake," she said, her eyes steady on his face. "They need to see the same face every day when they get up in the morning and when they get home from school. It's up to you whether it's a wife or a housekeeper or whatever."

"I'll get right on that. How do you advertise for a 'whatever'?"

The heat had gone out of his voice. Suddenly he felt her hand on his forearm. It was just a sympathetic touch, but it sent sparks of heat ricocheting through his body.

"Why don't we get engaged?"

He hadn't meant to say that, and she clearly wasn't expecting it. But he knew, immediately, that it would solve all his problems. His life was a shambles, and he could no longer afford to worry about whether marriage was right for a woman as young as Lucy or whether it would even last. He needed this now to get Maxine off his back, to settle the household so that he could focus on his work and to placate the kids. And he could move Lucy into his bed. That was the cherry on top. He excused himself for a moment and returned with a small box that he handed to her. She opened it and appeared to study the one-carat princess-cut diamond in the platinum setting.

"Did this belong to your ex-wife?"

He wasn't going to lie to her.

"Yes."

She nodded but said nothing.

"What d'you say, Lucy?"

"I'm thinking."

At least she hadn't rejected him out-of-hand. He decided to plead his case.

"We get along well."

"Most of the time."

"We're attracted to each other." She said nothing.

"You love the kids, and I think you love being in a family, too."

"I'll do it," she said, her voice flat, "but with two conditions."

There was a broad grin inside him, and it kept trying to break out. She'd said yes.

"Anything."

"You have to agree to talk to Maxine Slocum."

"What the hell?"

"The Slocums are the twins' grandparents, Jake. Sam and Lillie need them."

"Well, hell. What's the other condition?"

"It's a temporary arrangement."

"Of course, it's temporary," he snapped, still

focused on her first ridiculous condition. "It'll end as soon as we marry."

Her eyes, older and sadder, wrung his heart.

"Not in this case. The engagement is a bridge to more stability for the twins. Once that's in place,

we'll call it off."

He felt a weird hollowness under his heart. He'd wanted Lucy for keeps. But Jake, thirteen years her senior, knew that circumstances often took on a life of their own. Today, she was fake engaged. By next week, it could have turned into the real thing. Jake realized he wanted Lucy enough to take that chance.

"Deal."

His cell phone rang, and he held Lucy's gaze while he answered it.

"Langley."

"Hey, sailor, you're an hour late."

He grimaced. Christ. He'd forgotten about the make-up date he'd planned with Marilyn Hart.

"I'm sorry, Marilyn."

"I hope you're still planning to come. Believe me, I can make it happen."

Her crude joke elicited nothing in him but a vague distaste.

"I can't make it tonight or any other night," he said, staring into Lucy's hooded eyes. "You might as well be the first to know. I'm going to marry Lucy Outlaw."

****

Lucy studied the familiar ceiling over her bed. She wasn't sure why she'd done it. Instinct, probably. The incident this afternoon had scared the stuffing out of her. Sam could easily have gotten lost on his trek across town. He could have been hit by a car or, God forbid, he could have been kidnapped.

Something drastic needed to be done about the Langley household. If she left, she feared Jake would continue trying to piece together childcare. He'd continue the feud with his mother-in-law, and he'd continue to date nobody or inappropriate women like Marilyn Hart. The engagement would provide stability for the children and an opportunity to resolve the situation with the grandparents. If necessary, Lucy could steer Jake toward a better stepmom candidate. She grimaced and hoped it wasn't necessary, but she didn't waver about her decision to stick around. The children needed her and so did Jake. At least for now.

Lucy lifted her left hand and stared at the diamond ring. She'd agreed to wear the ring he'd bought for another woman simply because it was a concrete and constant reminder that Jake Langley didn't belong to her and that he never would.

****

Saturday morning someone shook Jake awake and he groaned, aware of a dull pounding in his head and a sharper, more insistent pounding in his groin that reminded him that Lucy had agreed only to a temporary engagement. She had not joined him in bed.

"Daddy, Daddy, Lucy's in the shower, and there's somebody at the door."

His mind, inspired by his morning erection, fixated on a picture of Lucy down the hall in the shower and he moaned.

"The door," Lillie said, tugging at his arm. "We're not s'posed to answer it by ourselves."

"Right." He started to fling off the tented sheet

when he heard Lillie's voice again.

"Where's your jammies, Daddy?"

"Could you hand me my jeans?"

She snatched them off the chair and handed them to him, her eyes curious and bright.

"Go join Sam. I'll be right with you."

It took him seconds to thrust his legs into the pants. It took a little longer to work the zipper up. He threw on a flannel shirt but didn't bother with socks or shoes.

"Damn," he said, quietly, when he threw open the front door. Coincidence? Or had the little witch planned this all along?

Maxine Slocum, dressed in a neck-to-ankle all-weather coat and a nylon rain hat with an enormous, Mylar-enforced brim, stood on the front porch. She was uniquely able to convey both accusation and determination in the same glare. A cold shudder ran through him. At least Maxine's arrival had banished what was left of his erection. Probably forever. The woman stepped over the sill without being asked, a battleship heading for port and was greeted with an excited chorus.

"Grandma! Grandpa!"

"Hello, Jake," Frank Slocum said. He'd barely noticed the silent figure who'd entered the house after Maxine. "Sorry to barge in on you like this."

The Texas oil man was not particularly tall, but he had the kind of muscular build developed from years of climbing oil rigs, the kind that can run to fat. Frank Slocum, however, had maintained a trim physique, and Jake could only assume that Maxine rationed his food.

"Frank," Jake said. He extended his hand, reluctantly. In a bitter custody suit, he'd have no illusions about the man's loyalty.

Maxine straightened to her full height of five feet. Jake was always shocked by her lack of inches. She was like a fierce terrier with a relentless bark that was definitely not as bad as her bite. She frowned up at him.

"Have these children been fed? It's nearly eight o'clock!"

Before he could answer he heard a cheery voice behind him.

"Maxine and Frank, isn't it? I'm so sorry I wasn't dressed on time to greet you. The children have had some orange juice and a banana, but we decided to hold off on the blueberry pancakes with real maple syrup until you arrived."

Since when had Cheerios, the Langley breakfast staple, morphed into blueberry pancakes? With real maple syrup?

"Maxine, will you help me make breakfast while Jake and Frank have a chance to catch up?"

It wasn't settled in the living room with mugs of hot coffee, the children watching TV on the floor, that it fully registered with Jake what had happened. Lucy had planned this. She'd invited the enemy to the house. His house.

"Did Lucy invite you?" Jake tried to keep his tone neutral.

"I believe she has some idea of brokering peace between you and Maxine."

Jake had never made the mistake of underestimating Frank's intelligence.

"Would that be so bad?"

Twenty-four hours earlier Jake would have answered with a resounding affirmative. Under the new plan, the fake engagement, it was different. For one thing, he'd agreed to try to get along with his ex-mother-in-law. For another, his presumed marriage should protect him from legal interference.

"They're your kids," Frank said, in a low voice. "We know it's tough raising kids alone though, and we'd like to help out. And get to know our grandchildren," he added, being an honest man.

"I'm willing to give it a try," Jake said, "but with the understanding that it will be here, in Eden. No ranch."

Frank looked disappointed but he nodded his agreement.

"Franklin!" Maxine's voice carried easily through the house. It was loud enough to wake Wiggles who'd been sleeping in a corner of the sofa. The cat jumped to the ground and scrambled down the corridor to Sam's room. "Come here this instant!"

Maxine was shaking her forefinger and her petite body quivered with anger when the men reached the kitchen.

"Sam ran away yesterday!" She was obviously trying to keep her voice under control.

Jake glared at Lucy, who shrugged, apologetically.

"I know I agreed to try reason first, but this is intolerable! These children aren't supervised or cared for properly. Either they're allowed to come with us, or we'll get a court order!" Her face was flushed under her frosted hair. She'd probably been attractive at one time, before her daughter's death and the loss of her grandchildren had turned her into a shrew.

Or maybe she'd always been like this.

"They're not leaving," Jake said, firmly.

"I agree." Frank's support surprised him.

Maxine's eyes narrowed into slits. "They need a mother!"

"They have a mother," Jake said. He pulled Lucy against him. "Lucy and I are engaged."

She extended her arm to display the ring just as someone knocked on the back door.

What now? Jake crossed the room in three strides and wrenched open the door.

A female body catapulted into his arms and feminine lips planted a smacking kiss on his cheek.

"Congratulations, brother-in-law," Hallie said. She detached herself and enveloped Lucy in a similar embrace. "I'm so happy for you!"

Once again there was a male left behind on the front porch. This time he was carrying a baby.

"Sorry to interrupt," Baz Outlaw said. He had the same sable-colored hair as Cam and Lucy, but his eyes were gray. Fine lines crisscrossed his broad face and white teeth flashed in his easy smile. Jake remembered a time, just a few months earlier, when Baz never smiled at all. Especially not at him.

"We just couldn't wait to congratulate you," Hallie interrupted. "Hi." She grinned at the Slocums. "Maxine and Frank, right? I know you must be thrilled about this. We want to have a party, of course. Maxine? You'll help out?"

The older woman gazed at Lucy. "You didn't tell me about this on the phone."

Lucy's expression was apologetic.

"It just happened."

"Is it real?"

Jake felt lightheaded, and he realized he was

holding his breath. Lucy had had all night to regret her actions. Would she let the cat out of the bag? Would she blurt out the truth?

"It's real," she said. She sounded so certain she almost fooled him. "I'm going to be Sam and Lillie's stepmom."

Chapter Eleven

Lucy scrubbed the frying pan hard enough to remove the enamel. She could hear Hallie and Maxine chatting as they stacked dishes in the cupboard, but she didn't listen to what they were saying. If she looked up from the sink, she could see the children playing catch with Frank and Jake in the backyard. Lucy Junior was sleeping in her cage, and Wiggles was underfoot looking for scraps. It was a thoroughly domestic scene.

And as fake as a three-dollar bill.

In twenty-two years of confusion, chaos, and screw-ups, she'd finally landed herself in the worst hornet's nest of all time. Why hadn't she thought this through? Sure, the scheme had placated the Slocums, but now Hallie wanted to throw a party. When the engagement ended, there would be so many people disappointed. Lucy could almost imagine a scenario where she and Jake would marry just to keep the peace.

He would marry her, too.

His proposal, lame as it was, had been sincere. Marriage had always been his objective, and it was still the answer to most of his problems. Even marriage to Lucy.

Could she do it? She loved the children,n and surely she could continue to work for Ed since they were in school all day. She loved Jake, too, and, therein lay the rub. He didn't love her. And what was almost worse, he didn't respect her. She knew very well that he had no intention of making her a co-parent. She'd be an assistant, fine for reading stories and providing an extra pair of hands and eyes, but she wouldn't be included in the decision making. She wouldn't be equal.

If she married Jake, she'd still be goofy, hair brained Lucy in the eyes of the town and, worse, in her own mind.

She couldn't do it.

She wouldn't do it.

She heard Hallie's voice.

"We'll have a formal party at the Grange Hall, of course," she said, "but tonight we'll have a picnic and invite everybody we know. This is huge." Oh Lord.

"I'm sure you and Jake were busy last night," Hallie added, with a wink, "but have you got any idea when the wedding's going to be?" There really was no way out.

"Christmastime," Lucy said. That gave her six months to convince Jake to respect her; half a year to make him fall in love.

That evening Lucy had served the children hotdogs, baked beans, potato salad, and lemonade when she heard her brother's voice.

"I need to talk to you. Come to the study."

She followed him, noting the way Maxine and Hallie were chattering with neighbors. Frank and Baz were playing horseshoes, and Jake seemed to be in a deep discussion with Ed Stiles. Just one cozy extended family, Lucy thought, sourly.

Cam poured himself a whisky and offered her one. She shook her head, surprised. Cam seldom drank around his daughter.

"About this engagement."

Lucy tensed. Cam was smart. He undoubtedly knew that Jake and Lucy didn't love each other. He undoubtedly believed, as Jake did, that she was too young for him. Too flaky. "Congratulations."

That was it? That was all?

"Uh, thanks."

"He seems like a good man."

"Uh, yup. He is."

Cam sat on the leather couch and leaned forward, the glass of whiskey in one hand. "Apparently I'm no longer a suspect." She blinked at the subject change.

"It seems Molly Whitecloud gave me an alibi."

"That's right. I was there."

Cam looked up at her and his blue eyes were dark.

"What happened? Why did she do it?"

Lucy studied her brother's flushed face. Surely he knew this story better than she.

"I think she was concerned. She didn't want you to be blamed for the murder. She told Jake that the two of you had gone over to the casino site and then, when you heard someone coming, you got back in the car and drove around the rez. She told Jake you'd fallen asleep on her sofa."

"And he believed her?"

"He's pretty observant, Cam. He believes there's still something between you and Molly."

He muttered a curse.

"Why is it a problem? Wasn't she telling the truth?"

Cam eased his legs out in front of him, and he slumped back on the couch.

"It's true. But there's nothing between us. Most of

the time we weren't even talking."

They were just being in the same space together. Lucy could picture it, and her heart ached for her brother. She owed him the whole story.

"I think she would have summoned Jake in any case, but her hand was kind of forced because I found one of her earrings out at the murder site. I gave it back to her. She chose to explain it to Jake."

Cam made a rough sound that might have been a laugh.

"She always was honest to a fault. Except about the important stuff." He drained his glass. "The trouble is her alibi places us both at the murder scene. If the sheriff can't pin this on anyone else, he'll come back to her. Or me. Or both of us."

"Jake won't do that," Lucy said, offended on behalf of her fake fiancé. "He's not a fool, Cam."

The blue eyes so like her own looked bleak.

"I'm the one who gets control of the casino project," he said. "And Molly's the one who wanted it in the first place. In the absence of any other suspects, those motives are gonna look pretty sweet."

"But you alibi each other."

Cam shrugged, wearily. "If Jake thinks there's still something between us, he'll suspect collusion."

"Is there still something between you, Cam?"

"Just memories."

Just memories. That's what Lucy would have someday if this engagement didn't work out.

"This alibi isn't going to help me with Sharon Johnson. I doubt if she'll be so understanding about my spending the night with Molly."

"Are you really interested in Sharon?"

"Of course I am. She's beautiful and kind and competent. She'll make a great stepmother for Daisy."

"You need more than a stepmother, Cam. You need passion."

"You don't understand because you're not a parent. Passion doesn't come into it. Everything has to be about the kids."

He was wrong. Lucy did understand. In spite of the warmth of the evening, she suddenly felt cold.

****

Distracted by the new direction of her life, Lucy forgot about her appointment to re-interview Shirley Packer until Monday morning when she left an apology on the woman's voicemail before she plunged into the two busiest days at the *Excelsior*.

She called Miss Otto, the twins' teacher, told her about Maxine and Frank and offered their services to help with Parade of Presidents. Miss Otto was thrilled.

"Guess you and the sheriff had some celebratin' to do this weekend," Ed said, with a lascivious wink. She couldn't think of a response quickly enough.

"Oh, come on, Luce. Engaged is as good as married these days. Besides, you spent that night together out on the rez."

"That was an emergency," she said, choking a little. She couldn't believe she was discussing intimacy—or the lack thereof—with her boss. "In any case, we're sharing the house with two young children."

"Ah, yes. I remember that problem. The secret is to drink lots of wine. Then you won't care if they hear you."

The dismal truth was that there was nothing to hear. Officially, if secretly, the engagement was still fake. Lucy had been prepared to point that out if Jake had made a move.

But he hadn't made a move.

They'd been polite to one another all weekend and had even joked about something at one point, but he had maintained a strict hands-off policy. She figured he was either attempting to respect the agreed-upon deal or he didn't want her anymore.

Either way, it seemed like a pity to waste whatever time they had together.

Maybe she should remind him about the flavored condoms.

****

If Jake's private life was spinning out of control, it was in direct contrast with the stagnating investigation.

The state boys, urged by the governor's office, checked in daily. The victim's wife, represented by her attorney, was eager for progress. There was little to report.

Jake had decided to concentrate on the three people closest to the victim, but even there, his constructs kept breaking down.

All three had strong alibis. None of them knew how to shoot a bow and arrow, although it was difficult to prove a negative. And, only Paula gained financially from Packer's death.

The Widow Packer certainly had the power to persuade any unscrupulous bowman to do her a little favor and eradicate her husband. Was that what had happened? Had she hired someone and suggested he steal the arrow from the Penobscots to implicate the tribe? She'd fulfilled the terms of her prenup by getting pregnant—if she was, in fact, pregnant. Maybe she was pregnant, but the child was not the desired boy. But couldn't she have just tried again?

Had the threesome, eager to be rid of the self-centered, dishonorable Packer, decided to combine Paula's ability to sell ice to an Eskimo with Shirley's brains and Moore's cunning?

Jake found he could believe the idea of a collaboration. He just couldn't find a strong enough motive for murder, not one that made sense. Thus far he had found no secret cache of cash.

Worst of all, Jake couldn't seem to keep his head in the game. He didn't trust Maxine, and he didn't like having her around his kids. The uncertainty about his future with Lucy gnawed at him, and his decision not to touch her until she gave him a sign that the engagement was real, was driving him insane.

Jake leaned back in his desk chair and brushed his fingers through his hair.

History had repeated itself. Once again he'd fallen for the wrong woman. The difference was that the last time he'd married her and this time she didn't want to marry him.

He forced himself to drag his feelings out into the light and to face the truth. He wanted Lucy to be the mother of his children, present and future. He wanted her in his life every single day. He wanted her in his bed every single night.

He was in love with Lucy.

Did he have the right to tell her? She was a tenderhearted creature. If she knew about his love, she'd agree to a real engagement and marriage. She'd give him what he wanted. She'd give up the plans she'd made for herself. Could he stand to do that to her?

Could he stand not to?

Jake knew one thing for certain. He couldn't continue like this.

He was, as Moonbeam would say, a hot mess.

After supper he sat at the kitchen table watching her work on the finishing touches to Lillie's Martha Washington costume. He stared at the mass of short curls on her bent head and watched her small, pink tongue as it emerged from her mouth during moments of concentration. This was the time to tell her how he felt, but lust was making him tongue-tied. He was grateful that the table blocked any view of his lower body even as he wondered how much more of this he could survive.

"I get the feeling there's something on your mind," she said, looking up from the sewing.

More like something in my pants. He kept the ignoble thought to himself.

"I think we need to talk about this engagement."

She put down the needle in her hand and stared at him. Her blue eyes were huge in her heart-shaped face, but he couldn't seem to read them.

"Saturday night's the party," he went on. "Everyone's taking this seriously."

"I know." Her voice was subdued. "I feel terrible about letting Hallie and Maxine go to all this trouble. I guess I didn't think it through. An engagement involves more than just the two people involved."

"In our case, the four people involved."

She scrunched up her face as if she were in pain.

"What do you want to do?"

"What do you want to do," he countered.

She picked up the sewing and pierced the heavy

cotton with the needle. He couldn't see her eyes.

"There's only one thing we can do," she said, evenly. "We have to call it off."

He knew he should have been prepared for that response but the words caught him in the gut. For a moment he couldn't breathe.

"Couples break up all the time," she said.

"People will understand."

"Sam? Lillie? Maxine?"

She looked up then, her eyes dark with distress.

"We announced the engagement to placate

Maxine," he said, carefully. "If we break up, I'll be back in the same leaky boat, with Maxine trying to get custody of my kids."

"I think you're wrong about that," Lucy said, seriously. "Maxine isn't a gorgon. She's just a grandma who wants the right to spend time with her grandchildren. That bit about getting a second wife, that was a smokescreen."

"The children need a mother, Lucy."

"I know."

"Are you telling me you don't want to be that mother?"

She lifted her eyes. They were even more beautiful filled with tears. He cursed himself for being a coward, for trying to manipulate her.

"Because I'd like you to be," he said, knowing it was too little, too late. "I'd like to make the engagement real. And the wedding, too."

She went very still. For a moment he thought she wasn't going to answer him at all. He was wrong.

"Why?"

Jake knew what she was asking. He knew, too, that

she had a right to know.

"I've had reservations about you and me. I'm thirteen years older than you. I've already married one woman who was too young, too unready for marriage. You have a bright future and you've barely tasted life outside Eden. It isn't fair to tie you down at such an early age. But the fact remains that I need you, Lucy. The kids need you. And they love you." He paused and plunged ahead.

"I love you, too."

The tears overflowed and streamed down her beautiful, heart-shaped face.

He'd said it quietly, without passion or emphasis. But he had said it. She wondered if he had any idea at all of what it meant to her.

And then she started second guessing.

Did he love her the way he'd loved the unfortunate Ariel? The way he'd loved Hallie? Was it a deep and abiding love or a love that would crash and burn if she screwed something up? Did his love include respect? Would he occasionally defer to her opinion on how to spend money? On the murder investigation? On the children?

Did he love her enough to have a child with her?

The questions were probably unanswerable. He probably didn't know yet how much he loved her, or how little. Love wasn't static, after all. He might love her a little today and a lot in five years. Or it could be the reverse.

She was aware of his eyes on her. They were very green.

He'd said he loved her.

That had to be enough for now.

She set down the Martha Washington dress, got up from her chair, walked over to him, and settled into his lap. He seemed a little surprised and a lot welcoming.

"I love you, too."

Suddenly his fingers were in her hair and one huge hand supported her back. Her arms came around his neck and she felt his lips, firm and warm against hers and she heard his breathing, hot and tight. His thighs shifted underneath her and she felt the hard, pulsing evidence of his desire against her bottom. Everything inside her melted, including her brain.

"Take me to bed," she murmured.

His grip tightened in her hair and his tongue was in her mouth and she sucked on it, hard, trying to get closer. She felt the groan in Jake's chest. She wriggled against him.

"Daddy?"

He ripped his lips away from hers and muttered one heartfelt syllable. "Fuck."

Lillie stared at them for a long, long minute before she spoke.

"Can one of you read me another *Fancy Nancy*?"

"No," he barked. "Go back to bed."

Lucy stiffened in his arms.

"But, Daddy…"

He cut her off with a curse.

"Back to bed, Lillie. Or no Martha Washington."

Lucy stifled her horrified gasp.

A tear trickled down Lillie's small face and Lucy bounded off her perch.

"Come on, sweetheart. I'll tuck you in."

"Will you read me a *Fancy Nancy*?"

"If you say yes," Jake said, his voice low and full

of menace, "the engagement is off."

For a moment Lucy couldn't move. She couldn't breathe. She could however deduce. At least she knew now what kind of love Jake was talking about.

The kind that didn't include respect.

She was tempted to head straight for her own room after she tucked the child in bed, but she fought the impulse. Running away wouldn't solve anything.

"I didn't think you'd come back," he said.

She shrugged. "I haven't finished the costume."

"Oh." He moved close to her, put his hands on her shoulders. "Look, I know I hurt your feelings and

I'm sorry. I was just, well, frustrated."

"I understand. I was frustrated, too."

"Really? Do you forgive me?"

She gazed at him.

"Is this what's going to happen every time you're frustrated or tired or we disagree about something?"

"No, no." He jammed his hands into his pockets and paced across the kitchen. "No. Of course not. It's just that I've been a single parent for a long time.

There's been nobody to contradict me."

"I get it."

He looked at her. "Do you?"

She found a grin for him. "I don't like it, but I get it."

His lips twisted into a half-smile.

"Let me ask you a question." She tried to keep any anger out of her voice. "Do you expect to share the discipline if we have a child of our own?"

"Certainly. But that's different. Sam and Lillie are my children."

"I don't think it's different, Jake. I don't think we

can have two sets of protocol in the same household. I don't think it will work for me to be an assistant parent with Sam and Lillie."

He frowned. "You have a point. I'll try to be less possessive, okay? Can you give me another chance?"

"Of course."

His grin widened. He stepped in front of her, took her face in his big hands, and brushed her lips with his. Her insides somersaulted.

Shoot-a-mile. She'd give him a million chances.

****

The following afternoon Lucy stared out the window of the *Excelsior*'s office. It had been another perfect spring morning, but the fluffy white clouds had stretched and darkened like milk spilled on the ground. She knew she should be feeling pleased with her efforts to integrate the Slocums into the household. She knew she should be pleased that she and Jake were not lying to everyone in Eden. She knew she should feel happy that she was actually going to marry the man she loved. And that he'd said he loved her.

The problem was, knowing wasn't feeling. She'd agreed to give Jake another chance to treat her as an equal, but she was afraid that wasn't something he could control any more than his gut instinct that she was too young.

Was the whole thing unrealistic?

At best it was a risk.

And then there was the investigation. She'd made up a few charts with the headings MEANS, MOTIVE and OPPORTUNITY. Bits of flotsam and jetsam were starting to coalesce in her mind. She had a favorite horse in the race for prime suspect, but there was no proof. Ideally, she should be able to discuss her idea with Jake but she couldn't see her way clear to do it and she knew why.

Sex. The issue of sex, or, more accurately, lack thereof, was gumming up the works.

If she and Jake were going to make this engagement work, they were going to have to blow out the cobwebs. So to speak.

Lucy clicked off her computer and pushed herself to her feet. Ed looked up from the *New York Times* crossword puzzle.

"If you don't need me for anything, I'm going out to the rez to pick up some crafts from Molly

Whitecloud's mother and the other ladies."

Ed gave her a long look.

"You don't sound like a bride-to-be."

"How does a bride-to-be sound?"

"Excited. Giddy. You know, turned on."

Exactly.

"Getting cold feet?"

"More like brain freeze. Everything seems kinda topsy turvey."

Ed shrugged. "Things have flip-flopped in your life pretty fast. Two weeks ago you told me you wanted to be a war correspondent. Instead, you're about to be an instant mama."

"It isn't that. I love Sam and Lillie. And I can still work for you. Right?"

Ed grunted. He looked over the top of his granny glasses at her.

"Learn to trust your gut, Luce. Mine invariably leads me to pizza and beer."

****

Jake couldn't concentrate on the investigation. Big surprise. He'd made a monumental error last night. A giant goof. He'd kissed his legitimate fiancée good night and retired to spend the night battling his frustration. He was an idiot.

And there was no excuse. He was thirty-five years old, and he knew what he wanted. He wanted Lucy. And she'd been right down the hall. Idiot. He jumped up from his desk, grabbed his hat, and headed for the Blazer only to find Lucy wasn't at the *Excelsior*, that she'd headed out to the rez.

Jake's lips curved into a slow, sensuous smile that he was careful not to let Ed see.

****

Lucy loaded the baskets, balsa-wood whittled animals, beaded bracelets and dream catchers into the Jeep. The items would constitute some of the first merchandise for the Maine Attraction, a crafts co-op sponsored by the Eden Chamber of Commerce. It was scheduled to open soon in the empty White's Department Store.

Cam was chairman of project that would become a link with the Blackbird Reservation. As Lucy watched Molly loading more crafts into the vehicle, she wondered why she hadn't noticed Cam's links to the reservation before.

Probably because she was focused on her own problems.

Thunder echoed across the woods and fields of the rez.

"Seems like it's always getting ready to storm when I'm out here," she said to the midwife.

Molly laughed.

"At least this time there won't be any snow."

Lucy headed down the lane, but instead of turning left at the main rez road, she turned right. Several miles later she headed north toward the casino site.

She wasn't sure why she'd come, but when she got out of the Jeep and felt the brisk wind against her face, she felt calm for the first time since she'd agreed to the fake engagement. It was almost as if the spirits of those who had lived here before had gathered around with bits of wisdom like "don't sweat the small stuff and it's all small stuff."

Lucy chuckled as she remembered one of her dad's favorite phrases. He'd been a good man, and she missed him. Jesse Outlaw, though, would never have sat on the floor and played Old Maid with Lillie or Chutes and Ladders with Sam. He'd never have taken Lucy and her brother to a Saturday matinee. Veterinarians worked on Saturdays. At least he did.

Jake Langley was a good man and a good father. Didn't it follow then that he'd make a good husband? What was she worried about? She stretched out her arms and twirled around like a leaf in the wind. Everything was going to work out. She was sure of it.

A thunderbolt exploded above her head, and the sense of peace was shattered. An instant later a shiver ran up her spine. She knew it had nothing to do with the threatening storm.

She watched as the Blazer tore across the empty field, and she was able to smell the scent of strawberry shortcake shampoo even before he got out of the vehicle. She admired the wide shoulders and the long legs, the easy stride. His eyes were the color of new leaves shot with gold flecks. Lucy shivered again.

When he got close enough, she lifted her arms, and he held her tightly and plunged his tongue into her mouth.

Everything was Jake.

Lightning cracked and split the sky.

"We need cover," she murmured.

"I need you."

He grabbed her hand, and they sprinted for the construction trailer as fat drops of rain splashed off their bodies.

"I'm sorry you got wet," he said. "I was late on the uptake." She put a hand on his chest and felt his heart thump hard.

"Now my outsides match my insides. They're both wet."

"Oh, baby, I need you."

"Back at ya."

She attacked the buttons on his uniform shirt.

His big hands closed around her rib cage. They felt warm and strong and when his thumbs brushed the undersides of her breasts she shuddered with pleasure. Jake groaned and recaptured her mouth. Every jab of his tongue made her jerk with pleasure. She abandoned the effort of removing his shirt and slid one hand inside his waistband. His hand spread across her buttocks and pulled her hard against him. She loved it that he wanted her so badly. That he needed her. She melted against him, absorbing his hard thrust.

"Sofa," he gasped.

They fell onto the cheap sofa in the late developer's office. Was it wrong to make love here? Lucy couldn't bring herself to care. Every nerve ending, every ganglion was focused on the man ripping away their wet clothing. She twisted her hips and arched toward him. She couldn't wait to hold him. Inside.

****

He'd lost every vestige of finesse but hell, that was nothing new with Lucy. It was hard to think when every ounce of blood in his brain had surged south. Just knowing she wanted him as much as he wanted her—if that was even possible—made him desperate.

He jerked down his zipper and came up over her, ready to pound into her until they were both mindless, but first he had to remove her jeans. Her wet, skintight jeans. He cursed and she laughed and together they wrestled the soaked denim off her long, shapely legs. He prayed for enough control to wait until she was ready. His fingers trembled as they slipped in between her soft thighs. Good God. And then her fingers found him, circled him, and squeezed.

"Don't do that, Lucy."

She let go immediately, and he cursed himself. Dammit, she was practically a virgin. She didn't understand. He found her fingers and placed them back on his body.

"I don't want it to be over before it begins," he gasped. "When you touch me like that, when you squeeze, it makes me come. I want to be inside you when that happens."

"Now," she said, urgently. "I want you inside me now."

A long, tortured groan ripped out of his chest, and his fingers shook as he made a place for himself and thrust. She flinched and he stopped dead.

"I'll try to go slower."

"No," she murmured. She wrapped her legs around his waist. "I want it hard. And fast." She captured his mouth and slid her tongue inside.

Jake's hips were like a jackhammer. He plunged and surged again and again, faster and deeper. He needed to come. He never wanted this to end. Her breathing hitched and she let out a series of breathy little sounds and then her fingernails bit into his shoulders and she screamed his name. He held her against his chest, his body wracked with unfulfilled need, his heart swollen with tenderness.

"Omigod," she whispered, when she'd recovered her breath. "That was amazing."

"I'm glad you liked it."

"Jake?" She must have noticed something amiss. Maybe it was the harsh rasp of his breath or maybe it was the fact that he was still deeply buried inside her. She tightened her legs around him again and slid her fingers into his hair. "Your turn."

He put his head down and drove into her. Once, twice and then the tension burst. He cried out and buried his face in her neck as he deliberately filled her with his essence.

Another child would be just fine with him.

Chapter Twelve

Breathing was overrated. It didn't even compare with the joy of holding his hard, heavy body against her, of knowing that she'd given him what he needed, of knowing that what he needed was her.

She felt so close to Jake—closer than she'd ever felt to anyone in her life. And she felt loved. They belonged together, and finally, he'd acknowledged it, in a manner of speaking. She grinned against his heavy shoulder. Everything would turn out now. She was glad to exchange her vague dream of journalistic fame for a family of her own and work on a weekly newspaper. She didn't need to prove her competence to anyone. And, anyway, once she was running Jake's household and helping to raise Jake's children, people would see that she was no longer scatterbrained.

A warm glow spread through her squashed chest. If life was a series of moments, this was one of the best.

****

He couldn't move.

Nothing had ever felt this comfortable. Nothing had ever felt this right. He felt a strong urge to just stay here forever, to drift into sleep on top of Lucy, but that was impossible. He could feel her struggling to inhale. And, anyway, they needed to talk. He had to make sure, one more time, that she was okay with the life he could offer, that she wouldn't have second thoughts when the going got rough. And he needed to do it before proximity to her delectable body tempted him into another bout of passion. God, she felt good. With a pang of regret, he started to heave himself off of her, but he froze when he felt her hand close around him and heard her voice in his ear. "Is that what I think it is?"

Desire surged through his veins.

"Mock me at your peril, witch," he muttered.

Her fingers started a sensuous massage.

"I'm not mocking, I'm admiring." Her voice was low and sexy. Heat streaked through him, and he was hard and needy, as if he hadn't had sex in a year.

"I can't believe what you do to me," he growled.

"I know what I want you to do to me," she whispered.

He made a rough sound and slid back into her.

"That's so good," she breathed, as he established a long, slow rhythm. "Don't stop."

It was an effort to talk. "Believe me, honey, I couldn't stop if a meteor crashed in the window."

Her giggle turned into a gasp, and she tightened her thighs around his hips. Jake buried his face in her neck and slowly but surely drove them both to ecstasy.

Later, when they were lying in a tangle of arms and legs and panting and blowing like beached whales, Jake realized he wanted Lucy to say she loved him. He knew it was true but, for some reason, he wanted to hear the words. He felt her suck in a breath and he smiled to himself as he waited for her words.

"Jake," she said, "do you think that maybe Shirley Packer or Claude Moore killed Nate? I mean, they both went on safari with him. Maybe they learned how to shoot, too, but decided not to tell us."

His disappointment surprised him given that he'd never been a big afterglow kind of a guy. "They both have alibis." He knew he sounded abrupt.

"Alibis can be set up, can't they?"

"Sometimes."

She shifted then canted up on one elbow.

"Who do you think killed Packer?"

"I don't know yet."

"But you must have a theory."

"I'm not ready to share it."

She peered into his face, her blue eyes thoughtful. "You're being an awful grump. A person would think you hadn't been laid recently."

"I hope you're not going to talk like that in front of the kids."

He sounded like a prim, pompous ass. What was wrong with him?

She sat up and swung her feet to the floor.

"If I slip up you can ground me. That's usually effective with adolescents."

"I'm sorry," he said.

She glanced back at him and nodded.

****

The morning of the engagement party dawned with a cloudless sky. It was one of those May mornings in Maine, the kind poets wrote about. Crocuses peeked out of the ground in most every yard and even along the highway. In some cases, daffodils had appeared already.

The beautiful weather, though, was not enough to distract Jake. He hadn't made things right with Lucy. He told himself there hadn't been time, but it was more than that. Her failure to mention love the day before had made him question whether she was ready for this step and, as always, he was wondering whether he was ready for it, too. She was just so young and impulsive. He frowned at the beauty of the new leaves on the trees that lined the interstate. Take the business with Maxine and Frank. They had taken up what seemed like permanent residence at the local B&B, the Garden of Eden, and it seemed like they were always at the house working with the children and Lucy on costumes for the play or baking cookies or whatever.

He'd agreed to let them have a role—a limited role—in the twins' lives, but Lucy was acting like they were her parents and Jake had seen, firsthand, that the children were smitten. He didn't like it. Not at all. Lucy was one of those woman who took a mile when given an inch. Jake's stomach churned. She'd just have to understand that he had a right to establish boundaries for his own children. He winced. Their children. He had to adjust to the new reality of sharing Sam and Lillie with Lucy. He did not have to share them with the Slocums.

This morning, though, he figured he'd better do some work and that started with re-checking alibis.

His first unannounced stop was the Packer mansion where he found the enticing widow entertaining her gynecologist, a young man who looked less like a practicing physician and more like *People* magazine's sexiest man in America. The faithful attorney was nowhere in sight.

"Where's your watchdog?"

"I sent him out to get me some Maine wild blueberry ice cream. It's made down in Lyndon,

Vermont."

Jake chuckled. The world might see Paula Packer as a brainless twit, but he knew differently. The woman was no fool. She knew how to take care of herself, and she knew how to get exactly what she wanted. Jake could respect that.

"I'd like to talk to your servants again."

The maid and cook stuck to their original statements. Mrs. Packer had gone to bed early the night of the murder. No one had entered or left the house between seven p.m. and eleven when the servants had retired.

It seemed that Paula was safe.

Shirley Packer wasn't home, but Jake was able to re-interview the across-the-street neighbor who had identified her car. The elderly man repeated his testimony word for word. At ten-thirty sharp—he'd just finished watching the local news—he'd gone out to move his trashcans and he'd seen her drive down the street and turn into her driveway. Since the house blocked the detached garage, he hadn't watched her pull into it, but he'd heard the door open and close. No, he hadn't actually seen her face, the windshield was tinted and it was dark out, but he knew Mrs. Packer lived alone. Who else would be driving her car?

Claude Moore wasn't home, either. It was Jake's second visit to the sprawling example of flat modern architecture. The entire, large structure was built on one level. Solar panels lined the roof and floor to ceiling windows lined one side of the living room. The house was open and airy and, of course, tastefully decorated with original artwork.

Margaret Monaghan had worked for Moore for a

dozen years since he'd moved into the house. She was an all-around housekeeper but had been hired for her cooking skills. She'd already told Jake that Moore was a man of no vices and regular habits. She always knew when he'd come in for the night because she could hear the buzz of the alarm system when he set it. The night in question she'd heard it at ten forty-five, which was pretty much standard. She repeated that Mr. Moore was a man of regular habits.

Jake sighed, inwardly. He hadn't been able to budge the needle on the alibis. The housekeeper walked him to the front door.

"Did you know Mr. Packer," he asked, suddenly.

"Not really. He was only here once or twice. Mr. Moore's a real, old-fashioned bachelor. His home is his castle."

"It's a beautiful home," Jake said, absently. "A lot of room for one person."

"Oh, I don't think so. He has the lower level set up as an office."

"The lower level? You mean the cellar?"

"It's not really a cellar," she corrected him. "More of a walkout basement. The house is built on an incline."

A walkout basement? Why hadn't he considered that possibility? Jake felt like a dunce. He also felt a surge of excitement.

"If Moore came in the basement door would you hear it?"

"Well, no. I wouldn't hear him come in either of the doors, you see, but he always sets the security system. That's what I hear."

That left the alibi intact. Moore had to be here at

ten forty-five to set the alarm. He made one last try for information.

"Mrs. Monaghan, you probably know Mr. Moore as well as anyone. Did he seem to be upset when Mr. Packer divorced and remarried and dissolved the partnership?"

"Upset? No. Mr. Moore never loses his temper.

He's always a perfect gentleman."

Jake nodded. "Okay. Thanks."

"He did get that look in his eye."

"What look?"

"The one where he's looking at you and talking to you, but his mind is somewhere else. My first husband got that look a lot. He tuned me out. At first I thought he was thinking about something important, you know?"

"Was he?"

She shook her head. "Nope. Turned out it was usually about his supper."

On the drive home, Jake shoved a Beethoven sonata into the CD player. The classical music relaxed him enough to stop his mind from racing and to let it, instead, sift through the information he'd gathered. The alibis seemed solid, but Lucy was right about alibis. Sometimes the perfect alibis were the most brittle and most easily broken. He decided to forget about alibis and concentrate, instead, on motive. By the time he pulled into his driveway, Jake had what he thought was a very promising theory, so promising that he called Homer and asked him to perform surveillance that evening. Follow-up would have to wait until tomorrow. Jake wasn't going to put any more stress on his somewhat fragile relationship with Lucy by missing the engagement party.

Two hours later he was knotting his tie when his daughter pirouetted into the room.

"Daddy! Daddy! Do you like my dress?"

She was a vision in pink lace and matching Mary Janes. Lucy had pulled her hair up into a ballerina's knot and decorated the little blonde bump with tiny rosebuds.

"You look like a Princess," he said.

"Princess Rosebud. That's what Lucy called me. She said the dress was too 'xpensive, but Grandma buyed it."

Jake frowned. He didn't want Maxine Slocum buying his children anything. Didn't Lucy know that?

"Can I wear this for my bridemaid dress?"

"If Lucy says so."

Lillie nodded. "Is Lucy the boss of you, Daddy?"

He winked at her. "Yep."

"Sam's gonna be the man maid."

"I'm not the man maid." Sam sputtered, as he entered the bedroom. "Lucy says I'm the Good Man."

Jake eyed the boy's blue blazer, khaki slacks, crisp white shirt, and red tie with trucks on it. He was a tiny echo of his father except for the trucks. Despite his irritation about Maxine, Jake's heart filled with love for the priceless children and for the woman who would complete their family.

"It's called best man. That's you, Sam. By the way, you look awesome tonight."

A moment later Lucy floated into the room. Jake had already seen her in the dress, half an hour earlier when he'd slowly, carefully, worked the zipper up the back of her silk, emerald green dress. The garment had built-in support so she hadn't worn a bra, and it fit her like a…well, it fit her like he fit her. Perfectly. He lived in anticipation of the moment, several hours hence, when he'd get to guide that zipper back down her beautiful back.

"Have I told you how beautiful you look?"

She blushed. "Several times. Not that I mind the repetition."

"It's true, you know. You are a beautiful woman, Lucy Outlaw."

She moved closer and brushed her lips across his hard jaw.

"And you're a beautiful, if stubborn, man."

He grinned and watched her swish out of the room, her full skirt belling out to reveal her beautifully shaped legs. Her dark curls were contained with rhinestone clips. She sparkled with light and life. Jake felt an ocean swell of possessiveness.

Lucy belonged to him.

****

The Eden County Grange Hall, built near the close of the nineteenth century and added onto at regular intervals, was located just outside of town. Nowadays area farmers grew fruits and vegetables for sale at local markets or they provided pick-our-own services for everything from berries to Christmas trees. They no longer had need of a grange. As a result, the hall had become a community gathering spot, rented for weddings and reunions and large parties during which the sober brick building would be transformed like Cinderella at the hands of her fairy godmother.

Hallie had spearheaded an effort to deck the place with thousands of twinkle lights, yards of tulle, and piles of white satin bows. She'd bought and arranged bouquets of flowers and had a banner made (Congratulations, Lucy and Jake!). Asia had made a tiered cake decked with pink sugar roses and inscribed with their names inside a heart. Many of the guests had brought food: macaroni, seven-bean salad, Jello salads, lobster rolls, fried clams, mussels, shrimp, johnnycakes stuffed with crabmeat, blueberry pies, and homemade rolls.

It was a feast and enough to feed an army. Lucy swallowed hard and blinked back tears. Hallie was so dear. Everyone had gone to so much trouble for her, goofy, brainless Lucy Outlaw. And for Jake, of course. Eden County had embraced their new sheriff.

She wondered. She stood by Jake in the door and greeted the guests as they arrived. Everyone seemed delighted by the engagement. How could she have considered moving away from Eden? This was her home. It was where she belonged. She'd been like the restless teenager in the Wizard of Oz, searching for happiness anywhere and everywhere when it had been in her own backyard all the time.

She knew Jake still had some doubts. She knew, too, they were because of his disastrous experience with his first wife. Lucy was prepared to cut him some slack on that. In time, he'd figure out that she wasn't too young, that she wasn't going to flake out on him. At the moment, he was particularly attentive, holding her hand, brushing a shiver-inducing kiss against her knuckles. She knew he was thinking about making love later in the big bed in his room.

She was thinking about it, too.

Lucy felt a moment of tension when Maxine and

Frank arrived, probably because of the muscle that twitched in Jake's jaw. He was perfectly pleasant to them, though. Nothing to worry about there. The relationship was almost normal, and Jake seemed to have accepted the twins' grandparents just fine. Lucy's heart swelled with love for the three generations of her new family, and she felt a stab of pity for Ariel, the woman who was missing it all.

"I think the guests have all arrived," Jake murmured to her. He slipped two fingers under her chin and brushed a kiss against her lips. The brief touch sent another round of shivers down her spine. "We can probably join the others. In a minute." He drew her closer and traced the seam of her lips with his tongue.

"Daddy, Daddy." Sam grabbed his father's hand and started to pull. "Hallie wants to talk to ya."

Jake winked at Lucy. "Hold that thought," he murmured in a throaty voice. "I'll be right back."

Lucy returned to the coloring table with Sam. Cam was there with his date, Sharon Johnson. They spent a few minutes admiring drawings by the twins and Daisy.

"Hey, Luce." Her brother, Baz approached.

"Where's the sheriff? It's time for a toast."

"Talking to your wife."

Baz flashed her a brief grin and pointed to the corner where Jake had stooped down to talk with Lillie.

"Your very young wife," Lucy amended. "I'll get him." She started across the room, but before she reached him, Jake stood and turned toward her. Lucy's heart stuttered. There was no mistaking the tension in the wide shoulders or the grim brackets around his sensuous mouth. The emerald eyes were as hard as the stones they resembled.

"What is it," she asked, when he drew near enough.

He didn't answer immediately. She saw him swallow, and she realized he was struggling with some emotion. She crossed her fingers and prayed it was love.

"Lillie says she and Sam are going to the ranch this summer. She says that you okayed the idea."

He didn't raise his voice. Only his glittering eyes revealed his fury. And his flushed cheeks.

Love wasn't what had him tongue-tied. It was anger at her. Nothing new in that.

"I told the twins it was up to you," she said. "But Lillie's right. I was okay with the idea. It seemed like a good one to me."

"Why? You tired of being a stepmom already? Christ, Lucy." He was quietly spitting nails. "The whole point of this engagement was so there'd be no chance of Maxine co-opting the kids. Now I find out you stabbed me in the back."

She held very still and reminded herself she'd known it was a risk. She'd probably pushed the relationship too far too fast, but she'd figured a visit to the ranch could take the place of a honeymoon. It would be fun for the kids, and it would make their grandparents happy. She'd clearly underestimated the extent of Jake's enmity toward his ex-in-laws. Her eyes narrowed on him.

"What kind of an example are you setting for these children, Jake? Don't you want them to know about forgiveness and second chances? Okay, so you have a history with Maxine, but that's in the past. You keep talking about how immature I am. Well, in this case, the situation is reversed. You need to grow up."

The ruddy color in his cheeks deepened, and his eyes flashed like lightning during a storm. Lucy half expected to see steam coming out of his head. She watched him grapple with the anger. Was he angry enough to ruin the entire party?

Just then Hallie arrived and slid her hand through his arm. Jake looked into her hazel eyes, and Lucy could literally see the anger seep out of him.

Her own heart felt like the limpest of dishrags.

"Time to toast the happy couple," Hallie said.

Chapter Thirteen

The interminable party finally ended. Sam and Lillie chattered in the backseat on the drive back to the house. Jake glared out the windshield, and Lucy tried to think about logistics. She wanted to get out as soon as they reached Cypress Street, hop in her Jeep, and disappear, but she couldn't do that. She had to make the transition as smooth as possible for Sam and Lillie.

"Now that you're 'gaged," Sam said, "can we call Lucy, 'Mommy'?"

A knife sliced through her heart.

"You'd have to rename the mouse."

"You mean Lucy Junior has to be Mommy Junior?"

"Right."

"That's dopey, Daddy," Lillie said. "You know Lucy Junior is a boy."

Finally, the children were settled in their beds. It was time for the showdown. Lucy knew Jake had a right to make decisions regarding the kids, but he was showing no effort at all to accept her as an equal parent.

Underneath it all, Lucy knew the argument wasn't about the ranch or Maxine or even the issue of co-parenting. At bottom, this was about Jake and his wariness to make a commitment to a much younger woman. He said he knew she wasn't like Ariel. She knew he thought he meant it but she knew, too, there was no chance of building a good marriage on the sand of his insecurities. Either he believed in Lucy or he didn't.

That question had been answered, again, tonight.

She didn't know whether he would apologize or insist, icily, that "we-have-to-talk" and she couldn't bring herself to care. She was tired of being treated like a mindless embryo.

He met her in the hallway as she closed Sam's door.

"Come on," he said, taking her hand and leading her toward her room. The words and his touch combined to make her heart pound crazily.

"What are you doing?"

He shrugged. "You need help getting out of that dress."

Practical Jake. He was right, of course. She let him unzip the dress. This time his hands did not linger on the silky, form-hugging fabric.

"I think we should discuss some ground rules," he said, "after you change." He strode out of the room.

So it was ice. That made her own decision easier.

Lucy pulled on her jeans and a sweatshirt. She removed her jewelry and hung the emerald-green dress in its plastic bag then she threw her underwear and clothes into the suitcase she'd stored in the closet. This part of it seemed like adding insult to injury. A decision to separate was gut wrenching enough. A person shouldn't have to go through the packing up and fifty-five trips out to the car.

But then, this wasn't a divorce. She'd never intended to stay. Not really.

Her heart was beating like a trapped bird and she

felt lightheaded. In the end, she just couldn't deal with the suitcase. She left it behind and walked out to the living room.

Jake frowned at her.

"I thought you'd get ready for bed."

He'd changed into jeans and a T-shirt, too, but then he didn't own any pajamas.

"I'm not planning to sleep here tonight."

She hadn't known she was going to say that until the words were out.

Shock registered on his handsome features. He flopped on the sofa and gazed, broodingly, at her face.

"You're overreacting, Lucy. It was just an argument."

She knew better, but she couldn't explain it to him, not tonight when there was a cannonball stuck in her throat.

"Step relations are always difficult," he said, wearily. He pushed his fingers through his hair.

She felt a wave of sadness. She'd become a too-young, trouble-toting step relation. There was nothing left of Lucy in this engagement.

"Do you even want to be a mom, Lucy? Or do you want a career?"

She gaped at him. Had she expected him to argue? Had she expected him to plead? He wasn't going to do it. He agreed with her unspoken assessment that this wasn't going to work. He'd taken her apparent rebellion and shoved it back in her teeth. He wanted her to walk out.

"This isn't about mom versus career. I like being a reporter, and I love you and the kids. I think I can wear two hats. What's going on between us isn't mom versus career. It's about what I want."

"Which is?"

She couldn't believe he didn't know.

"To be treated as an equal, Jake. It's that simple. And that complicated."

She walked toward the door, her keys in her hand.

"Where are you going?"

His voice sounded hoarse, raspy. Well, why not? He was exhausted. So was she.

"I'm going home to get some sleep."

"This is your home, Lucy."

It was an excellent opportunity for a withering and final exit line, a perfect chance to rip off the engagement ring purchased for another woman and fling it in his face. She couldn't bring herself to do either.

"I need some time alone," she said.

Lucy sat in the veterinary clinic parking lot and stared at the darkened building. She couldn't bear to climb the stairs to her lonely apartment. She knew she wouldn't be able to sleep, and if, by some miracle, she decided to wallow in the painful breakup, there wasn't even any ice cream there.

She could let herself into the Outlaw family home, but no one would be up to talk to, and anyway, she didn't want to talk. She didn't want to think anymore either.

Mostly, she didn't want to feel.

It was after midnight and the temperature, in typical Maine fashion, had dropped to the low forties. Lucy shivered. She couldn't just sit in the Jeep all night unless she could think of somewhere to drive it. Without making a conscious decision, she switched on the ignition and backed onto Walnut Street. Minutes later she was on the interstate driving east—to Bangor.

****

Jake stared at the blank screen of the television set. Somehow, he hadn't expected her to walk out, but her absence gave him plenty of time to critique his own behavior.

He'd treated her like one of those punching bag clowns, knocking her over, pushing her down, over and over and every time she'd absorbed the blow, gotten back on her feet and forgiven him. She had seemed to understand his fear of getting burned again. It had taken him too long to understand how important she was to him, too long to find the courage to risk another mistake. Each time he thought he was ready, he'd get cold feet and push her away.

He thrust his fingers through his hair. Okay, so he'd treated her badly and he was sorry for it, but dammit, she had no right to agree to send the children to Maxine's. Christ! It was like shipping them off to a concentration camp—they might never come back!

Except to Lucy, it wasn't some grisly final solution, but a chance for them to visit the grandparents who loved them.

He was the one with the problem, not Lucy. He was the one afraid of getting hurt. He was the one who was immature.

Dammit all to hell.

Lucy. He closed his eyes and dropped his head against the back of the sofa. He pictured the twinkling blue eyes, the animation in her face, the warmth of her smile and his heart jerked. He felt the eager touch of her hands and his body throbbed. He heard her voice as she

215

read a bedtime story. He heard her breathy, little sounds as she accepted him into her tight, untried body. He felt a surge of lust followed by a surge of grief.

Lucy. Jake had never been a man who dithered but he'd dithered with his temporary nanny. He hadn't been able to decide whether he had the right to keep her or not and so, he'd lost her.

Emotions gathered in his throat and tears pricked the backs of his eyes. He hadn't cried when his mother died or when Ariel left. He hadn't cried since he was Sam and Lillie's age. He felt like crying now.

****

Clouds scudded across the sky so that crisp, clear moonscapes alternated with shadowed darkness. It felt odd to be out at night with no one around and no place to go. Sort of like a helium balloon cut loose from its string. Sort of like soaring in a Cessna two-seater in an empty night sky.

It felt both empowering. It felt desolate.

Mostly, it felt good not to be anywhere.

Lucy didn't turn on the radio, partly because the only local station that stayed on the air all night played exclusively country western tunes and partly because the silence helped her feel more like part of the ghostly scrub-pines that lined the highway and less like Lucy.

She passed the turn off to Overmyer, a tiny village three miles down a dirt road. It was exactly here that she'd met Jake that first time. She'd been heading after Christmas and he'd stopped her because of a burned out tail light. He hadn't been interested in the fact that she'd just gotten out of school and didn't have a job and thus, no money to replace the light. He'd scowled at her and told her to do it.

Even back then he'd been dictatorial. She should have known better than to fall for him but she'd taken one look at the glittering emerald eyes in his masculine face and she'd been a goner.

Silly girl.

A sign for Bangor routed her painful personal thoughts toward the murder investigation. She never had gotten back to Shirley Packer, but she still thought the first wife, the spurned wife, was the key to the whole puzzle.

She'd go see her now.

Lucy parked along the curb in front of the Cherrydale house. Enough neighbors had left their porch lights burning that she could see her way up the flagstone walkway even though Shirley's house was dark as pitch. Mrs. Packer was probably upstairs asleep in her bed. If Lucy had a grain of common courtesy, she'd turn around and leave as quietly as possible.

But she didn't have a grain. That was well-documented.

She stepped up on the porch and pushed at the front door. It creaked and opened a few inches. Lucy gasped as a shiver crawled down her spine.

Something was very wrong.

A part of her mind felt all the folly of entering the unlocked house of a murder suspect. Another part of her mind was caught up in the excitement. Was she about to discover the quintessential clue? The biggest part of her mind felt reckless. Whoever was inside the house couldn't hurt her as much as she'd already been hurt tonight and she was a reporter. There was a story here and she intended to report it.

Even so, she took the precaution of sprinting back

to the Jeep and extracting the long-handled flashlight Jake had given her after their snowbound night. He'd said, prophetically as it turned out, that he wouldn't always be around to rescue her.

A gust of wind carried with it a splash of water against her cheek. She looked up, surprised. She hadn't expected rain. Her heart thudded hard as she pushed the front door wide enough to enter the dark foyer. It occurred to her, belatedly, that Shirley Packer would never have gone to bed with her door unlocked. Lucy sprinted back down the path, found her cell, called 911 and reported the break-in. The dispatcher said they'd send a car.

The rain had picked up. Lucy could hear it dancing on the roof like quarters pouring out of a slot machine. At least it masked her footsteps. She didn't turn on her flashlight but moved deeper and deeper into the thick blackness. The hair was standing up on the back of her neck now. She tried to decide on a plan. If she found no one downstairs, should she risk climbing to the second floor? Shirley Packer would probably be tucked in bed, with a loaded pistol under her pillow.

Lucy knew that wasn't the real risk. The greater likelihood, was that she'd be a sitting duck, trapped on the second floor.

She and Flynn had turned right at the end of the corridor into Shirley's living room. This time she turned left and found herself in a small butler's pantry. She pushed open two sets of swinging door and then she was in a kitchen. And the darkness had eased.

Lucy glanced at the window. There was some kind of light out in the yard. She tiptoed across the tiled floor and peered out. Slanting rain restricted her vision but she was able to make out the source of the glow. It was coming from the interior lights of a car.

A sports car.

A mauve Bugatti Veyron.

Not that she could see the color, but she'd have her fake engagement ring that she'd guessed right. Why was Claude Moore's car parked in Shirley Packer's driveway at one a.m.? Were they lovers? She dismissed the thought immediately. Impossible. Co-conspirators? Maybe. She peered into the backyard. Maybe she'd interrupted a getaway scene. She slipped her hand into her pocket intent on calling Jake, but before she could punch in his number, she glanced out the window again.

This time the light reflected a cap of salt-and-pepper hair plastered against a woman's skull. The woman's brows were knitted as if she were angry and she moved jerkily. It didn't take long to figure out why. Almost at once, Claude Moore's slender figure came into view, and Lucy watched him shove Shirley hard enough to make the woman stumble and hit her head on the doorframe. Lucy heard a faint cry and a masculine curse. For an instant, she froze. This wasn't a getaway scene.

It was an abduction.

Claude was kidnapping his erstwhile partner.

Good grief!

There was no time to call Jake or anyone else. If Lucy didn't act immediately, Moore was going to get away with it. She had to do something—fast. If only she'd thought to park in the driveway. She hadn't though. She couldn't walk out the backdoor in full view of the villain. Lucy sprinted back through the house and exited through the front door. Then she ran through the rain, ducking behind bushes when she got closer. Claude was attempting, with limited success, to stuff Shirley's lower body into the low-slung seat of the sports car. Lucy moved closer, trying to stay hidden as long as possible. It was difficult to see with the rain needling against her face. On the other hand, the downpour provided cover for any sound she might make. She worked her way to within a few feet of the pair. She heard a sudden harsh groan followed by growled words. "Damn bitch."

It sounded like Shirley had kicked him. Someplace where it counted. Lucy gave a mental cheer.

"I'm not going with you, Claude." Shirley's voice was calm and even and Lucy could hear it clearly even over the rain. "If you want to kill me you're going to have to do it here."

"Don't tempt me," Moore panted. "You deserve a bullet, damn you. Get your feet into the car."

Lucy caught the glint of metal an instant before she heard a sickening thud as whatever it was—a gun, probably—slammed into Shirley's skull. The woman slumped and the attorney bent down out of sight. Suddenly, he cursed again.

"Goddammit, Shirl! You made me drop the gun."

Lucy's breath caught. She controlled the urge to turn on her flashlight to blind him. Light might confuse Claude, but it wouldn't stop him. He might be in pain, but he was closer to the dropped weapon than she. On top of that, Lucy was beginning to develop a strong suspicion that he knew how to use the weapon. She slipped up behind him as he bent over to search for the gun. She saw him jerk with excitement and knew he'd spotted it. This was her best chance, possibly her only chance. She lifted her flashlight and launched herself at the attorney swinging frantically. Her first attempt whiffed, and Claude looked up. Shoot-a-mile. Lucy settled for a shorter backswing. This time she connected with a sickening crack, hard enough that her own body reverberated with the shock. Her fingers opened, and the flashlight released onto the ground as Claude let out a howl.

"What the fuck!"

An instant later Lucy felt cold metal against the side of her neck. The gun barrel? He screeched, "Don't move!" But it was unnecessary. She couldn't even seem to breathe. She imagined Jake's reaction to the sight of her cold dead body on the morgue slab.

Always was too impulsive. Should've waited for help.

No one in town would argue with that.

"I take it you've decided to join us, Ms. Outlaw."

She wanted to challenge him. She wanted to ask him why he was terrorizing Shirley Packer.

"Not exactly," she muttered. "Not so full of questions tonight, are we?" She saw his arm lift, and she winced.

"Just wiping the blood off my face," he said, conversationally. "I'm not at all pleased that you've ruined my suit. It's one of my best, you know."

She risked turning an inch and saw that blood was pouring out of a wound above his temple.

"You should get stitches."

"Thank you for your input. Get in the car."

Her heart sank. Well, it wasn't as if she hadn't expected that.

"There's no room." She pointed at the woman who was half in and half out of the Bugatti, like Winnie-the-Pooh and the honey tree.

"Shove her over."

His voice sounded thin. She risked another glance. Was he turning chatreuse? It was hard to tell in the darkness. He doubled over, suddenly, and retched. Had she given him a concussion? Guilt warred with a sense of triumph. Maybe he'd pass out.

"On second thought," he sputtered, "get in on the driver's side." He shoved the gun barrel harder against her neck. "Now."

"I've never driven one of these."

"Get in the fucking car before I put a bullet through Shirley."

There was no missing the menace in his voice. Lucy circled the car and got in under the wheel. Shirley must have realized he meant business because she let him shove her up onto the console. He got in after her and closed the door.

"You ever driven one of these before?"

According to Flynn, only three hundred Bugattis had been sold in the whole world. It was an idiot question.

"No."

"Any stick?"

She figured it wasn't the time to mention the deal she'd made with her behind-the-wheel instructor in high school. *I'll pass you, Lucy, if you promise never, never to drive a stick.*

"Sure." The pistol, she noticed, lay loosely clasped in Moore's hand. He could discharge a bullet through Shirley's brain—or hers—in less time than it would take for her to turn the ignition.

"This is a seven-speed. Non-synchronized gears but a standard 'H' configuration, just with an extra 'H.' Reverse is outside the 'H' on the left-hand side."

Lucy shoved the stick into what she hoped was reverse and the gears squealed. Moore swore, savagely. He'd probably really enjoy killing her when this was over for what she was doing to his car.

"The clutch, Ms. Outlaw. Don't forget the clutch. Left foot."

Ah. She'd forgotten about the clutch. Briefly, she recalled the way she'd bumped and ground her way down Main Street during her less-than-successful driving class. She stomped on the clutch and tried to shift again.

"Hit the gas with your right foot."

The car jumped, exploding down the driveway like a shooting star. Claude Moore would have made a good driving instructor if he hadn't been so busy killing people. She turned the steering wheel when she got to the street. It, too, responded like a thousand-dollar-a-night hooker. How to get it to go forward?

"A standard 'H,'" he barked, as if she could understand him. She heard the strain under the words. The man was hurting. Just then he retched again.

"You should probably lie down."

"You should probably shift into first, if you're interested in continuing to breathe."

Lucy shoved the stick forward. The car bounced. "The clutch, Ms. Outlaw! The clutch!"

She had the distinct impression that the anguish over his car was diverting him from his roiling stomach.

"This is not an Easter ham. It's a two-million-dollar vehicle and requires a light touch." He retched but didn't vomit. The Bugatti was starting to take on an unpleasant scent.

"Car practically drives itself," he continued, like a father bragging about his child. "You'll see when we get on the country roads."

The country roads? Where were they going? And what did Claude intend to do with them when they got there. Uneasiness clawed at Lucy's stomach. Or maybe it was the stench.

"Why are you kidnapping Shirley?"

He growled as the car stuttered again. "Move up to fourth gear, dammit."

A distraught Claude, she thought, was marginally safer than a cocky Claude. She depressed the accelerator but deliberately didn't use the clutch.

"Goddammit, Ms. Outlaw! Can't you do anything right?" The effort of yelling at her had him bent over. For once, though, the familiar comment didn't hurt.

"You know," she said, feeling sassy, suddenly, "you're in the midst of kidnapping two women, and you probably murdered your best friend. Seems to me your car isn't your biggest problem."

"It's not a car. It's a Bugatti."

"Yeah, well if anything happens to Shirley or me, the Bugatti is gonna be scrap metal. My fiancé will take it apart with his bare hands."

"Nothing will happen to you," he snapped. "Shirley was insurance. You're just a pain in the ass."

"I've heard that before."

"Shocker."

The car leapt forward even with Lucy's less than competent driving skills. It really did drive itself. And it really was a pleasure to be behind the wheel. For an instant, Lucy forgot about the danger she and Shirley were in.

"Turn at that light," Claude directed. "You'll have to downshift through all the gears. Just keep the clutch in while you're doing it."

She focused on his instructions. This time the car obeyed without the convulsions.

"Not bad."

Faint praise from a murderer. Lucy felt absurdly proud and cocky. She decided to go for broke.

"Why'd you kill your best friend?"

"Shut up."

"Come on, Claude. You must have had a reason."

He shot her a look of hate, and he didn't answer but Lucy knew. It wasn't only women who could be scorned.

Nate Packer, debonair, self-assured and careless, had betrayed Claude Moore when he married Paula, dissolved the original company and the original friendships along with it. It was as simple as that.

She shivered and shifted to a higher gear.

Chapter Fourteen

Jake stepped back into the kitchen and heard the faint trill of chords that indicated someone had left a message on his cell phone. He'd missed the call because he'd wandered out on the back porch in an effort to clear his muddled brain. Apparently he'd succeeded because he hadn't responded to the phone in his pocket or the sudden gusts of rain.

Finally soaked, he returned to the house and dripped on the kitchen floor. The cell squawked again. This time he heard and he answered.

"Sheriff? Homer, here. We've got a situation." Damn. He'd forgotten about the surveillance. Had the suspect made his move? Jake's pulse quickened.

"Shoot."

"Mrs. Packer's been kidnapped."

"What? You were supposed to be watching her."

"Not that Mrs. Packer. The other one. The ex."

"Shirley? Shirley's been kidnapped?"

Jake knew he sounded like a confused parrot. Homer was infinitely patient.

"I was watching t'other one. But that lawyer fooled us, boss. Our best guess is he's aimin' for the Canadian border. The Bangor patrol noticed the sports car heading north out of town."

"Let me get this straight. Moore kidnapped Shirley Packer, right? How did you find out?"

"Call to Bangor 9-1-1. A civilian went to the Cherrydale house and interrupted the kidnapping."

A shiver of premonition worked its way up Jake's spine.

"What civilian?"

"It was Lucy."

Tension knotted Jake's chest. He could barely breathe. Why the hell would Lucy be in Bangor at this time of night? It couldn't be Lucy.

"It can't be Lucy," he said, voicing his thoughts. "Lucy's home."

"She's there with you?" He heard the relief in his deputy's voice.

"No." Jake hated to air their dirty laundry but everyone would know soon enough. "She's back at the Outlaws."

"Well her Jeep's settin' in front of Mrs. Packer's house on Cherrydale."

"Where's Lucy now?" Even as he asked the question, he knew.

"We think Moore's got her, too."

For an instant, panic paralyzed him. Then he jammed on his sneakers, grabbed his gun belt, and scooped the car keys out of the fruit bowl near the back door and sprinted to the Blazer.

"I'm on my way."

He heard the tires squeal and felt the vehicle sway as he gunned the motor and shot backwards onto the street.

"Sheriff?"

He hadn't realized he was still on the phone.

"Yeah?"

"You leave anybody home with the kids?"

Goddammit! For an instant he considered leaving them home alone. Lucy needed him. And he needed to know she was all right. His gut twisted.

"Call the Garden of Eden Inn. Ask Ms. Johnson to send the kids grandparents over to the house."

"Roger, boss."

"Homer."

"Yeah, boss?"

"Call me back a.s.a.p."

"You got it."

In the jumble of confusion and fear something came to Jake. A gift from a forgiving God. Moore was an amateur pilot. He wasn't heading to the border. He was heading to that little airstrip on the north side of town. When the cell buzzed again, he reported that to his deputy.

"I'll meet you out there. You and any other backup you can round up."

"Roger, boss."

When this was over and Lucy was safe, he was gonna have to cure Homer of using that expression. He scowled at the rain spattered windshield. When this was over and Lucy was safe, he wasn't gonna care about anything else. He stomped on the accelerator, oblivious to the slippery surface of the road or the limited visibility. He'd never been so scared in his life.

His fear-triggered behavior had pushed her out the door and now she was in danger.

If anything happened to her, he'd never forgive himself.

He'd been a damn fool about that woman. He was still a damn fool, but at least now his eyes were clear. He'd rescue Lucy this one last time and then, come hell or high water, he'd go on rescuing her for the rest of their lives. And he'd let her rescue him, too.

Jake forced himself to try to get inside Moore's skin. Moore had shot up to the top of the suspect list within the last day or two as soon as Jake had discovered a few large deposits in Moore's bank account. It seemed likely he'd been siphoning funds out of the business since Packer's death. Jake had been concerned that if Paula suspected the thefts, she would be at risk, so he'd had Homer surveilling her house.

The thing was that, unlike Shirley Packer, Moore hadn't suffered much financially when Packer had dissolved the partnership. He'd lost some stock options in a stumbling business, but more than that, he'd lost face.

Shirley hadn't seemed to mind Nate's defection, but Claude Moore was a different kettle of fish. He was more image-conscious, more compulsive, more needy. In Jake's mind, Moore would have been wounded and infuriated. It was a tailor-made setup for revenge, a powerful motive for murder.

Moore had been with Packer at the Tribal Council meeting that night, so he had opportunity, too. The alibi that had looked so solid, seemed flimsy now. How hard would it have been to trick Mrs. Monaghan?

Then there was means. Death by bow-and-arrow. That clinched the deal as far as Jake was concerned. The irony of using Packer's favorite killing weapon to kill him seemed perfect for a revenge murder. And the bow and arrow was symbolic of the trips that had marked Moore and Packer's long friendship. He Packer understood? Probably. Jake couldn't imagine the calculating attorney not seizing the opportunity to make sure his victim understood.

What he didn't understand was why Moore had kidnapped Shirley or what had taken Lucy to the Cherrydale house. At this point they were hostages, and once Moore got to the airport, he'd have no more use for them. Jake's fingers tightened on the steering wheel, and he pushed the accelerator to the floor.

Twenty minutes later the cell rang.

"Me and the Bangor cop are at the airport, if you can call it an airport," Homer reported. "No one's around."

Jake felt a twinge of uncertainty. Had he guessed wrong? "Get out an all-points bulletin, Homer, instructions not to stop the Bugatti but to keep an eye on it. Meanwhile sit tight out there. If he shows up, remember he's probably armed and desperate, and he'll probably try to jettison his hostages." Jake's throat was dryer than a Maine drought. He could barely get the words out.

"I hear ya," Homer said, sympathetically. "Roger, over and out."

This time Jake didn't think about Homer's habit. He didn't think about anything except getting Lucy out of danger and back into his arms.

****

Lucy felt oddly calm, and she wasn't sure why.

It might have been because of the car. Driving the Bugatti was almost like flying. If she'd been with anyone but a murderer, she'd have shared her sense of exhilaration.

It might have been because, in a weird way, she controlled her fate. She'd gotten so tired of the rollercoaster relationship with Jake. This situation was about as far from emotions as it was possible to get. She'd need to rely on her wits, she knew that. In spite of his protests, she was pretty sure Moore intended to kill them both. They were just excess baggage.

Lucy figured she had a half an hour—the length of time it would take to reach the border—to figure out how to rescue herself and Shirley. She was banking on the injury to help. Moore had begun to moan, softly, and to clutch at his head.

Lucy knew from experience there was nothing worse than a pounding headache, unless it was urgent nausea. The lawyer seemed to be suffering from both.

"Turn at the next right." She made a face. The man sounded dismayingly clearheaded. "And downshift. It's a dirt road."

The last command came just in time. Lucy jammed her foot on the clutch and moved the gear stick from seven to six to five to four." She took the turn a little too fast, but the car cornered beautifully.

She heard Moore gasp and glanced at him. The car's dashboard resembled the Starfleet Central command. In the light it generated, Lucy could see a sheen of sweat on the attorney's face. He looked like he was in pain, and she thought blood was still oozing out of his head wound.

Shirley, draped over the console, barely stirred. Had she been drugged? Or had she decided there was no point in conversation or argument?

"The next turn is in five hundred yards." Moore's voice was little more than a gasp.

"Downshift to two."

Suddenly Lucy realized where they were.

"Omigod," she breathed. "The airport."

He said nothing as she clutched and downshifted and turned down the short road that ended at the airfield's unpaved parking lot.

"Drive up to the third Cessna on the right," Moore said, "then stop."

His breathing had gotten heavier and ragged. She glanced at him again. The bones seemed to stand out on his face as if to remind the world there really was a skeleton under his skin.

"You should see a doctor," she said. Distracted, she forgot to clutch before she stopped. The Bugatti shrieked and stalled, and Lucy felt a sharp blow against the side of her head.

"Just a reminder to keep your mind on your task."

Just a reminder, she thought, to forget about Claude's health and focus on the fact that he'd killed Nate Packer and was probably planning to kill her and Shirley. The realization unaccountably, made her bold.

"You killed those animals, didn't you? It wasn't Packer."

"Start the car and park over there."

She did what he asked. "Nate probably didn't even know how to shoot a bow and arrow."

"He was a poseur. A coward, in fact. Get out of the car, Ms. Outlaw, and into the Cessna. Pilot's seat."

"We're going to fly? At night? In the rain?"

Stupid questions considering they were already at the airport. He didn't bother to answer. He opened the passenger side door.

"Do as I say or I will shoot Shirley. I think it's unlikely I will miss from here."

Lucy got out of the car and climbed into the Cessna. She was relieved that Claude joined her in the co-pilot's seat without discharging a bullet into Shirley.

"Are you expecting me to fly this?"

"It isn't difficult. You handled the Bugatti."

Lucy was absurdly pleased by the compliment.

"Thank you."

He responded by doubling over and vomiting on the Cessna's floor.

The rain had eased up, but the sky was very dark. Lucy knew how dangerous it was to fly this kind of aircraft at night. She knew, too, how dangerous it would be if she simply refused to fly. Claude was sick and probably dizzy, but he was functioning enough to shoot both her and Shirley. She had to go along with him until she got an opening of some kind. Unfortunately, she couldn't really imagine what that would be.

"Turn it on," he said. He pointed to the plane's ignition. Lucy turned.

"Now what?"

"It takes a few minutes to warm up." He dropped his head against the seat rest but he didn't close his eyes and he didn't let go of the pistol. Lucy figured she might as well try to get an explanation, and she sensed that he wanted someone to understand. It had been an emotional response, Lucy felt sure of that.

"Why'd you kill him, Claude?"

The lawyer swallowed convulsively, as if trying to control the nausea.

"He betrayed me. I gave him all those years, all that loyalty. He wanted a dynasty." He spat. "A dynasty of cowards. All right. Step on the gas and start taxiing out to the runway."

"You do realize I'm not a pilot."

"I am. I can talk you through it. Use the throttle on

the console to give it gas."

Lucy felt a flash of fear. This was going to happen. She was going to have to try to get the Cessna into the air and keep it there. A million things could go wrong, not the least of which was that, at any minute, the attorney could decide to kill her. She'd never see Jake again.

The prospect was almost too bleak to contemplate.

"We'll line up there," Moore said, gesturing behind them, "then make a run up to the end of the airstrip."

"What about the trees?"

"We can go over them or through them, Ms. Outlaw. Your choice." A low moan followed the dry comment. Moore clutched his stomach again. Suddenly, Lucy panicked.

"What happens if we're airborne and you pass out?" A scene from *Six Days and Seven Nights* flashed before her eyes. "I won't know how to land. Or where. I don't know where the brake is." She figured there was no point in giving him any hope that she could do this.

"The brake is the pedal on the floor. Advance the throttle now in a slow, steady motion."

His head lolled back again. Behind his glasses, his eyelashes fluttered. She prayed he'd pass out before they left the ground.

"Now taxi down the strip giving it more gas until you reach the last barricade, about fifty yards from here. That's when you'll pull back on the yoke. The plane will lift off the ground."

"The yoke?"

"The steering wheel."

It was an effort for him to speak. "Then what?"

"Then you're in the air. You climb until you've

cleared the tree line and then fly straight. North." He pointed a shaking finger at the compass.

Lucy's hands were shaking now, and her chest was tight. Claude's condition had worsened but not enough. He wasn't going to pass out. He was going to sit there, calmly ordering her to fly to Canada, and if she didn't smash into a tree and kill them first, he'd kill her when they landed. If she could figure out how to land. She had to do something. Now.

She forced her foot down on the accelerator then she stomped on the brake.

Chapter Fifteen

As the Blazer plunged down the turnoff into the airport parking lot, Jake's pulse raced. He could hear the drone of the Cessna's engine, and he could hear the hum of the propeller.

Was Lucy in the plane?

All he could think about was stopping the aircraft before it lifted into the sky. Maybe he could block Moore by driving the Blazer in front of the plane. Of course, if Moore didn't stop, they'd all die in a fireball.

Sweat poured off Jake's forehead and slid inside his shirt. It trickled into his eyes. He'd never felt so helpless. He couldn't let her die. He couldn't bear the thought of a world without Lucy.

Had he told her he loved her? Maybe. Had she believed him? Probably not. Christ.

He spotted the Cessna turning near the terminal, preparing to take off. Too late, then. He pushed the pedal to the floor. The Blazer bounced and bucked and caught up with the Cessna, but he couldn't swerve in front of it. He didn't dare. For a few absurd seconds the plane and the SUV drove next to each other, like the drum majors in a marching band.

Inevitably the plane nosed ahead. In minutes, no, seconds, the crate was going to lift into the air, and Jake would be left on the ground watching the lights disappear. Fear gripped his heart. There was nothing he could do except pray. He sent up a clumsy, out-of-practice but very fervent prayer.

Keep Lucy safe.

He'd just grabbed his cell, intending to direct Homer to contact all the potential landing sites just over the border, when the lights on the Cessna bounced up and down and up and down again, like a damn gymnast on a trampoline. What the hell?

Jake gunned his own motor and raced after the plane. It hiccupped a couple more times then stopped, dead.

Jake was out of the SUV in an instant and racing across the grass when the pilot's door opened. Lucy's face was pale and her eyes wide. She looked scared to death and cold but she was alive.

"Thank God," Jake muttered as he caught her in his arms and held her against him as though she were the most precious thing in the world to him, which she was, as if he'd never let her go, which he wouldn't.

"Moore?" His voice was hoarse.

"He bumped his head. Hard." She spoke into his shoulder. "I only meant to make him sick enough to drop the gun, but I may have killed him."

"How?"

"I alternated the gas and the brake. It made the plane jerk."

"I saw. Very enterprising." His voice was muffled now by her hair. "What about the gun?"

"Here." She pushed away from him and raised her right hand. Goddam if she didn't have the weapon. He took it out of her fingers. The safety was off.

"Shit, Lucy."

He set the safety and slipped the weapon into the

back of his waistband. He needed his arms to hold onto the girl he loved.

"We need to call an ambulance."

His heart stopped. "Are you hurt?"

"No. It's for Claude. And Shirley."

Fuck Claude. Fuck Shirley, too. He kept the ignoble thought to himself. "Ambulance is already here."

He took her to the Blazer and set her gently on the seat, and then they drove back to the terminal.

"Sheriff?" It was one of the ambulance attendants. "We should check her over. Let me take her off your hands."

He looked at the E.R. attendant and shook his head. He didn't plan to let the little witch out of his sight. Ever.

"If you can get the other two to the hospital, we'll meet you there."

****

Lucy was dazed and tired, the adrenalin rush of the last hour completely gone as she sat on the examining table in the Bangor Regional Hospital. She'd never forget the look of pure anguish on Jake Langley's face when she'd appeared in the door of the Cessna. He looked shattered. Probably she should feel flattered that he cared that much. Instead, she felt guilty. Once again she'd gotten herself into a world of trouble. Once again, he'd rushed to the rescue. The whole thing was getting old. She eyed Jake slouched in the molded plastic chair. He looked more exhausted than she felt and she felt a sudden, overwhelming need to cry.

"Who's with the kids?"

"Maxine. And Frank."

He said it so naturally, as if, hours earlier, he hadn't intended to send them out of town on a rail. It was a good sign. Maybe Jake had begun to understand that it really did take a village to raise a child. Or, at least, an extra set of grandparental hands. The guilt receded, a little.

The intern who'd applied salve to the side of her head where Moore had clocked her, packed up his things. He told her to stick around for a little while, that he'd be back to make sure she didn't have a concussion. She stared at Jake's beloved face.

"I'm sorry," she said.

"For what?"

"I shouldn't have gone to Shirley's house tonight."

He shook his head. "I had Homer watching the mansion. I sensed Moore was about to make a move, but I figured any danger was to Paula because she was the cause of his split from Packer and because he'd been stealing from her." He paused. "If you hadn't interfered, Shirley might have died."

"Or not." Lucy had had time during the long wait at the hospital, to think through the consequences of her actions. "I think Claude had decided he needed a hostage, and Shirley seemed like a good candidate. She'd figured out what had happened, that Claude had killed Nate, and why."

"He couldn't afford to leave her behind."

"I think he was wrong. She wasn't going to rat him out," Lucy said, thoughtfully. "Shirley knew Nate had screwed them both. I think, fundamentally, she felt sympathy toward Claude."

"Revenge," Jake said. "Not as common as greed

239

but still a damn good motive."

"Could you check on Shirley?"

"I did. When the doc was examining you. She's got a slight concussion, and they're keeping her overnight. She'll be fine."

"Good. And Claude?"

"He's babbling."

"Omigod! Because I hit him?"

"Indirectly. He's dehydrated. He'll be all right in a few days. Healthy enough to face a long, long prison term."

It was a sad thought. Suddenly she felt Jake's warm fingers under her chin. His green eyes were full of an emotion she hadn't seen before.

"Forget about Claude Moore," he murmured. "The guy doesn't deserve your sympathy." He set his palms on either side of her face and brushed a butterfly kiss across her lips. "The important thing is that you're all right, Lucy." He kissed her again. "And as soon as you're released, I'm taking you home."

"My car."

"We'll get it later. Right now I want you in my home, in my bed, in my arms." He shook his head. "I can't tell you how I felt when I saw that Cessna disappearing down the runway. I may never
recover."

"You came after me," she said, with a little smile. "You're my knight in shining armor, Jake. You gonna spend the rest of your life rescuing me?"

"Yes," he said, dropping another kiss on her lips. "I am."

The vow should have made her happy, but she felt another wave of guilt. She wasn't the second wife that

Jake wanted, but he cared for her, and more than that, he felt responsible, just as if she were a third child.

Lucy didn't fight him, though, when he turned the Blazer down Cypress Street. Morning would be soon enough to finally end this ill-fated relationship.

Maxine and Frank, dozing on the sofa, accepted a very abbreviated version of events then left, promising to come back the next day.

Jake put his arm around Lucy's waist.

"A better man than I would leave you alone tonight," he said, in a rough voice, "but that's not gonna happen." He led her into his room. "If I fall asleep, I need to know where you are the instant I wake up."

"Jake."

He shook his head. "I know we've got stuff to iron out. No more talking tonight. Just, sleep with me, Lucy."

Weariness surrounded her, sucked her in.

"You don't have to ask twice," she said, stifling a yawn. "This is where I want to be."

He peeled off her sodden clothing and his own then turned on the shower long enough to shampoo her hair and warm her chilled skin. He was efficient but thorough.

"You're so good at this."

"Lots of practice," he said, wrapping her in a fluffy towel.

She glanced up at him. "Practice?"

"With Sam and Lillie." A smile flashed in the eyes that had been too solemn all evening.

Lucy was too tired to smile, and he seemed to sense it. He bundled her into one of his T-shirts, not bothering with a trip down the hall to her bedroom, scooped her into his arms, and deposited her on the clean-smelling sheets.

She shouldn't be there. It was misleading and not right. But it felt right to be next to him just as it always had.

Jake," she started to say.

"Shh." He rolled over and pressed a warm, dry kiss against her lips then he pulled her against him, spoon fashion. "Just sleep."

She was aware of the male arousal pressing against her hip, but she closed her eyes and slept.

There wouldn't be a last time, after all.

****

Jake returned to consciousness with a sense of contentment that quickly morphed into raw need when he became aware of the soft, sweet-smelling body next to him. He slipped his arms around her waist and moaned as she snuggled backwards and into the cradle of his thighs.

Predictably, the bedroom door opened with a sharp bang, and he found himself looking past the dark curls and into two pairs of curious, emerald eyes.

"Hi, Daddy," Lillie said. She put her small fingers on Lucy's dark curls. "Grandma said you and Lucy was heroes last night."

"Lucy was the real hero," he said. He cleared his throat, hoping his daughter wouldn't notice the huskiness in his voice. "Go on back to the kitchen and I'll join you. We'll let Lucy sleep."

But Lucy must have heard her name. She scooted back against him, and heat exploded in his body. He bit back a curse.

"You look funny, Daddy," Sam said. "Kinda red."

"I'm hot."

Lucy lifted her head, stared at him, and then smiled at the children.

"He is hot. You guys hungry?"

"Grandma made us pancakes," Sam said. "She said you and Daddy is sleepyheads."

Lucy canted up on one elbow to talk with the children. At the same time, she rubbed her backside against his front. The little witch. He was fast approaching the point of no return and apparently, Lucy knew it.

"Could you help Grandma make more pancakes for Daddy and me while we get dressed?"

Lillie nodded. "Coffee, too, okay, Sam?"

"Okay, Lucy. Want me to bring Lucy Junior in to see you?"

"What I'd really like," she said, in a hushed tone, "is for you to read a story to Lucy Junior. Daddy and I will come find you when we're dressed."

"Okay, Lucy," Lillie said.

"Okay, Lucy," Sam said.

She blew them air kisses which they returned and then they fled.

"You have a nice touch with the kids," Jake said. He needed to roll away from Lucy before he did something unforgivable.

"I have a nice touch with their dad, too." She flipped over so that her mouth was inches from his.

She slid her foot down the outside of his leg.

"Lucy," he groaned.

"We have a little time," she said.

He wasn't going to slide into sex, not until they'd worked out their future.

"We need to talk first." He realized he didn't sound very resolute.

"I think," she said, finding him with her fingers, "we need to talk second. Come on, Sheriff. A little reward for a hero?"

His spine stiffened. "A reward?"

"For me, silly. I'm the hero, remember?"

"Hmmm." Her fingers were stroking with just the right amount of pressure, and she smelled so good.

"Please, Jake."

He hadn't meant to make her beg. He flipped her onto her back, and with a long, low moan of infinite satisfaction, he slid into the place where he most wanted to be.

Moments, before he could even move, she headed for the door, and her bedroom down the hall.

"Hang on," he gasped. "One hand washes the other, remember?"

Her eyes widened.

"You wanted to make love, so we made love. I, on the other hand, want to get married."

Something went out of the blue gaze, and he suddenly felt very cold.

It's too late, isn't it? I've ruined it."

She hurried back over to the bed. "No, no, of course not. It's not that. It's just that I've had second thoughts about my future." Her words were halting but clear. Jake couldn't believe what she was saying. "I've realized I really want what Ed would call 'the big canvas.' That wouldn't work with a family, Jake."

He must have looked as stricken as he felt because Maxine took one look at him and spoke to her husband.

"After breakfast, dear, I wonder if you and the

children could drive Lucy back to Bangor to get her Jeep."

When they were alone, Maxine made him a fresh cup of coffee and sat down at the table.

"Tell me," she said, "what's wrong."

He told her. Part of him couldn't believe he was baring his soul to Maxine. The other part of him prayed that she could help.

"So," she said, when he'd finished, "you've convinced her you don't really want to marry her."

"She wants a career."

"Forgive me for contradicting you, Jake, but a woman can have both these days, and that particular woman loves you and the twins. You need to tell her she's got it wrong." The older woman made a little face. "That's not an easy message to convey or to accept, but Lucy's battled that bubblehead message for too long. She's not an airhead. You know it and I know. Now you have to convince her."

"How?"

"Simple. Find a way to convince her that you can't live without her, Jake."

Maxine regarded him for a long moment. He knew she was trying to tell him something, something he was too much of a thick-headed male to understand.

He shook his head. "She's an adult. I can't make her marry me."

She shrugged. "Then I guess you'll just have to let her go."

His back teeth ground themselves together.

"Never."

****

Lucy thought the day would never end.

All she wanted to do was retreat to her apartment and bury her head under her pillow.

Instead, she had to talk to the Bangor police about what had happened with Claude and Shirley, then she had to interview both of them and Paula Packer and, worst of all, she had to call Jake to find out what charges he was bringing.

Even then she wasn't finished, because the family, of course, wanted to hear her version of the attempted kidnapping. At least the latter occurred after a filling meal of Asia's beef stew and homemade bread.

"You never told us you were taking flying lessons," Baz said. "Very enterprising of you."

"And way to spike Moore's guns," Cam added. "I'd never have thought of that."

"You were so brave," Hallie pointed out. "Enterprising and brave. I think we can safely say nobody's going to confuse you with 'I love Lucy' anymore."

Lucy found a smile for them then she settled down to a half hour of Pigs and Ladders, a variation on the game created in honor of Daisy's pet pig, Wilbur.

When it was time to say goodnight, Lucy allowed Hallie to walk her back to the apartment. Hallie pulled Lucy's arm through hers.

"I'm not going to ask what's going on between you and Jake," her sister-in-law said.

"Very noble of you."

"Very," Hallie agreed, "considering I was the one who threw the engagement party."

"Touché."

"I just wanted to say one thing, sweetie. I know it has bothered you that Jake and I dated for a bit. I want you to know that I was fond of him and I think he was fond of me. He thought I'd make a good wife."

"You do make a good wife."

She laughed. "Thanks." Her smile disappeared in favor of an earnest expression. "I wouldn't have made a good wife to him, though, and I think we both knew it. I didn't love him, Lucy. And he didn't love me."

"I think you're wrong."

The veterinarian shook her head.

"I've seen the expression on his face when he looks at you, and I recognize his feelings. They're the same feelings I have toward Baz. That sense that you've found your mate."

"I appreciate you telling me that, Hal."

"But…"

"But it isn't just about love with Jake. It's more important for him to find the perfect stepmom for the twins."

"You are the perfect stepmom, Lucy. No one could love them more than you do. Look at the way you brought Maxine and Frank into their lives. That's pure love."

Lucy shook her head. "Jake thinks I'm too young and ambitious to settle down."

Hallie peered at her. "Is he right?"

Lucy shrugged. "I don't honestly know anymore. I just know that I'm tired of trying to prove myself." She hesitated. "When I turn my story into the *Courier* in a couple of days, I'm going to see if they have any openings."

Hallie clasped her hand. "We're all behind you, Luce, whatever you decide."

Her cell phone rang just before she climbed in bed.

She felt the familiar tingle against the back of her neck and knew it was Jake. A lump formed in her throat at the sound of his deep voice.

"You okay?"

"I'm fine. And you?"

"I miss you." The lump got bigger. "How are the kids?"

"They miss you, too."

She didn't know what to say.

"I'm sorry, Luce. I know that everything that went wrong between us, well, it was my fault."

"That's not true."

He went on as if she hadn't spoken.

"I was just like everybody else in town. Worse. The thing is it wasn't really because I thought you were incompetent. I realize now it was a defense against the feelings I had from the first time I saw you."

"You tryin' to tell me it was love at first sight?"

He didn't laugh.

"I don't know. I never really tried to understand. I felt something powerful around you, and it scared the crap out of me. And then you came to stand in for Mrs. Peach, and well, you got under my skin."

She wanted to cry.

"You got under my skin, too."

"We sound like a coupla bed bugs."

There was a long, awkward pause.

"I need some time, Jake." Another awkward pause.

"I understand."

"Thanks."

"I actually called to tell you the arraignment's scheduled for tomorrow morning. We're gonna hold it at the hospital at eleven. Thought you might like to attend."

"I would. Thanks."

"Need a ride?"

"I'll come with Flynn. We'll need photos."

"Right." Another pause. "You sure you're okay?"

"I'm fine."

"Well, goodnight, then."

This is what happened in a disintegrating relationship. There got to be less and less to talk about until the partners were reduced to total inanity. It was beyond depressing. She fell into bed, certain she wouldn't be able to sleep.

Fortunately, she was wrong.

The next morning she put on a dress she'd bought the previous spring when she was still in college and worked part-time at a boutique. It was silk, lightweight and floaty, a checker board of blue and turquoise with some defining black lines. She wore black boots with it, the kind that came partway up her shin. The dress was too fancy for a hospital arraignment, but Lucy knew it looked dazzling on her and she needed the boost. She met Flynn at the *Excelsior* office.

"Wow," he said, smacking the heel of his hand against his forehead. "You could give the merry widow a run for her money in that get-up."

Lucy wrinkled her nose. "Thanks. I think."

She spotted Jake the instant she stepped off the elevator. He was surrounded by a group of uniformed cops, all of them young and attractive, but he was the only one she saw. He saw her, too. His green eyes widened, then narrowed when he noticed Flynn.

One look at Claude Moore sent everything else out of Lucy's head. Even allowing for the hospital gown replacing his high-priced suits, he looked terrible, old, yellow, and wrinkled. It was almost as if the bitterness that had lived inside him since his best friend's betrayal had become visible. Lucy felt a deep pity.

First Jake laid out the facts of his case and then a prosecutor from Penobscot County questioned Moore about the details of the murder.

Nate Packer's former best friend held nothing back. In a dull, quiet voice he spoke about talking with Nate at the Tribal Council meeting. He said he had something important to tell him, but it had to be in private. They'd agreed to meet at the construction trailer at the casino site. Moore got there first, parked, out of sight on a fragment of an old logging road, hid behind the trailer with his bow and arrow and waited for his prey to arrive. Lucy thought Molly and Cam must have heard Moore while they were talking on the spot where he would kill Nate a few minutes later.

Claude admitted he'd taken the arrow from the Penobscot museum as a diversion for investigators. He said that he, not Nate Packer, had killed all the trophy head animals in the Packer Mansion. Nate wasn't interested in the killing, only the reputation of great white hunter.

After the murder Claude had driven back to Bangor. He'd considered setting Mrs. Monaghan's clock back by twenty minutes and risk having her notice, but he'd decided, instead, to trust the Bugatti. His trust had been rewarded. The speed of the sports car, combined with the luck of nearly empty roads, had gotten him back to his house by ten forty-five.

"I understand how you killed your ex-partner," the prosecutor said, dryly. "The question is, why?"

"He betrayed me. He betrayed Shirley, too."

"How did he do that?"

"He dissolved our partnership and formed a new one with his new wife. He was obsessed with the idea of creating a dynasty, and it didn't bother him at all to sacrifice a lifelong friend. Shirley understood."

"You were friends with the first Mrs. Packer, too?"

"Of course."

"But you threatened her life the other night, along with that of Ms. Outlaw."

Lucy felt Jake's eyes on her.

"I needed Shirley for protection. It wasn't personal," Claude said, wearily. "I'm tired now. Are we finished?"

Moments later Jake walked Lucy and Flynn to the elevator.

"It's almost like he's proud of what he did," the photographer said, scratching his head.

"It was a revenge killing," Jake said. "He felt justified in what he did. He wants everyone to understand."

"I would have understood if it had been the first wife," Flynn said. "It's kinda weird that a guy would take a bust up so hard."

"He'd sacrificed a lot for Nate," Lucy said. "He hadn't married. He'd sublimated his own hunting skills to let Nate take whatever glory is associated with slaughtering innocent animals."

"C'mon, Lucy." Flynn laughed. "Tell us what you really think."

They all chuckled.

"I think it's just a difference in personality types," she said. "Claude probably always cared more about

Nate than Shirley did. He's just more passionate."

"Seems like that passion didn't serve him very well."

Lucy shook her head. "It may not be the best basis for a relationship."

"Yeah?" Flynn looked skeptical. "What's better?"

"I don't know. Belief in the other person's integrity? Trust?"

Flynn made a face. "Give me passion any day. Say, Luce, don't let me forget to stop for ice cream on the way home."

Chapter Sixteen

Wednesday the banner headline on the *Excelsior* topped a story about the murder case along with a first-person sidebar. Lucy did not write it from the perspective of a heroine. Instead, she included some self-deprecating humor, including a description of how she stumbled into the kidnapping that was already underway.

The following morning, a longer, more detailed version of the story appeared under her byline again, this time on the front page of the *Hartford Courier*.

That afternoon, Ed Stiles swung his feet down from his own desk and perched his bulky form on the corner of Lucy's. First he praised her for her work, and then he stared at her a long moment.

"What would you say to taking over the *Excelsior*?"

"You feeling the need of a vacation?"

The older man sighed. "A permanent one. My wife and my doc are teaming up on me. Retirement looks inevitable."

Lucy stared at him. It was hard to imagine the *Excelsior* without Ed.

"The *New England Observer* chain wants to buy me out. I've had a standing offer from them for a long while, but frankly, I'd a lot rather keep this in the family. If the chain takes over, the paper will be filled with generic stuff from all over the state." He shrugged. "A small town paper's the heart and soul of the community, you know that, Luce. Next best thing to the grapevine. Without a paper, there's nothing to line the birdcages." His voice trembled slightly. Lucy felt tears prick the backs of her eyes. Ed was talking about giving up the career he'd loved all his life.

"How 'bout it, Luce?"

"I can't do it."

"Empty pockets?"

"As well as an empty head. I've got less than fifty bucks in my savings account and less than two weeks of actual newspaper experience."

The editor shrugged his beefy shoulders.

"Let me hang onto the paper, and I'll pay you to manage it. If you decide you like it, you can buy me off gradually. I'll give you a fair price. And as far as the rest, well, that's all in your head, you know. You never were flakey. Just impulsive. You've shown you've got talent and guts and drive. Everything you need. Besides, you'll need a job in town now that you're gonna get hitched to the sheriff."

Lucy swallowed. "That getting hitched thing. That's on hold. And, anyway, I've got an offer from the *Courier*."

"Oh? They sending you to Kabul?"

"Just the copy desk. But it's a start."

Ed looked at her for a long minute. "Wedding's off?"

"I'm ashamed to say it, but it was never really on. The engagement was fake. Jake needed to impress his in-laws. Now that everything's okay between them, there's no hurry for him to marry. And, I'm too young."

Ed scratched his head, but he didn't offer an opinion.

"All right, Luce. The offer's open. Think about it. There's a lot worse places to spend your life than in a newsroom, just like there's a lot worse places than Eden. For my money, this is where you belong."

Lucy felt the exasperating lump in her throat again. Good grief. She'd been on the verge of tears more in the last couple of weeks than in the first twenty-two years of her life.

****

Jake tried not to think about Lucy while he was in his office. He figured if he didn't think about her he wouldn't miss her so much. He tried not to think about her when he was in the Blazer making traffic stops or when he was on the phone with the Penobscot County prosecutor. He tried not to think about her when he was with his kids and their grandparents.

None of his efforts were successful. He couldn't stop thinking about her. He couldn't stop missing her. He wracked his brain for something he could say that would change her mind but even if he'd thought of one, he wouldn't have been able to use it.

Maybe she did want a career. Lucy wasn't a liar.

Maybe she'd been telling him the truth.

The night before the presentation of Parade of President, he was tucking his daughter into bed when her small mouth straightened into a grim line and her green eyes flashed.

"Sam and me has come to a decision, Daddy," she said. "We want Lucy to come back."

Jake's gut clenched.

"She's busy."

"Not in the night. She gots to sleep someplace. Why can't she sleep here?"

"We miss her," Sam said, from the doorway.

"And she misses us," Lillie said.

"How do you know that?" It was an absurd question. He had no doubt that Lucy missed the children.

"She told us so," Sam explained. "At the rehearsal."

"You've seen her?" He couldn't believe he was jealous of his own kids.

"She tole Grandma she's moving away." Sam's lower lip started to tremble.

"Moving away?"

"To Hartford. Lucy got another job cause she's famous."

She hadn't told him. She hadn't asked him if he'd mind. She'd meant what she'd said. It was over.

He re-tucked the children in their beds then he stepped out onto the porch. It was nearly the end of May, and the evening air was pleasant and mild. Jake stared at the apple tree remembering the night Lucy had rescued Wiggles and he had rescued her. The night he'd kissed her for the first time. His chest tightened, painfully.

She belonged with him. With them. It had been clear from their first encounter. She was more mother to the twins than their own mother had ever been. She belonged to them and they to her. And she belonged to Jake. If she didn't understand that, he was just going to have to make her understand. He was going to have to do something drastic, a game-changer. But what?

Suddenly, in the still of the May night, inspiration

dropped into his lap, like a benediction from on high.

Suddenly, Jake knew what he was going to do.

****

Lucy was all packed. Now that she'd decided her future, there was no reason to procrastinate. It was time to start her new career, her new life. She planned to Sunday, right after the Saturday night production of Parade of Presidents.

There was still an hour until the performance so, even though she'd said her goodbyes at a family dinner the night before, she wandered back toward the house. Hallie was working in the garden with Daisy. Wilbur on a blanket in the shade next to Robert in his baby seat. It was such a sweet, domestic picture, it brought tears to Lucy's eyes.

She hunkered down by the little girl.

"Ladies slippers, bachelor buddons and forgetme-dots."

"Great. I remember planting flowers with Asia. It was always lots of fun."

"Didn't you got a mommy, neither, Aunt Lucy?"

Daisy was not a deprived child. She was much loved and cherished, and yet the question cut Lucy to the heart. Maybe it was guilt about abandoning Sam and Lillie. Maybe it was grief.

"No. But I had a daddy and brothers, and now I have a darling little niece." She found she couldn't leave Robert out. "And nephew."

"And pig," Daisy said, with a giggle.

"Maxine told me she and Frank are thinking of renting a house in Eden for part of the year," Hallie said. "That should be nice for Sam and Lillie. And Jake."

Lucy nodded.

"I don't got a grandma, neither," Daisy pointed out.

"Why don't you run in the house and get a cookie for you and Wilbur," Hallie said. The idea appealed to the little girl, as Hallie had known it would. She turned to her sister-in-law.

"Is this really what you want? This job in Hartford?"

Lucy couldn't seem to speak. She couldn't even nod. She hated being so emotional all the time.

"I know you love Jake."

"It's not enough."

"I think it is, sweetie. I think love is always enough. When you get down to it, love is everything." "It wasn't everything for Baz. Not at first."

Baz had been afraid of his feelings, too, just like Jake, but eventually he'd come around.

"Baz never had any reason to doubt your feelings for him," Lucy pointed out. "I'm sure Jake thinks he's being noble now that I have the *Courier* job. He's not going to ask me to stay, Hallie. Not

again."

"Couldn't you tell him what you want?"

Lucy shook her head. "I don't know how to explain it. I need him to understand me well enough to just know how I feel. Anyway, I've accepted the

job. It's too late."

"Oh, honey." This time the tears were in Hallie's hazel eyes. "I just want you to be happy." Lucy hugged the shorter woman.

"I'm happy that Baz came to his senses. I'm happy to have a sister."

****

A live stage play, even a first grade effort, was a big event in Eden, and The Parade of Presidents was well attended. Audience members mixed and mingled in the corridor outside the Eden

Consolidated High auditorium, their spirits high as they anticipated the performance. Jake heard Lucy's name murmured by several theatergoers. Naturally. It was the first such gathering since Miss Violet's Ode to the Seasons. Would there be unruly bells? Flying feathers? Explosions of any kind?

Everyone in Eden knew the sky was the limit when Lucy Outlaw was involved.

Sam and Lillie were backstage with Frank and Maxine but Jake, hoping to avoid the inevitable questions about his engagement, slipped through the crowd at the last minute. He had one last shot at this and he had to make it count but there were no guarantees. Lucy was softhearted, but she was no pushover. She'd begun to understand her own power. She'd become a woman, not a girl. The change made her even more interesting. It also made her more unpredictable. Would she buy what he was selling?

Jake's palms were moist, and his throat was dry. This was like the most important job interview of his life. He figured he'd get about three minutes of her time before she cut him off. He had to make it count.

He would make it count.

The future of his family depended upon it.

Outside the auditorium he accepted a program from a solemn-eyed girl who came up to his knee. He nodded and grunted at people as he found a seat and dropped into it. He couldn't feel Lucy's presence. She wasn't here. What if she didn't come? What if she'd decided to ditch the play and she was already on the road to Hartford. Jake forced down a feeling of panic. If she was on the road, he'd catch up to her. If she was already there, he'd go to her apartment or her office.

The houselights went down, and a diminutive narrator stepped out from the curtains to introduce the play. When she'd finished speaking the audience clapped. At the same time, Jake felt a shiver rumble up his spine. She was here. She'd just come in. He turned to catch her eye, to motion her to sit by him.

Somewhat to his surprise, she did.

"Hey," she said.

His heart crashed into his ribs.

"Hey, yourself." He forced himself to grin.

The curtain rose to reveal a plywood rendition of Mount Vernon. Sam, dressed in white pantaloons, a cutaway jacket, and a tri-cornered hat, stood on the stage opposite Lillie, whose ankle-length blue gown frothed with lace at the neck and sleeves. There was a distinct lack of jingle bells. No doubt some audience members were disappointed.

"The nation wants me to serve again," George Washington said in a familiar piping voice. "But all I really want to do is stay home with you, my dear."

"But George," Martha said, a scowl on her face, "what about your duty? The country needs you."

George removed his hat revealing a head full of blond curls. "I hate to leave you to raise the children alone, Martha, my dear."

"Hmmm," Martha said. "I have an idea! The children and I will come to Washington with you!"

George picked up her hand and kissed the back of it. "With you by my side, Martha, my dear, the nation will get a much better president."

Jake's heart swelled with pride and then he felt Lucy's hand on his.

"They're so wonderful," she said, her voice trembling. He lifted her hand and pressed his lips against it. She made a little noise, a whimper and his blood heated. He forced himself to be patient, to focus on James and Dolley Madison as they removed a wagonload of silver from the White House and rescued a portrait of George Washington during British invasion of 1812.

Honest Abe, wearing a stovepipe hat, brandished a piece of paper and a quill pen and announced that he was "'mancipatin' the slaves." William Henry Harrison came on stage just long enough to die in his bed and Theodore Roosevelt strode across the stage with a stuffed teddy bear under one arm and a bull moose under the other. Franklin Roosevelt, pince nez falling off his nose, held out a long cigarette holder and declared war on Japan and Germany and afterwards, Harry Truman ended that same war with a decision to drop an atom bomb.

"Maxine made that costume," Lucy whispered, when Jackie Kennedy appeared in a pale yellow suit with a pillbox hat to support her husband's creation of the Peace Corps.

"Nice," he said. He wondered if she could hear the strain in his voice.

The play ended with the unfurling of an oversized American flag and a gathering on stage of all the first graders waving battery powered flashlights and singing "This Land is Your Land." The audience stood, clapped, and whistled, then bolted into the hallway to congratulate the cast members. Jake stood behind Lucy waiting for the aisle to clear. He fought the urge to put his hand on her waist. Too soon. He bent his head to speak into her ear.

"I'd like to talk to you." She turned her sky blue eyes up to him, and his heart ached. The eyes had lost their sparkle.

"Well, Lucy," said a strident voice. "I understand you have taken a job at the *Hartford Courier*. It's a fine offer, but you will be missed in Eden."

"Thank you, Miss Violet." Her voice shook.

"A career is a wonderful thing for a woman," the older woman continued. "It is unfortunate that it is so difficult to combine one with family."

"Difficult," Jake said, seizing the opening, "but not impossible. Most women today work outside the home. There's no reason that Lucy can't have a career at the *Courier* and enjoy our family life at the same time."

He'd gotten their attention. Both Lucy and Miss Violet stared at him.

"There's one problem," Lucy said, a little edge in her voice. "The job and the family aren't in the same town."

Jake nodded, dismissively. "A minor problem, my dear. That will be corrected within the next few weeks, when I've moved the twins to Hartford."

"What?"

"I've listed the Cypress Street house with Marilyn Hart, and I've contacted the Hartford city police. I've got an interview Tuesday, but it shouldn't be much of a problem to get hired. After all, I've just solved a local murder."

"You've solved it!"

She sounded indignant. He grinned at her.

"I'll admit I had a little help."

She'd barely been able to keep her mind on the play with Jake sitting next to her, his shoulder brushing against hers, the scent of strawberry shortcake shampoo in her nostrils and her awareness of his big, masculine body so close by.

She'd felt his pride in every molecule of her being when Sam and Lillie had performed. She'd felt his essence in every ounce of her blood. This would be the last time they were together. She closed her eyes at one point trying to imprint the moment in her memory. She no longer felt like crying. The emotions were like dead ashes. It was a step toward recovery, she was certain. She was doing the right thing. This had to be the right thing only it was queer that the right thing hurt so much.

Jake picked up her hand at one point, and she wanted to squeeze it. She wanted to tell him how much she admired him, how much she'd loved getting to know him.

How much she loved him. None of that was appropriate now, though, so she said nothing at all.

Suddenly the play was over, and they got up to leave. Lucy fought the panic that rose in her throat. She heard Miss Violet talking to them, but she couldn't seem to focus. This was it. The last few minutes she'd have with Jake. She nodded and smiled and hoped her responses wouldn't offend anybody. She knew they probably didn't make sense.

And then she heard him say something about moving to Hartford, about selling the house, and getting a job with the police department.

"There are fine schools in Hartford," she heard him saying to Miss Violet, who was staring at him as if he'd suddenly sprouted horns.

"And, of course, the children's grandparents will be with us often. That helps a lot, you know, to have extended family." He grinned at Lucy and then at Miss Violet. "It takes a village."

"Pardon me," Miss Violet said, "but did I hear you correctly? Are you truly going to move to Hartford?"

"Of course." He sounded as if it weren't the most harebrained scheme imaginable. "That's where my future wife's career is. Of course we're moving to Hartford."

"Daddy, Daddy," Lillie said, making a beeline down the aisle toward her father.

"Mommy!" It was Sam. He threw his little arms around Lucy's waist. "I can call you that," he said, with his shy smile. "Daddy said so."

Tears filled Lucy's eyes. They splashed down her cheeks. She lifted Sam, aka George Washington, up into her arms.

"You can call me anything you want, darlin'."

"We're gonna go to Har'ford with you," Lillie said, from her perch in Jake's arms. "Wiggles and Lucy, Jr. don't wanna leave our house, but we told them it's important. That's what Daddy says. You have to follow your heart."

Lucy looked at Jake's laughing green eyes, and she read the sincerity in them.

"You are my heart," he mouthed.

The tears plummeted down her cheeks and onto the child in her arms.

"My goodness," Miss Violet said, pulling out a

handkerchief. She held it to her nose. "My goodness."

"What do you say, sweetheart." Jake gave her a rueful smile and she returned it. There was no point in waiting for privacy. "Do you like the plan? Can we come?"

"Do you have your heart set on the Hartford Police Department?"

"No, Luce." His voice was low and intimate, in spite of the audience. "Only on you."

"Then I'd like to stay in Eden. I'd like to run the *Excelsior*. I think a small canvas is more my style." She grinned at him, and she knew her heart was in her eyes. "A small canvas and a big family."

Jake's kiss involved no hands. It was chaste and brief ,but he managed to convey the promise of much more to come.

"I love you," he said.

Lucy, still holding Sam, moved into his arms for another kiss. An instant later she realized they'd been joined by Maxine and Frank.

"It's all right that they're kissin'," Sam explained to his grandparents. "'Cause Daddy loves Lucy."

A word about the author...

It doesn't have to be a dark and stormy night for me to enjoy a mystery story and a mystery mixed with romance is even better. My idea of fun is an evening spent with Patricia Wentworth, Lord Peter Wimsey, Inspectors Alleyn, Morse and Lewis, Sandra Brown, Jayne Ann Krentz, Janet Evanovich and Margery Allingham. I've tried to bring some of the delicious tension of those authors and works to my own romantic suspense.

There's no mystery about me. I'm from Ann Arbor, Michigan, a town that, it turns out, was not named for me, but now live in Northern Virginia. I'm an ex-reporter, a sometime teacher, wife of a longtime Associated Press reporter who loves to read as much as I do, and mother of three perfect adult children and two equally perfect children-in-law.

www.annyost.com

~*~

Other Ann Yost titles
available from The Wild Rose Press, Inc.

ABOUT A BABY
EYE OF THE TIGER LILY
THAT VOODOO THAT YOU DO
FOR BETTER OR HEARSE
THE EARL THAT I MARRY

Thank you for purchasing
this publication of The Wild Rose Press, Inc.

If you enjoyed the story, we would appreciate your
letting others know by leaving a review.

For other wonderful stories,
please visit our on-line bookstore at
www.thewildrosepress.com.

For questions or more information
contact us at
info@thewildrosepress.com.

The Wild Rose Press, Inc.
www.thewildrosepress.com

Stay current with The Wild Rose Press, Inc.

Like us on Facebook

https://www.facebook.com/TheWildRosePress

And Follow us on Twitter
https://twitter.com/WildRosePress

www.ingramcontent.com/pod-product-compliance
Lightning Source LLC
Chambersburg PA
CBHW070326260626
47160CB00003B/959